The Ex-Factor

Helena

GIBSON SQUARE

First edition published by Gibson Square

info@gibsonsquare.com
www.gibsonsquare.com
Tel: +44 (0)20 7096 1100 (UK)
Tel: +353 (0)1 657 1057 (Eire)

ISBN   9781908096562

For my two favourite Chelsea boys:
Leonardo Wright and Frank Lampard

The Ex-Factor

❦ 1 ❧

"How on earth are you ever going to explain in terms of chemistry and physics so important a biological phenomenon as first love?"
Albert Einstein

November 2010

At *The Chronicle* just off Baker Street in London, the daily news meeting is signalled by what the staff call the 'Vagina monologues' echoing down the hall from the office of Cameron Knight, the 55-year-old editor-in-chief.

Normally it is a tirade of abuse heaped on Les Moore the news editor, better known in the newsroom by his nickname Les Misérables. On a good day he only gets called a c**t once, but most days are not good, and poor old Les gets what has become termed a double or even a triple c**ting.

Most other staff who have come into contact with Knight have been double c**ted at the very least.

Sometimes the whole newsroom gets treated to a heap of abuse as he wades through it after a long lunch, ripping up pages and yelling about scoops they should have had and that are now on their competitor's front pages. Just so no one feels left out.

A newspaper office is run like a medieval fiefdom. There are the slaves, consisting of most of the staff, especially the down-table subs whose job it is to make sure that all the facts printed are correct, or if not, that they're wrong by design. Most of the unfortunate reporters fall into this category too. Then there are the managers, or the section editors, such as the news editor, the travel editor and the features editor. They command a little more respect than the slaves, but also get more abuse. There is a coffee-stained embroidered cushion in the staff tearoom that reads 'With responsibility comes retribution' bought by some section head long since fired and forgotten.

Slightly removed from the majority of the staff are the columnists, a rarified breed only exposed to limited abuse. Among these there might be one favourite, a court jester, who is allowed liberties others can only dream of, whom the editor listens to, and who has worked with the editor long enough to remember when he or she was a mere mortal.

Finally there is the editor – the king, or queen, a kind of god whose word is law and whose favour you must have if you are going to survive more than a morning. The editor's favour is not, unlike a mother's love, unconditional, and it has to be won on a daily basis.

The battle for the editor's approval repeats itself every day at *The Chronicle* at the 11am conference, the meeting where it is decided what will go into the next day's newspaper, and where abuse about that day's edition is meted out.

Although Marina Shaw has not yet had a bad run-in with Knight, she knows it is more certain than death and taxes. But it may take a while. She is a columnist, so already at an advantage, and there are three additional reasons she has avoided abuse: one, Knight recently poached her from *The Chronicle*'s main rival so sees her as a prized asset; two, he finds her not unattractive with her long curly dark hair and voluptuous figure; and three, probably most importantly, she usually only comes to conference once a week, the day before her column, This Life, appears in the paper.

"Right, today we're all about Wills and Kate, obviously. They're engaged in case you hadn't heard," says Knight, putting his feet on the desk and leaning back in his large leather chair. "Features, got any good ideas for a change?"

he directs his gaze at Hugo Willoughby, the old Etonian strawberry-blond features editor.

Knight is rather pleased to have an old Etonian to boss around, mainly because he wishes he were one. At least his sons will be.

If he had ever asked Hugo about his education though, he would have been told that he had more or less hated his time at Eton. In fact he had hated much of his schooling; there is no lonelier place than a cold English prep school when you're seven years old and your mother is in another country.

Hugo immediately sits upright like a schoolboy being asked to recite his timetables.

"Yep, lots of ideas," he smiles with his habitual charm and confidence. "Over to you Millie." He nudges his deputy, a rather scrawny Glaswegian who blushes and looks at her notebook.

"Yes, well, we had a thought…"

"One thought?" interrupts Knight, shooting himself forward in his reclining chair like a cannonball. There is a sweepstakes in the office on when he will either come shooting out of it, or fall backwards. You can get good odds on either happening before Christmas.

"One thought for eight pages? It had better be good." He looks around the room as the assembled staff laughs dutifully, but they all feel sorry for the hard-working Millie, who has put up with being Hugo's slave for more than a year without a word of complaint. The man has an extraordinary talent for delegating, which he gets away with, mainly because he's so charming.

"How about a look at other famous university romances that have flourished, or even floundered?" she goes on.

"Crap," says Knight.

"We also considered other royal relationships, how they started, where they went and so forth."

"Been done."

"Right, well, we quite like the idea."

"That's enough crap ideas for now. Anyone else?"

Marina feels the butterflies in her stomach as she prepares to speak. However many times she goes to conference, she never quite gets over her nervousness.

"I was thinking about something for my column about first love," she begins, squeezing her toes to contain her nerves, then she pauses, half-expecting to be shot down. But Knight is silent and looks at her with a sort of grimace that could almost be taken for encouragement.

"Well," she continues. "Remember when they split up in 2007, I always thought they would get back together. I mean look at what happened to Camilla and Charles. We all know the old saying; first love never dies…"

"Yes!" Knight interrupts Marina and is up now and pacing, his chair spinning from the speed of his departure. "Make it personal. I mean, did you have a first love?" he glares at her. She opens her mouth, but he cuts her off before she has a chance to answer. "Of course you did, we all did. How many in here can remember their first love? Come on, hands up."

Reluctantly at first, the assembled gang of 20 or so of Fleet Street's most hackneyed reporters raise their hands. Some even get a sort of glazed look normally only witnessed at the Rose & Crown round the corner just after last orders.

"You see," shrieks Knight. "And the nation will be the same. We all remember our first love, whether we want to or not. And in this Facebook age, your first love is only a click away. This is great. Let's do one of those fatuous on-line polls. Where's that c*** Bill? Rosemary!" he bellows at his secretary through the intercom, although she can probably hear him through the wall. "Get that c**t Bill in here, we need an online survey. And health, how about something on the physical manifestations of first love? What is that thing that happens?"

"Emotions?" asks William Mount wryly, looking up from his BlackBerry for the first time this morning. He has only had a BlackBerry for three months and they are still in the flushes of a first romance.

"Steady," replies Knight. William Mount is the only man that is allowed to joke with the editor. He runs the daily gossip column at *The Chronicle*, along with the dippy aristocrat The Honourable Miss India Drayton-Fox. He joined the paper with Knight ten years ago.

"Do you remember your first love Will?" asks Knight. "Looked her up on Facebook yet?"

"I'd be amazed if she's heard of Facebook," replies William in his barely detectable Yorkshire accent, softened from years of living in the south. "But I do remember she was an extremely attractive young lady from Harrogate, by the name of Rose, Rose Summerton." He savours the name as if he sucking on one of his favourite Werther's Original caramel sweets.

"How about a spread of quotes from celebs about their first loves?" suggests Hugo, saved, once more, by whatever guardian angel it is that looks after Old Etonians.

"Great idea," Knight, sits down again and reclines in his chair. "Get a good mix, some film stars, some fashiony people. What's that self-publicist woman called who built up some fashion empire mainly by selling sexy shoes and underwear? Katie something or other…"

"Katie Tomlinson," says Marina. "Her name is Katie Tomlinson."

"That's the one, stupid cow, always in the gossip columns. Can we get to her?"

Marina looks down at the ground. The last thing she wants to do is to contact Katie Tomlinson. And like all good editors Cameron Knight has spotted her reluctance.

He continues. "Well can we, Marina?"

Marina nods.

"Splendid, Marina you get hold of her and you features c**ts can find another ten or so, that'll work well. Now what have you c**ts on news got for me?"

As the vagina monologues moves to news, the rest of the staff traipse out of the office and back to their desks. Marina walks down the corridor and through the newsroom towards her spot alongside the features team.

"Here you go love, try not to spill it." Flora, one of the tea-ladies, has arrived with her morning cup of coffee. Her rotund sidekick Jo, who is never far behind, laughs but doesn't take her eyes off the knitting she always carries around with her. "Poor mite, give her a break," she snorts.

"Thanks," smiles Marina and takes the coffee. Much as she hates to be reminded of her clumsiness, Flora has a point, and it would be an annoying start to the day.

"Don't mind Little and Large," says Felicity, one of the less cutthroat features writers, once they're out of earshot. "They think they're incredibly amusing. But they're just not."

"Great nicknames, really suits them," laughs Marina, sitting down at her desk, then wonders briefly what her own nickname is. Maybe she hasn't been there long enough. At her last job she was known as Mourinho because of her love of Chelsea football club.

She pretends to stretch just to make sure no one is behind her before logging on to Facebook. Her profile picture comes up; there she is, smiling into the camera. Just below the profile picture is her husband's. 'Married to Mark Chadwick' reads the tagline. Below that her friends and the couple's friends, 210 of them. A few 'likes' mainly linked to Chelsea football club.

She scrolls down to her friends; she will need to talk to a few of them for her first love column. She has five or so favourite sources, friends who always have something interesting to say on a topic. Her closest friend Ulrika is among them – she can always rely on her for a fairly outrageous quote. She changes their names when it comes to quoting them, and they appear again and again as anonymous Rachels, or Sarahs, or whatever name happens to pop into her head.

Today though there is only one name that keeps popping into her head: Tom Stamford. She moves her cursor to the search facility and taps in his name. Her hands are shaking, which makes her feel like an idiot. She is a 33-year-old professional woman with a husband who works as a heart surgeon. She is no longer an impressionable teenager. How can a name send her into such a state? Or can she blame the large coffee she has managed to drink as opposed to spill?

Then she remembers that she has agreed to write an article about precisely this topic by 2pm and congratulates herself on creating such a good intro. As her first editor always told her: "Everything is copy."

She just hopes her husband won't mind.

"From the cradle to the coffin underwear comes first."
Bertolt Brecht

As Marina contemplates the best way to approach her, Katie Tomlinson is in her penthouse office overlooking Knightsbridge wondering how to seduce the opera singer she met last night. Katie is a workaholic and rarely allows herself any time off, apart from the odd yoga session. But when she really needs to relax, she finds seducing people the most satisfying way of doing it. Each conquest is like a boardroom coup, and good practice for her business too.

"It doesn't help," she tells Cherry, her personal assistant and closest thing she has to a confidante, "that he is married to the stunning soprano who sang the role of Zerlina. Although I could have sworn when he sang that romantic aria with her, you know the one where he seduces her, *La ci darem la mano*, that he was looking right at me."

Cherry doesn't know the aria; she will have to Google it later, like so many things her boss mentions, or people she dates, or places she holidays in. What she doesn't know is that most of the time, her boss does exactly the same thing.

"I was right in the middle of the front row, natch, so he could hardly miss me," she smiles, remembering the feeling of the music flowing over her, seducing her with every note, just like the young Zerlina on stage who falls for the scurrilous Don Giovanni. "Especially as I was wearing our latest off-the-shoulder blazing red full-length number and vertiginous stilettos. I swear I saw a glimmer of recognition when we were introduced at the post-performance cocktails. God, he's amazing, an opera singer with the body of an athlete, unbelievable. Apparently he works out with a personal trainer for three hours a day. I think it would be rude not to let him show me how fit he is."

"But married?" says Cherry.

Katie stands up and walks over to the window. Today her slim frame is clothed entirely in beige, her preferred colour for board meetings, not too ostentatious or too much in your face. But she always wears the best bright-red signature underwear to give her extra confidence. If she is floored by a tricky question by one of the dreary bean-counters, she just imagines how powerless he would be in the face of her red matching underwear and floors him right back.

"Thank you Cherry, for pointing that out. But as we both know, that hasn't stopped me in the past and it won't stop me in the future. Can you get the head of costumes at the Royal Opera House on the line for me? I want to talk about the contribution I can make to their next production. And don't forget I fly to Milan this afternoon after the board meeting. Arrange the car will you? – my favourite driver, not some moron who tries to tell me about his dreary life or discuss the latest football results. Anything else?"

"There's a reporter from *The Chronicle* who is trying to get hold of you for a quote about your first love. Can I tell her to call later?"

"Yes, have her call me at 12 sharp." She turns back to the window, signalling to Cherry that it's time for her to leave.

She gazes down towards the street below. What should she tell the reporter? That her first love was someone who barely even noticed her because he was in love with another girl? No, not good for the image. She needs something that will be useful to her, either to increase her glamorous aura, or to further the brand in some other way. The brand, KT, and she have become almost inseparable. She loves it like some women love their children. In fact she can't imagine loving anything more. She can barely remember what she was like before she became founder and CEO of her eponymous clothing and accessories empire, now valued at more than £20 million, sold in all the best places across the globe, and copied in the worst.

So she had some help from daddy to set it up, but apart from the starter capital the empire is her doing entirely. She worked every hour she had and then some, and she was good at it, better than most people imagined she would be, including daddy. Sometimes she still surprises herself by how good she is at her job. Her phone rings. She sees from the number that it's her global head of retail. Probably calling to complain about some dreary shop manager.

"Yes Grace?"

"Morning Katie, look we've got a situation here, Kate has been photographed in the Anna dress, you know the one with…"

"I know the one Grace, I personally oversaw its design, you don't name a dress after Anna Wintour without making sure it looks bloody good. So what's the issue?"

"It's selling out everywhere and our customers are

frantic to get their hands on it from New York to New Delhi. We need another 5,000 pieces and we need them now."

"So, get the factories to churn them out."

"There's not enough time, we need to outsource. I have someone who can handle it and have 5,000 to us by the end of the week but there's one small snag."

"Which I am assuming you are going to share with me?" says Katie.

"There is a suspicion that he uses child labour."

"Right."

"What do you think?"

"Don't use him. Are you fucking kidding? I can see the headline now; Child labour feeds fashion empire. No thanks. Find another way, but no children. And no animals either," she adds just to be on the safe side.

She slams the phone down. Honestly, stealing someone's husband may be one thing, but using child labour? Quite apart from the danger of adverse publicity, it makes Katie Thomas feel extremely uncomfortable, and that's not a feeling she is used to.

Now, back to the first love interview. Should she say something cheesy like 'my first love was clothes'? No, she needs something sexier, something more in keeping with KT.

She sits down and takes a sip of her ginger and apple smoothie. Her first love, how many years ago was that? Fifteen? She remembers the first time she saw him, in that pizzeria on the King's Road. It seems like a different life, like she was a different person. In a way she was. But look at her now: for all her fame and fortune, she is still single. *Single*.

She hates that word even more than she hates chatty drivers. She just can't bear to hear it. Unattached is better – it makes it sound like a choice you have made, not a situation you have ended up in because no one has asked you to marry them. But single is almost a synonym of loser, and it has the same connotations. Strange that after all these years of so-called equality a single man manages to sound sexy, but a single woman, at least over the age of thirty, still sounds desperate and lonely.

Is that what she is? She looks around her office; redecorated for the tenth time in as many years to keep up with trends and give her a new landscape to live in. How can she possibly be either with everything she has? She thinks back fifteen years. Who else from that crowd she used to hang out with goes to the *Vanity Fair* Oscar party? Who else has slept with more film stars and pop stars than they can remember? She doesn't even know what happened to them, apart from Marina, whose byline she sees sometimes in the papers while she is looking for more interesting stories about herself.

She is about to be thirty-three. If she is ever going to produce an heir to her empire she has to get on with it. Maybe she has been too picky? Perhaps she should just settle for something that feels good, and not hold out for great. Maybe this true love thing is all a myth, or at least once you hit thirty it is. She is running out of time. "What's that noise," her brother teased her last time they met. "Tick tock, tick tock, it's your biological clock."

If she were a business, her stock would be going down. "It's time to act, fast," she tells herself sternly. "Before I fall out of the FTSE 100."

Katie sees her phone blinking.

"Yes?"

"Marina Shaw from *The Chronicle*," says Cherry.

She catches her breath. Talk about a blast from the past. Or rather a chill wind from the past. "Put her through."

There is a moment's silence. Katie quickly decides she is in the driving seat here. After all they want something from her, and why should she be intimidated by Marina?

"Marina…long time no speak. How are you?"

"Fine thanks, how are you?"

"Great. We really must catch up. Do you see anyone else

from the old days? Whatever happened to Mark and Tom," she asks, trying to sound casual. "And what about Ollie?"

"I'm not sure about Tom, or Ollie," says Marina. "But I'm married to Mark."

Now it's Katie's turn to be silent. "Wow, well congratulations, how amazing. I always thought you were mad about Tom."

Marina doesn't speak.

"What can I do for you?" Katie continues.

"We're after a quote about your first love, who he was, what he meant to you and how you feel about him now," Marina explains.

Katie Tomlinson takes a deep breath. Marina is the last person on earth she would ever tell the truth to. "Happy to help. But I need to have final say on the image you use, is that agreed?"

"I don't deal with images," says Marina. "Just the words…"

Katie interrupts her. "Just ask the picture editor Kevin to call me, he knows me."

"OK, will do." Marina is tense. If it weren't for the fact that she can see Cameron Knight's reaction if she comes away empty-handed she would tell Katie to sort her own fucking images out. Typical of Katie, still bossing everyone about.

"So here's my quote. 'I don't have a first love story to tell you, because I have never been in love. I have yearned for love, searched for love and longed to find that special person, but so far, I have failed. I implore someone out there to rescue me from my solitude and come and sweep me off my feet.' OK with that?"

"Perfect," says Marina. She knows the game, this is utter tosh, but Katie will be using it to get publicity. "Thank you very much."

"Thank you," says Katie. "And say hi to Mark." She hangs up. Her own words still ringing in her ears. "Say hi to Mark." She had sounded oh so casual. But Katie was an expert actress, her talent honed on the stage of England's most exclusive girls' boarding school. There are many things she has wanted to say to Mark for a great number of years, and "hi" is not one of them. Especially not via his wife. She wonders what Marina looks like nowadays, she was always quite plump. Someone more generous might call her voluptuous. Katie wanders over to the window and gazes at her view. The Russian opera singer is already forgotten, her sights now set on someone else's husband.

Her buzzer sounds and Cherry announces the arrival of the car. Time to fly to Milan and prepare for the media frenzy when she gets home tomorrow to the first love story. Some people like nothing better than their family meeting them at the airport. Katie Tomlinson's idea of a good homecoming is hundreds of flashbulbs and a media circus. Now, what to wear….?

3

*"Love is the state in which man sees things most
widely different from what they are."*
Friedrich Nietzsche

Flashback, New Year's Eve, 1995

There were five of them sitting in the middle of the road
playing cards. It was 3 am so there wasn't really any traffic
on Ladbroke Grove. Not that they were worried about
being run over. They were young, between eighteen and
twenty years old, and oblivious to danger. Added to
which they had each taken a tab of Ecstasy, which made
them totally invincible. Or so they thought.

On top of this they had taken industrial amounts of
nutmeg, because Tom Stamford, a 20-year-old university
drop-out with thick jet-black hair and all the combined
charm of his Irish ancestors, had told them it would give
them an additional high.

"It's totally wicked," he said, mixing a whole jar of
Schwarz grated nutmeg with hot milk in his small

basement kitchen. "We're going to get totally wired. Manic."

The gang agreed to try it, partly because anything Tom said went, but also because it was a lot cheaper than real drugs.

There was only one member of the gang who wasn't in Notting Hill that night to get wired. Marina was there because she was in love with Tom. And Tom loved drugs more than anything, so if she took some, she reasoned, he might love her too. Or at least notice her.

It seemed ridiculous even to her teenage mind that she had been in love with Tom for two years already, and that almost nothing had happened between them. The whole situation made her feel stupid. But every time she made up her mind to move on, he would give her hope. He would do something, such as tell her she looked lovely, or even have sex with her, as he had three times, the first on her birthday last year.

It wasn't the earth-moving experience Marina had expected it to be. She was so nervous she could barely breathe, and Tom was disengaged, like he wanted to be somewhere else. But afterwards she rationalised the sex as progress, of a kind. The other two times had been better, but still not the sublime experience she had built it up to be, mainly because she was too nervous to relax.

Marina was not the only member of the gang who was in love with Tom. There was Ollie as well. Not in a homosexual way, but in just about every other way. He worshipped Tom; for Ollie, Tom was like a god. They were best friends, but it was hardly a balanced friendship. Ollie just did whatever made Tom happy and Tom rewarded him by hanging out with him.

"Let's try another game," suggested Katie, pulling her long blonde hair into a ponytail, which she tied with the scrunchie she kept around her wrist. "We're all too wired for poker."

Everyone agreed. The cards were dealt. Marina watched them being placed on the tarmac. She could control the speed at which they moved, which was part of the reason she wasn't worried about any cars running them over. It was as if her brain had turned into a video camera and she could replay the action in slow motion, or speed things up at will. She didn't much like the sensation, although it did give her a certain power.

"Snap!" shouted Katie and Tom, their eyes meeting, flirting, smiley. Marina saw all this in slow motion and wished she hadn't. She knew this would happen. Before Katie had been invited to their little drug-taking party, she was the only girl. Now she had to compete with Katie's pretty face, long hair and impossibly flat stomach. She and Katie didn't get on. Marina couldn't help it. She liked most people, but there was something about Katie that irritated her. She had asked herself the obvious question of whether it was because Katie was thinner and richer than her. And that might have had something to do with it. But it wasn't just that. There were plenty of people who were thinner and richer than Marina, and she didn't dislike all of them.

Tonight Katie was wearing 501s with a thin leather belt and a white cropped t-shirt, so her trimness was doubly obvious. Tom was clearly impressed. He probably imagined snorting coke off the flat surface of her stomach.

"Snap!" yelled Mark. "Marina – snap, wake up."

She had been staring at a weeping willow moving in the wind, its branches like the arms of a ballerina, graceful and elongated. She could almost hear the music to Tchaikovsky's *'Swan Lake'* as she watched it. She hadn't been paying attention to the game.

Mark smiled at her. No, he REALLY smiled at her. She smiled back but tried not to look encouraging. She didn't want to be a tease; there was nothing worse, and she was too honest for that. She had suspected he might like her for some time. The drugs had given her clarity. It was as if she could see the truth and this was it: Tom once again had failed to notice her, despite the £10 tab of Ecstasy and the mug of disgusting nutmeg-milk she had forced down her throat as if her life depended on it. He had, however, noticed Katie with her concave stomach and expensive loafers.

Mark was clearly keen on her, but this was no consolation for Marina. Mark was not Tom. Mark was blond and skinny and intense. He was eighteen years old and had just left school. He wanted to study medicine and would soon hear if he'd got in to university. This was his last summer of freedom. He was not a habitual drug taker, but doing ecstasy in Notting Hill Gate was another thing to tick off the list of experiences to have. Another thing to get out of his system before he grew up and settled down, like losing his virginity and opening a bank account.

Katie was not really bothered about drugs either. In fact, life didn't really bother her, nothing much vexed or worried her, a bit like Jane Austen's *Emma*, her mother always said. She knew she would always be all right. But she was vaguely amused by Tom's attention and would probably sleep with him, simply because she could, much in the same way that she would buy a designer handbag she didn't need. Mark interested her more, at least he had some ambition.

"It's getting light," said Ollie. "Let's go inside."

Dawn was to be avoided at all costs. They walked back into Tom's basement flat and drew all the curtains to keep the day out. Marina tried to anticipate where Tom would sit and pick a spot close to it. But Tom didn't sit, Tom was wired. He put on a record. It was a love song.

"Oh I can't forget this evening, and your face as you were leaving," sang Harry Nilsson. Tom sang with him, serenading them each in turn. Ollie reciprocated and sang with him, swaying around the room in vague time to the song. Even serenading Nilsson Tom managed to look cool. Ollie did not.

Mark laughed nervously when Tom approached him, Katie, who was sitting next to him, looked serene. When it was her turn Marina felt all the discomfort a teenager feels when exposed. If she could see the truth so clearly that night, she was sure everyone else could.

"I can't live," sang Tom, standing right in front of her, moving his hips slowly, his brown eyes focused on her face in mock intensity "if living is without you."

She perched on the edge of the sofa, twiddling her

pink scarf and tried to look nonchalant; to pretend that she didn't want more than anything for him to mean what he was singing. That for her those words were completely true. She was also holding her stomach in, which made breathing difficult.

The song ended.

"My turn," said Ollie, jumping up and swapping Nilsson for Pink Floyd's *Dark Side of the Moon*. For a few minutes everyone just sat and internalized the music, feeling every beat and every word with extraordinary intensity.

No one spoke and no one except Marina noticed Tom leave the room. All she worried about was that Katie would follow him and they would not come back. Katie didn't move from her spot next to Mark and Tom didn't come back. Had they agreed to wait for a bit? Was he waiting for her in his bedroom?

"Hey," said Mark, walking towards her. "You OK?"

"Fine, thanks," she smiled, half-wishing he would leave her alone, but touched that he cared.

"How are you enjoying the trip?"

Tom was back, standing in front of her, grinning, and holding a gun to her head.

She knew what happened next because her filming

mind slowed it all down. Mark rushed at Tom, grabbing his arm and yelling. The gun went off and a bullet hit Ollie in the stomach. He looked surprised and hurt, his expression saying "Why did you shoot me? All I've ever done is love you," as he fell over and the blood slowly trickled on to the cream carpet.

"Fucking hell man, I was just kidding, I wasn't going to shoot, you stupid fucker," Tom was yelling. "I didn't even think it was loaded."

Mark was trying to stop Ollie bleeding but Ollie was slowly turning white.

Katie walked over to the telephone. Marina couldn't hear what she was saying but assumed she was calling an ambulance, followed by Daddy, or possibly Daddy's lawyer. Pink Floyd played on. "I'll see you on the dark side of the moon" they sang.

Everyone else was on real time. Only Marina had the luxury of slow motion.

Less than an hour later Marina was in a police cell with Katie. Marina can't think of anywhere she'd less like to be. An officer was talking to them and pacing the cell. It looked a bit like a sauna but made of concrete instead of wood.

"There's a boy in hospital who will probably be dead

before long and a stash of cocaine in my top drawer, found at the home of Tom Stamford, a convicted druggie. We want some answers. What the hell were you fuckers up to and who shot the boy?"

"Is my lawyer here yet?" Katie demanded.

"Yes, and your father. But no one is getting out of this cell until I have a confession. And if no one owns up, I'm charging Mr Stamford with attempted murder and possession of drugs and a firearm. He could go down for twenty years, more if the boy dies," he said, and left the cell.

For a few minutes they were quiet, then Katie spoke. "It's up to us, if one of us owns up to it we can say it was an accident, my lawyer will secure the absolute minimum sentence, I'm sure we could even avoid prison. They'll look upon us favourably, but they'll take Tom to the cleaners. He already has previous convictions for drugs, his whole life will be ruined, and by the time he gets out he'll be an old man."

She was sitting on a concrete bench lining one wall; her petite frame made the cell seem even more austere and uninviting. "We need to do something," she continued. Marina could almost hear her brain working. Suddenly she stood up. "But what about the gun?" she asked. "His fingerprints are on it."

"No they're not," said Marina. "I wiped them off with my scarf."

The two girls looked at each other and although neither of them spoke, the decision was made.

❧ 4 ❧

"There are no ugly women, just lazy women."
Coco Chanel

Marina is so busy counting her pelvic floor squeezes that she almost loses track of the conversation, or rather the monologue of the man sitting next to her. He is talking about commuting. He tells Marina that he is an anesthetist at the hospital Mark works at. Maybe he won't notice if I fall asleep, she thinks. Must be a bit of an occupational hazard.

If there were a premier league of dinner party topics, Marina has always maintained, commuting would be number one, closely followed by childcare and then possibly the weather. Why does anyone bother having dinner parties, she often wonders, if that's all they talk about?

They should have said no, but it is impossible to say no to Mark's boss, especially as Charles Parton is one of

Mark's best friends. As a close friend, he doesn't impose too many dinner parties on them, but they get invited once every three months or so to lower the average age of the guests or when the Partons have a last-minute cancellation. Marina often feels these evenings are stolen evenings, as with so many dinner parties. At least if you stay home you know you won't be bored; there are countless books, a comfy sofa, *Downton Abbey* or some football and white wine in the fridge. At a dinner party you are at the mercy of your hosts, who can expose you to any kind of bore and often inedible food to be eaten at a time of day when any self-respecting digestive system has closed down. And you can't even decide when to go home – if dinner is still going on at midnight, then so are you.

Marina hates wasting time, so here she is, trying not to fritter away the whole evening by improving her pelvic floor muscles with intermittent squeezes as her fellow guests discuss the pros and cons of the District Line.

Someone mentions what they read on their daily commute. Most of them of course read *The Guardian*. Possibly *The Economist*, or the latest Ian McEwan novel. Marina can feel what's coming next. She has the same dread she used to get at school when the teacher would read out her name in the register. For some reason her fellow pupils picked on her name to make up endless little rhymes such as 'Marina Shaw is a bore' or 'Marina Shaw what a chore', so every time her name was read out giggles were stifled all over the classroom.

"Marina, what's your column about tomorrow?" the voice of Victoria Parton rings out across the table. An heiress as well as the wife of the chief surgeon at St Thomas's Hospital, she is, as usual, wearing Chanel and covered in diamonds. Somehow neither of them ever seems to make her very happy; "glittering and glowering" is how Marina describes her.

This evening though, she is quite cheerful, or maybe her face has just been Botoxed into a cheerful expression. Never leave to nature what you have some control over is Victoria Parton's motto.

"I never read *The Chronicle*," she says. Oh goodie, thinks Marina, downing her red wine, the ritual humiliation of working for the country's top tabloid is about to begin. "Absolutely dreadful rag. But I do read your column, you have some great insights."

"Oh, do you work for *The Chronicle*?" asks her District Line commuting neighbour. "I'd better watch what I say," he laughs at his own wit.

Every time she hears that joke, Marina is tempted to respond, "No one would be interested in what you have to say with the possible exception of your mother." Or in this case the CEO of London Underground. But as usual she stops herself and instead responds to her hostess's question.

"It's all about first love," she explains. "Pegged to Will and Kate's engagement."

There is a collective 'oooh' around the table. Finally the District Line has lost its allure.

"Such a fascinating topic," says Victoria, taking a sip of wine. "So, what are we going to discover?"

"Well, there is a theory that we imprint on our first loves, that's why the feeling never dies. We are like Konrad Lorenz's geese," says Marina. "We follow our first love around blindly like a baby goose."

"Is that why you're still following me around?" says Charles Parton, looking at his wife. Marina has always rather liked him because he reminds her of Hugh Laurie as Dr House, all tall and angular, with a wry sense of humour and cut-glass accent. His wife looks at him indulgently.

"Have you written about your first love?" Mark asks her.

"Yes," she nods. She was going to tell him later, warn him really, but she didn't want it to seem like a big deal. She never normally tells him what is going in her column. Why would she today?

"Surely it was you?" says Victoria, glowering as far as her forehead will allow in Marina's direction. She doesn't like many people, but she is extremely fond of Mark.

"No, it was a boy called Tom," Mark replies. "A rogue, a very good-looking rogue, who was part of a gang we used to hang out with. I knew Marina at the time, but she only had eyes for Tom. I think in part because his surname was Stamford, like Stamford Bridge."

"I don't believe it," says Victoria with indignation. "Marina, how could you ignore this gorgeous young man?"

"She was a silly goose," says Mark before she has a chance to answer. There is collective laughter. Marina pretends to join in but actually feels like kicking someone. Mainly her husband.

"Happily at university I was able to take her mind off Tom," adds Mark, smiling across the table at her.

Marina wonders briefly how successful he would have been if Tom had decided to follow a life in academia as opposed to one of dissolution. Or if Mark had got into Oxford and not had to settle for Bristol.

It wasn't as if she went for second best with Mark, and after a year of being good friends in Bristol she finally realised that he was the man for her. But there was no doubt that back in those days whenever Tom was in a room, every other man blended into an insignificant background.

"Whatever happened to the rogue?" asks Victoria.

"The last we heard was almost fifteen years ago. He was very interested in recreational drugs and went off to Italy. We don't really know what happened to him, do we?" Mark responds.

"No," says Marina. "No idea." She doesn't mention that she spent most of the afternoon on Google and Facebook, seeing exactly what did happen to Tom Stamford.

In the taxi on the way home Mark takes her hand and kisses it.

"How was your end of the table?" he asks.

"Quite dull, we talked about commuting for most of the evening. But at least I only dropped a fork this time and not my entire plate."

"That's progress," he laughs, before adding. "So I guess your pelvic floor is in good shape?"

"You know me too well," she smiles.

"But seriously, it's great that you're exercising it."

Marina looks at him. "Why exactly?"

"Well, you know, getting it ready for a baby."

Marina stiffens. She has begun to lose count of how

many times they have had this conversation.

"Mark," she sighs. "You know bloody well I'm really not sure I'm ready, even if my pelvic floor is."

"I don't mean we have to go for it this minute."

"Oh the cabbie will be relieved," she snaps.

"Very amusing. But I have been thinking about it more and more recently. It would be great if we are still relatively young when they're growing up, and if we start thinking about it now then we have a chance."

"A chance of what? Total and utter chaos? Not to mention the expense. And to be honest, after my crap childhood, I'm not sure I want to inflict it on anyone else."

"I know, I know all that. And you think we might regret it. I know all your arguments."

"My view is: if it 'ain't broke then don't fix it'. Having a child is something you can't undo. What if it ruins our lives? Our relationship? Who's going to get up in the middle of the night to feed it when we're both working? And more importantly, who will look after it when there's a Chelsea game on TV?"

Mark laughs. "Seriously though Mina, how many people do you know who say having children has ruined their lives?"

Marina thinks for a moment. "No one. But there's

always a first."

Mark sighs and takes her hand. He kisses it gently.

"I'm not saying we need to decide now, but please, Mina, just think about it."

Marina can feel a column coming on. How many women try to convince their husbands NOT to have children?

But she just doesn't want to, she never did. Added to which, now she has just got her dream job and needs to focus on that. Even if a lot of their snootier friends look down on the paper, it is still read by almost two million people a day and she loves the fact that she can reach such a wide audience. And she gets paid an enormous salary to voice her opinion.

"I know we've got time," Mark continues. "You're only thirty-three, but I don't think it gets any easier with age. And you don't even know if you can get pregnant."

She doesn't respond. Instead she looks out of the window at the rain pelting down outside. She loves the sound of the rain falling on the taxi roof. It's such a London sound; you really couldn't be anywhere else in the world.

Mark is wrong. Those words echo something an angry NHS nurse said to her as she sat in a cold consultation room in 1996, having just turned nineteen. As

Marina wept, she had snapped; "At least you know you can get pregnant. There are plenty of women out there who can't, you selfish young lady."

She hates to be reminded of it, especially when the whole conversation has left her feeling uncomfortable. She feels claustrophobic and slightly panicked, as if she can't breathe, a little like she used to when her mother forced her to play with a child she didn't know. The feeling of claustrophobia is not helped by Mark putting his arm around her and drawing her closer.

"Don't be stressed darling," he says, kissing her head. "Let's talk about it another time."

Marina nods and tries to relax. She puts her head on Mark's shoulder and breathes in the smell of him, lime aftershave mixed with some residual hospital smells and body odour that is never unpleasant. He must be the only man she has ever met whose feet don't smell. That would definitely be on a list of his top attributes, along with intelligence, humour, great cheekbones, slim legs and perfect surgeon's hands. All are things that she still loves but somehow can't seem to get excited about any more.

He strokes her hair and kisses her forehead.

"I could check out your pelvic floor muscles for you when we get home if you like," he whispers.

"Thanks for the offer," she smiles. "I'm quite tired though."

It's only half a lie.

5

"I wouldn't recommend sex, drugs or insanity for
everyone, but they've always worked for me."
Hunter S Thompson

Out of the corner of his eye he can just make out the upper wall of the Coliseum. He is lying on the bench that Audrey Hepburn collapses on in the film *Roman Holiday*. He knows this because he has spent hours watching old black and white films. Not that he can remember every detail or even every plot. But he does remember the bench.

He closes first one eye and then the other, so the view of the monument changes. What a great energy-saving tip – no need to move one's body, just change your vista with a blink of an eye.

It is getting light and the traffic is increasing. Soon he will probably be moved on by the police. They don't like commuters being exposed to Rome's underbelly, to the down and outs, the ugly side of the eternal city. He closes both eyes and tries to focus on the day ahead. He needs to earn some money; he needs to make things up with Carla, but most of all he needs to have a shower. He has been in these clothes for three days now, and they weren't even that clean when he put them on.

He must fall asleep because he is woken up by the clatter of heels on the pavement. The sun is shining and Rome is awake. He sits up and adjusts his dishevelled shirt. "Asleep on a park bench," he can hear his mother's voice. "The shame of it. How did you sink so low?"

It's a fair question. And one to which he doesn't really have an answer. He is now thirty-five years old. A ridiculous age to be a no-hoper. Except he never really saw himself as a loser – he was having fun, lots of fun. But then the years just raced away in a blur of drugs, girls and classic films and suddenly he is in his mid-thirties. Not a great age to be sleeping on park benches with no money in your pocket and no home to go to. You can get away with it as a floppy-haired boy in your early twenties, when everyone thinks it's just a phase that you will grow out of. But now? When does a phase turn into a lifestyle?

He runs his fingers through his hair. At least he still has that. There are plenty of old school-friends who will be both bald and fat by now. But they probably have families and lawns to mow every weekend, as well as jobs and hobbies and all the other things that go with a life that isn't dominated by addiction.

At least drug addicts don't get fat, he says to himself. Look on the bright side. But what exactly do they get?

"Dead mainly," he answers out loud. And it is just this sort of moment of lucidity that sends Ollie over to his dealer's house every day to beg for more credit.

"First love never dies," Mark reads out over the breakfast table. "Here I am, palms sweating as I look up my first love on Facebook. I haven't seen him for almost fifteen years, but the thought of him…"

"OK, OK, I know what I wrote," says Marina, trying to put her mascara on and eat some of her crunchy-nut cornflakes before they go totally soggy. "It's a job Mark. I warned you this would happen with a personal column, it's inevitable."

"But is that really how you feel?" he asks looking up from behind the paper rather shyly. She is relieved, she had expected him to be angry, even though she keeps explaining to him it's just a job, which, unlike most people's jobs, involves telling more than two million readers about her personal life. There are limits of course, and more often than not she follows the first rule of journalism: simplify and exaggerate. But in all her columns there is some truth, which Mark is too clever not to understand. Although this is precisely the reason they don't discuss them before the paper goes to press. Mark would find too much to object to and it would stifle her writing.

"No, well, I mean of course I still have some feelings for him, which is the whole first love phenomena thing, and of course nothing to do with him as a person. I doubt I would even recognise him in the street. What I say in the article, if you read on, is that first love is an illusion, a memory that was never tainted, an unattainable ideal."

Mark spreads some marmalade on his toast with a surgeon's precision. It was one of the things Marina used to love about him – how precisely he did everything, whether it was cutting an onion or an artery. She watches him insert the knife into the middle of the bread to clean it. Another thing she used to find charming, but now it just annoys her. It is something she longs to write about but doesn't quite dare. The transformation of lust to love mingled with irritation and occasionally on very bad days a feeling akin to some kind of loathing.

Is this how everyone's marriage is? Surely not. It must be possible to live happily ever after. Otherwise why would anyone bother trying? How come it had happened so quickly with them? They had only been married for five years, even if they had been together on and off since their early twenties. And they had known each other for much longer. Had they simply been together too long? Did he feel the same way? Are there things about her that make him want to reach for the scissors and stab her? Or even his scalpel?

Mark is reading the paper again, thankfully having moved on from her column to the sports pages. She looks at him. She knows every gesture, every intonation, every mood he has. She can almost see what he is thinking from his body language. They have grown up together, almost like siblings. He has been her closest friend for so many years, as well as her boyfriend, then husband and, if he has his way, father of her children.

"Must dash," she says, kissing him on the top of his blond head. "We're not going out tonight are we?"

"No," he smiles. "We can stay in and chill and watch the football. I'll put some wine in the fridge."

"Heavenly," says Marina, grabbing her coat and bag and walking out of the door.

On the Tube on her way to work, Marina does her usual glance around to see who is reading *The Chronicle*. Only one lucky winner this morning. There it is – a huge picture of Katie Tomlinson on the strip on top of the front page and the headline "Will you be my first love?" underneath it.

The reader has yet to get to Marina's column. Not that she would recognise her, at least not from her picture. A well-known anti-ageing trick columnists use is to have a photograph of themselves in the paper that is at least ten years old. There are male writers at *The Chronicle* who are bald as coots but have more hair than a young Bob Dylan in their portraits, and one woman who has been a columnist for more than thirty years but still doesn't look a day over eighteen.

She shuffles out of the Tube with the other commuters, who move en masse like a herd of dumb animals, only half-aware of their surroundings, hands dug into pockets, arms clutching handbags, going through the same routine day in, day out. Ah, the joy of commuting – and then some people want to talk about it all evening as well.

It is a short walk from the Tube to the offices of *The Chronicle*. The building stands out among the other Victorian stone ones on the street, with its glass façade through which one can see long escalators leading up to the newsroom and the large seating area with a café that makes up the first floor, where meetings take place that determine careers, headlines and who is sleeping with whom, both within the building and in the celebrity world that dominates the pages of the paper.

As she walks towards her desk she can hear Les Misérables being yelled at in the middle of the newsroom floor by Cameron Knight. Only 9.30am and already a double-c***ing. Poor man. The newsroom at least is relatively empty. Most people work until after 9.30pm when the paper 'goes to bed', so they don't tend to come in before 10 o'clock. She is looking forward to seeing Hugo today, they have much to discuss about the Chelsea game tonight and the team in general. He was the first person to befriend her when she joined the paper, he knew she was a Chelsea fan from columns he had read, so they had that in common. He even blue-toothed her his Chelsea BlackBerry ringtone. The sort of gesture that can engender boundless loyalty from a fellow fan.

She sits down at her desk and turns on her computer. A picture of Mark and her on a beach in Wales last summer comes up as the machine prepares itself for the day's action.

He has been talking about children more and more recently. She wishes she could change her mind, if only to make him happy, but the whole thought of it terrifies her.

She just doesn't want to do it. Not only because she has no maternal desire herself, but because she doesn't like what it does to most of the friends she has who have had them.

Part of her envies women who find their children endlessly fascinating and can talk about nothing else – life must be so simple. But she is never going to be one of them, and will probably even make an effort to avoid them. In fact, she feels another column coming on.

As people start arriving, there is a real buzz this morning in the newsroom, with plenty of talk about the Katie Tomlinson scoop, even if everyone knows it that it was more of a plant. Still, it will annoy the competition and that's the main thing.

"So you've no idea where he is then?" Millie from features is at her desk nursing a large latte.

"Who?"

"Tim, if indeed that is his name, your first love?"

Marina smiles. "No, no idea. Who was your first love?" she says, changing the subject quickly.

Millie laughs. "If you mean 'first fumble behind the bike shed at Lanark Comp', then it was a boy called George Flynn. He had red hair and sweaty palms – enough to put you off sex for life."

"Did someone mention sexy?" says a voice from the

door. "I can only assume you're talking about me." Hugo Willoughby strides across the room towards them, wearing his trademark pink shirt and beige chinos. It's a uniform shared by thousands of men like him, adopted not really to impress but because it is safe. Blazing exterior self-confidence is another part of the uniform, along with hidden interior doubts.

Millie turns to greet him. "Yes Hugo, we were talking about bad sex, something you probably know all about."

Hugo, as always, is totally unfazed. "My dear Millie, bad sex might be something you get up to north of the border, but down here it's all about total and utter pleasure. Now come along, we need to out-scoop ourselves tomorrow. What have you got up your rather substandard nylon sleeve today?"

"Wouldn't you like to know?" says Millie laughing and following him to their desks on the other side of Marina's table.

Marina smiles as they walk away. Hugo always makes her smile; she misses him when he's not in the office. She envies his confidence, and often wishes he could transfer a dose of it to her. She sometimes wonders what she might have achieved had she been more out-going and sure of herself.

She opens her inbox. As always on the day the column

comes out, there is more mail than usual. Some readers agree with her, some are angry; the more abusive ones don't get forwarded by the letters desk. Marina tries to answer them all, and tries to make them all personal. Sometimes she gets emails back saying 'I didn't expect you to respond', which makes her smile and wonder why they bother to write at all. There is an email from Ulrika, her best friend, asking if they are still on for lunch. "Longing to hear if the rogue has written to you saying it was all a huge mistake and he wants you desperately," she writes.

Marina replies that they're on for lunch but there is no word from the rogue, at least not yet. A tiny part of her, well actually not that tiny, is disappointed. She wondered if he might see the article and try to contact her. For some reason she hoped he would. She might admit that to herself, but only just, and she certainly won't be sharing it with two million readers, or even her most fervent reader, her husband.

"I'm glad you're here," says Carla, as she opens the door. "Come in."

Ollie walks in, apologizing for his behaviour over the past... how many days was it? Three, maybe four, maybe more.

"I'm going to change," he says, sitting down on the red sofa in her studio that doubles as a bed. "I really am."

"I know you are," says Carla, leaning over to stroke his cheek and looking deep into his eyes.

He's not sure how she can be so confident, but he is grateful that she is.

He has been to see his best friend, his only friend really, unless you can count drug dealers among your friends. He has showered, washed his hair and borrowed some clothes. He has invested in just enough stuff to make him function, to make him seem normal, to stop the shakes and the sweating. He feels good, this is good, Carla is important to him; he can't believe she sticks with him. She is beautiful, clever, and above all Italian, a fact that makes a woman attractive in itself. He has lived in Italy since the accident fifteen years ago, and is still stunned on a daily basis by the women there.

Ollie met Carla when she walked into the bar he was working at in a side-street off the Piazza Navona. It was one of the jobs he'd managed to hold down for the longest – almost two years. He was never going to get promoted but it was a steady income and the hours suited him – a late enough start to sleep off the excesses of the night before, finishing just after midnight so there was plenty of time to party. She had sat at the bar and ordered a glass of Pinot Grigio; he had given her a light for her cigarette and they started talking. She had the most incredible green eyes and thick black hair. She had stayed at the bar all evening and they had spent the night together getting high and talking. Sex happened at about six in the morning.

"So you could hardly say I slept with you on the first date," she had joked. He wasn't that worried about the etiquette; he was in love.

That was almost a year ago, and now he is sitting in her apartment with an uncomfortable feeling there is something going on. She looks like a woman who is about to tell him it's over.

"I need to talk to you, *caro*," she says in her soft Italian accent. He looks at her. She is smiling, so maybe she's not about to finish with him. But why isn't she sitting down?

"There's someone here to see you," she begins. He doesn't like the vaguely guilty look on her face. Should he run? Has she called the police? Why would she do that?

He stands up and heads for the door. "Don't," Carla says calmly. "There's no point."

He opens the door to flee and runs straight into his mother. He thinks briefly about bulldozing through her but he was never that brave. Added to which, his brother has suddenly appeared as if by magic, along with his best friend.

"It's over, darling," says his mother. "We've come to take you home."

He pretends to find it funny. "Why? There's nothing wrong with me, is there Carla?"

He turns around for support but she's gone.

"Come on mate," says his brother Jack, taking him by the arm. His mother and Tom are behind him. "The game's up, no one wants to see you destroy yourself any more, it's time to come home."

The four of them leave Carla's apartment and go down to the car that is waiting to take them to the airport. Carla cries as she watches them go from the window.

He doesn't really register the journey, doesn't speak, he feels like he is watching himself on a cinema screen. Who is this man in the car? And where are they taking him?

Check-in happens in a daze and they are at passport control.

"Bye then," says Tom. "Good luck, I'll come to London to see you soon. Don't be angry. I did it because I couldn't let you go on."

He looks at him but finds it hard to talk. Part of him is ashamed that his best friend and girlfriend are in cohorts with his mother to save him from himself. What kind of a loser is he?

"Thanks sweetheart, for all your help, he'll be fine,"

says his mother, hugging Tom goodbye. "Oh, and I picked up *The Chronicle* this morning on the flight. There's an article about first love written by that girl Marina you all used to know. She's going on about some man called Tim, but I think it's you, Tom. Wasn't it you she was always so mad about?"

✨ *6* ✨

"A man who has not been in Italy is always conscious of an inferiority."
Samuel Johnson

Tom Stamford walks slowly towards the train station to catch the Leonardo Express back to town. Life without Ollie in Rome will be strange; they arrived here practically at the same time all those years ago to escape the repercussions of the shooting, as well as the nagging expectations of those at home to get a job and stop acting like life was there to be inhaled. But things had got out of hand.

Tom always felt partly responsible for Ollie's downward spiral into drugs. His best friend had only started taking drugs because he did, but then he seemed to find it impossible to stop. The accident had made things much worse. Tom, after a year or so of playing around in Rome, had a wake-up call when he was arrested and badly beaten up in a Rome police cell. He realised he could do better with his life and stopped immediately. He spent the money he had left from the sale of his London flat and checked himself into rehab for a month. Shortly afterwards he got a proper job and an apartment and the other things that go with being a grown-up. Ollie stayed high.

Tom had hoped that meeting Carla would change Ollie, and it did to a certain extent, but finally the drugs seemed to have much more pull than even a hot Italian primary school teacher with breasts like two over-sized buffalo mozzarellas.

Maybe that was Tom's saving grace; that he had always found women more addictive than drugs. Maybe his love of women and desire to seduce them was an addiction of another kind, but at least it didn't kill you.

He finds a window seat and opens the newspaper Ollie's mother thrust into his hands. He rarely reads the English papers any more. Not that he reads the Italian ones either; he keeps up with the news online. He flicks impatiently to the article he is looking for. He recognises Marina's picture before he sees the headline. The curly black hair and dark-brown intelligent eyes. She is half-smiling, looking straight at the camera, straight at him.

He starts to read:

"First love never dies. As William and Kate finally bow to the inevitable, here I am, palms sweating as I look up my first love on Facebook. I haven't seen him for almost fifteen years, but the thought of him still makes me nervous.

I remember the first time I met Tim. It was in Pucci Pizza on the King's Road. The restaurant doesn't exist any more, but our relationship does, at least it does to me. After more than a decade of no contact, I am still wondering what he's up to, where he is, and if he ever, even just fleetingly, thinks about me.

Rewind fifteen years and I was a shy, scared seventeen year old being introduced to the most handsome man I had ever seen. He stood by the bar, smoking and grinning, with dark floppy hair and deep brown eyes. I fell deeply in love. Instantly. Irrevocably.

Sadly I didn't have the same effect on Tim. Although my utter infatuation was to last for another four years until I fell in love with my husband, the only man who could eclipse my first love, Tim never fell for me.

No, our relationship basically consisted of me following him around like an adoring puppy and him more or less ignoring me. We did end up in bed together a few times. It was a bit of a disaster. I was so nervous I almost fainted and he was slightly disinterested. He also once told me that if he ever had to get married, he would marry "someone like you". Not much of a compliment. But enough to keep a desperate teenager hooked.

Despite, or maybe in part because of his indifference to me on a romantic level, I just fell more deeply for him. We were friends and every time we laughed together or went to a party or hung out there was hope. I even tried to make him jealous once by parading a boyfriend in front of him.

"Is that your boyfriend?" he grinned rather conde-scendingly, pointing at him. He knew he still had me.

We lost touch after a rather disastrous New Year's Eve fifteen years ago, the details of which I will save for another time. I went off to university and in my last year I started going out with my husband, who finally over-shadowed Tim.

But still the power of his memory on me is astounding, ridiculous really. Why does he still mean anything at all to me?

There is a theory that we imprint on our first loves, rather like Konrad Lorenz's geese; that however unsuitable they are or downright dodgy they turn out to be, we always think they are perfect, because the power of that first love is so strong that it eclipses everything else. In other words, we remain giddy teenagers when it comes to that particular person. It's probably just as well I haven't made an effort to find him again."

Tom leans back in his seat and sighs. The Italian countryside whizzes past. In the distance he can make out cypress trees lining fields and hilltop villages. The woman sitting opposite him complains about the lack of heating in an effort to strike up a conversation. She is not bad looking – typically Italian with dark features and thick, glossy hair. There's a subtle scar just to the left of her lip that he briefly imagines kissing. But he decides against chatting to her and smiles politely, holding up his English newspaper as a barrier.

Soon they will be back in Rome, his favourite city in the world. He will, as he has been since he first moved here, always be taken back by its beauty, the buildings, the fountains, the antiquity, the fact that anywhere you walk you are likely to stumble upon a hidden treasure that in most cities would be in a museum but here is just part of the furniture.

He arrived fifteen years ago, running away from any possible legal implications of the shooting, even after the girls' heroic efforts that saved him. Ollie followed as soon as he was out of hospital. They spent a year or so exploring the Roman drug scene, which was much like London's, if slightly less aggressive and with prettier girls, until Tom had his run-in with the Italian police force.

He didn't have any qualifications, apart from A-Levels, but he managed to get a job in a photographer's studio where he worked his way up to become one of the most in-demand fashion photographers in the city, surrounded by models day and night. In a job he loves, with a beautiful apartment in Trastevere, overlooking the Tiber, woken up every morning by the sound of car wheels over the cobblestones on the streets below. He never has a day when he doesn't think 'This is where I want to be', even if he can't always remember the name of the person in bed next to him.

But despite meeting more beautiful girls in a week than most men do in a lifetime, he has never been in love. He picks up Marina's article. "I fell deeply in love. Instantly. Irrevocably." He envies the fact that she felt it, even if it was never reciprocated. He yearns to know what it's like, to cross over from lust to love, even just for a minute – to finally understand what all the fuss is about. To love someone so much you would do what she did for him. Because while the sex is all good fun and the girls extremely charming, after all these years what he has is a bit like eating in the best restaurants and not really tasting the food.

"Do you mind if we eat in the canteen?" says Marina, kissing Ulrika hello. "It's too bloody cold to go out."

"Not at all," says her friend. "I just want to see you, don't care where the fuck I eat. Or what for that matter."

"You'd fit in well here, with your foul language. The 'vagina monologues' wouldn't even faze you."

Ulrika laughs and throws her head back, shaking her long blonde hair, which looks like it comes straight out of a Timotei ad. The action has the male staff walking past them entranced.

"How are things?"

"I have had to go back to work at the family firm, can you fucking believe it?"

"Good," says Marina as they walk towards the escalator. "You were always too bright to do nothing. Why the change?"

They walk towards the canteen and find a table. Ulrika undoes her coat and puts it down on a chair with a sigh. Marina puts her bag on the table and it immediately falls off. Ulrika catches it with one hand and puts it on top of her coat. Years of hanging out with Marina has taught her to be prepared.

"Well, you know Ben's family sold the company and we got some cash and then set up the marketing thing on his own?"

"Yes."

"Of course he's not making any money, useless fucker. Hasn't got a single client, and we've got nursery fees for the twins, the mortgage, the car loan. Basically we're fucking broke."

"Can't you take them out of the private nursery?"

"And put them where? There are no places in state nurseries, added to which they only speak Hindi in most of them. Can I smoke in here?"

"No, you can't, and you really should give up, it's terribly ageing."

"Oh fuck off."

Marina laughs. "OK, but don't blame me when you're a wrinkled old trout."

"At least my eggs won't be shriveled up. When are you and Mark going to have some sprogs? I want to be an evil godmother."

The waitress comes to take their order and they both opt for the Salade Niçoise.

"A bit too healthy for me," says Ulrika, "but it means I can have crumpets for tea. So?"

"What?"

"When are you going to start breeding?"

"Oh now you can fuck off."

"Oooooh. I don't often hear you swearing like, well, like me. What's wrong darling?"

Marina rubs her forehead as if to clear her thoughts. "I just don't know what's the matter with me. Most women yearn to have babies, they just can't wait. But I just don't want to do it, the whole thought terrifies me, makes me feel trapped, claustrophobic and just, well, in a panic."

Ulrika rubs her arm. "Sweetpea, you know you don't HAVE to reproduce. It's not against the law to stay childless."

"But that's just it, Mark is SO desperate for me to get pregnant, I just know he's itching to convince me every minute. It's like the elephant in the room, he tries not to talk about it but then it just comes out and I feel so bad because I just don't feel the same way AT ALL. It's got to the stage when I don't even really want to have sex with him. Is that normal? I mean he's such a lovely husband but I just can't seem to get excited about him. Do you want to have sex with Ben?"

"Ew, hell no. But that's because I hate him, and he's a twat. Shame I only just realised now after seven years of marriage. But you and Mark, you're so lovely together, he so adores you and he is great for you, so grounding and kind, and hot as hell in his surgeon's kit."

"Aaarrggghhhh. I know, I know, which is why I feel so desperate. He is all that so why can't I just be grateful and in love and give him what he wants?"

"Do you think maybe that's it?"

"What?"

"You don't love him?"

Marina stares at Ulrika in shock. "Of course I love him. At least, I think I love him, I mean we're happy and all that…." She trails off.

"Are you still hankering after the cad?"

"Noooooo," Marina shrieks. Ulrika raises an eyebrow.

"Are you sure? I don't believe you didn't go looking for evidence of his hot ass on the internet, go on, tell me."

"Ok, ok, I admit it, he lives in Rome, he's a photographer."

"And…? Pictures? Is he still hot?"

"Identical," sighs Marina. "But of course I am now an old married lady and not affected by cads."

"Here we are ladies," says the waitress plonking their food down.

Ulrika looks at it. "You sound as convincing as this salad looks. Can't you do your clumsy thing and knock it off the table?"

Marina laughs, pokes her salad around and sighs. Ulrika's phone rings.

"It's Kitty," she mouths to Marina, who nods. Kitty was Ulrika's nanny and is now ninety-six years old, living alone in Brighton. Ulrika calls her every day without fail. Marina hears her tell Kitty she will call her back in an hour.

"Right, where were we?"

"Look, I do love Mark, I just don't feel terribly, well, excited by him...I love him, but..."

"Oh no you don't," interrupts Ulrika. "You're not going to come up with that shitty old 'I love him but I'm not in love with him' crap cliché?"

Marina pokes at her salad. "Well, it's a cliché but you know that might just be it. Clichés only become clichés because there's some truth in them. Like all Swedish girls are sluts. "

Ulrika laughs, "Yes, and extremely good in bed." She chews a lettuce leaf and nods. "Well, at least you have the fact that you love him going for you. I don't love Ben, and I'm not in love with him either. The twat. I've got to do something drastic. As far as I see it, I have five more good years, if that..."

"Less if you keep smoking," Marina interrupts.

"Ok, shut up, and in those years I need to bag a

seriously, stonkingly, hideously rich lover who can release me from my heinously dull, flat broke life, at least for an afternoon or two a week."

"Nice lunch, ladies?" They look up to find Hugo Willoughby standing there.

"No, hideous. I'm Ulrika," she says stretching out her hand to shake his.

"Hugo," he smiles at her, taking her hand. "What an unusual name, where does it come from?"

"Sweden, my father's Swedish."

"Ah, hence the blonde hair and good looks," smiles Hugo.

"Vom," says Marina, barely under her breath.

"I know a much better place," he continues, "just round the corner. Next time you'll have to allow me to show you."

"Thanks Hugo," says Marina, trying her best to dismiss him with her tone. This can only end one way, and it's not good.

"So what do you do for this esteemed organ?" asks Ulrika, smiling.

"I'm the features editor."

"Oh, how perfectly fabulous. I work for a small family business that is just about to celebrate its 200th year. We make bespoke jewellery for the royals among others, everything from rings to tiaras. I was wanting to talk to someone about maybe getting an interview with my father, the grandson of the founder in one of the papers. He's such a character, a real old-school type and terribly outspoken, as well as best friends with all sorts of celebs."

"Here's my card," says Hugo, grinning. "Do email me and we'll talk further. In fact we could all go out for a drink to discuss. How about Friday night?"

"Sounds good," says Ulrika.

"Marina, will you come along?" asks Hugo.

Marina nods reluctantly. "Yep, sounds good to me too."

"Great," Hugo takes Ulrika's hand again. "Ulrika, it was an absolute pleasure to meet you, and I look forward to Friday."

"Me too," says Ulrika, standing up mainly so Hugo can see exactly what he has to look forward to.

"I thought you were looking for a rich man, not some pompous toy-boy in chinos and a pink shirt," snaps Marina once he's gone. "Honestly, if you think I'm coming out Friday to be some bloody gooseberry, think again."

"Well, you could just come along for a drink and then, well…"

"Bugger off basically. Really Ulrika, he's about ten years younger than us."

"I know, but he's utterly delicious." Ulrika smiles and Marina knows the fight is lost. They have known each other since university and she knows that look. Ulrika has spotted her prey.

"What will Ben say?"

"Oh, I wasn't planning on telling him," she laughs.

Marina laughs in spite of herself. It must be wonderful to go through life like Ulrika, stunningly beautiful, totally invincible and adored by every man you meet. Even if she is married to a twat.

7

The idea of organising a reunion suddenly comes to her just as they are landing in London. She is woken up by the 'cabin crew please take your seats for landing' announcement and it is there, lodged in her head like a new dress design.

They would have another evening, like the one all those years ago, but preferably without the Ecstasy, the nutmeg and the shooting. It will be like a Fellini film – the past encroaching on the present, old scores settled, maybe even old romances rekindled?

But then she wonders if it's wise to get them all together, after what happened. There could be repercussions. But it was so long ago, Katie reasons, and they are all grown up now. And surely it is better to finally close the whole episode, even if it is painful.

The idea grows on her by the second. She hasn't felt this excited since she opened her first store in Milan or Anna Wintour picked her as 'one to watch' in the September issue of American *Vogue* all those years ago.

Yes, it's a fabulous idea. She will be the one to provide that closure, to bring them all together again. It's almost like playing God. And who knows what might come of it?

She's sure she can get a private detective to track them down; in fact she probably doesn't even need to do that. Marina is easy; she has her number at *The Chronicle*. And she has seen Tom Stamford's byline in some fashion magazines; he's a successful photographer now. She knows all the editors of the fashion mags so that's no problem. Tom would know where Ollie is. And of course Mark is married to Marina. She wonders what Mark is doing now, probably a surgeon as he always said he would be, he was the only one of the gang who had some ambition and knew what he wanted to do.

If she's honest with herself, and she rarely is because she normally feels that complete honesty is overrated, Katie would have acknowledged that part of her motivation is to show them all how far she has come. Marina and Mark may have gone to university, something Katie failed to do, but how many of them could now afford to entertain them all on a yacht in Positano? Or should she take them to her villa in the hills above St Tropez? It would have to be at least a weekend thing, maybe even longer, somewhere warmer than London – well, just about anywhere was warmer than London at this time of year, with the possible exception of Canada, and who in their right mind would ever go there?

But when should it happen? They are now in early December. Most people will have plans for Christmas. Maybe New Year? A New Year's party to remember? Like the last one – she laughs ironically to herself. Or does she already have something at New Year? She switches on her iPhone to check the diary. The flight attendants are all sitting down now anyway, and she just doesn't believe that her looking at her diary could possibly interfere with anything, except perhaps her own mood if it doesn't look interesting enough.

She looks at the month of December. She is meant to be at Richard Branson's island for New Year, but frankly, she's had enough of his parties. In fact all those so-called A-list parties are the same.

Katie understood pretty quickly, once she became the

red-carpet dress, shoe and bag designer of choice for film stars across the globe, that once you get on the celeb party circuit you end up seeing all the same famous faces all the time. And actually because everyone is there to be seen, no one really relaxes. So the parties aren't ever much fun. Unless you got chatting to Charlie Sheen, of course, or someone else whose career was nose-diving. But the successful ones are so obsessed with their own image that they barely drink, or laugh, let alone dance or fuck.

Katie flicks through her address book for the email of Franca Sozzani, editor of Italian *Vogue*. 'Ciao bella, can you please send me a contact number or email address for a photographer you use a lot, a Tom Stamford? Baci – KT' she writes.

"Sorry madam, but the captain hasn't given his permission to turn electronic items on yet," says a voice in a whiney estuary accent.

Katie looks up at the stewardess. You'd think in first class they would be told to leave the punters alone. She has two choices – either get her fired, or try to take her yoga teacher's advice and exude good vibes, whatever *they* are.

"Maureen," she smiles sweetly, reading her nametag. "How right you are. I hadn't noticed. I'll switch it off immediately."

Maureen blushes. "Oh, don't worry, really, he'll make the announcement any minute. It can't do any harm now."

'Then why the fuck are you harassing me?' she wants to yell, but instead she breathes deeply and thanks her. Imagine what a sordid and drab little life the poor girl must have if her idea of a good time is to tell millionaires to switch off their phones. Makes you think.

"So, what are you going to do?" asks Marina, although she knows the answer already. It's Friday evening; she and Ulrika are sitting in The Horse's Head drinking far too large glasses of wine. Ulrika has moved Marina's a safe distance away so she doesn't knock it flying – "it might drown me," she jokes. The topic, as it has done for the past fifteen years, turns to men.

When they first met in Bristol it was boyfriends or one-night-stands, then it was serious boyfriends, then it was 'Will he won't he propose?', then it was getting married, and then it was husbands and how much we love them, soon to be replaced by husbands and how much we hate them. It seemed they were about to embark on the next phase: lovers.

"I'm going to fuck him, of course," smiles Ulrika. "I'm going to get in touch with my inner floozy and just go for it. I deserve it; it's my little treat. I can't afford to shop any more thanks to my useless twat of a husband, we will probably have to sell our house, which I paid the deposit for from my own money, and the next thing to go will be my car. If all that doesn't earn a woman the right to some side salad then I don't know what does."

Marina takes another sip of wine. It feels good, the way it seeps down and relaxes her body. It's a good way to start the weekend. It's another thing she would have to give up if she got pregnant. Tomorrow she will go to yoga and then have an afternoon sleep – her day is entirely hers. How do women with children plan their weekends? Around the playground probably, and dirty nappies.

But for some reason, the thought of Ulrika and Hugo together is vaguely uncomfortable. It might be that a tiny part of her feels sorry for Ben, or that he's her friend and she knows he will be chewed up and spat out. And for all Hugo's confidence and aplomb, if he falls for her, he will get hurt. And she wouldn't want him to be hurt.

"What about Ben, and the twins?"

"They won't know the difference, I'll tell Ben I was with you and sneak into bed while he's asleep. The twins will just be thrilled that mummy is in such a good mood after her night out."

"Don't you feel guilty?"

"I haven't even kissed the man yet! But no, guilt is not an emotion I anticipate feeling. Lust, ecstasy, joy, even a brief moment of youthful exuberance and surprise at how agile I still am, yes. Guilt, no."

Marina laughs. "You so have to call me and tell me all about it. I can't imagine what Hugo will be like in bed, and I'm not sure I want to. I mean he is cute, but just a bit too public school for me. I was put off those public schoolboy types at Bristol, such cads and all deeply superficial."

"That's my kind of man. He's perfect for this little adventure, just what I need. Confident, young, cute and lots of floppy blond hair. And enough of a bastard not to show up on my doorstep proclaiming never-dying love. Which would just be too tedious for words."

"Just what your husband used to be," says Marina, realising too late that it's possibly too incisive a statement.

Ulrika strides over it. "Yes, precisely. Have I changed? Have I suddenly become a fat, frumpy, yummy mummy type with nothing to say? Do I wear hideous clothes from Laura Ashley? Has my hair been cut short to save time and have I stopped wearing lip-gloss 24/7? No, I don't think so. But he's changed: he's got fat, and poor. Both of which are utterly unforgiveable." She finishes her wine. "Same again?"

Marina smiles. "Yes please, but don't worry, when your side salad shows up I'll be off. I don't want to go to yoga with a hangover. And I don't want to stick around watching Hugo's charm offensive either, entertaining as I'm sure it will be. He is always that, if nothing else."

Hugo arrives shortly afterwards, looking dashing in a white shirt and red jeans, when they're halfway through their second glass of wine. As Marina predicted, he is entertaining, charming and full of good newsroom tales. He gazes at Ulrika as if she is the most exotic creature he has ever set eyes on, which is something Marina has seen men up and down the country do – most men in fact, every time she goes anywhere with Ulrika.

The first time she saw her was during fresher's week at university and she too was taken aback by how beautiful she was. "Far too pretty to be friends with," said Carol, her mate from school. Marina had agreed but then bumped (literally) into Ulrika in a bookshop a day later where they were both looking for the same Tom Stoppard play they had to read as their first assignment. There was only one copy left so they decided to share it.

"You read it first and I can crib all your notes," laughed Ulrika, handing Marina the book.

She did just that, and offered to do the same for Marina with the next book. By the end of the first term they were best friends, and Marina just got used to being the 'not as pretty' friend, although she was nice looking, tall and curvaceous with brown eyes and brown-black curly hair, and would probably have had more attention had she not insisted on hanging around with the university's most stunning girl.

She was well aware of this, of course, but Ulrika was the most amusing girl there as well as the prettiest. She had an ability to make Marina laugh that was too good to miss, added to which she was always invited to everything, because where Marina went, Ulrika went.

At the beginning of their third term at university, Mark had asked Marina out to the cinema. Of course she had known him since they were hanging out in London together as teenagers, so she assumed he must have asked her in order to meet Ulrika. He came to pick her up from her digs and she walked out with her blonde friend.

"It's lovely to see you," said Mark. "But did you have to bring your ugly friend?"

The three of them collapsed laughing and by the beginning of the following term Mark and Marina were an item.

They split up during Marina's final year at university but stayed good friends throughout their twenties. It was at Ulrika's wedding, a rather posh do at her family's showroom in Knightsbridge, that they got back together again. For Marina it felt like coming home, for Mark it was the culmination of a dream he'd had since he was seventeen and first met Marina at a pizzeria on the King's Road.

Marina leaves the pub and walks towards the bus stop. Her feet seem to be beating out a rhythm on the pavement. 'Thirty-three and childless, thirty-three and childless' they keep repeating. She does need to get on with it if she is ever going to become a mother. Ulrika has the twins, now aged almost three, and almost all her other married friends have had children too. She and Mark are beginning to be the odd ones out. Even now, when women have children later and later. When is the cut-off? Definitely forty. Who wants to be older than sixty at their graduation and mistaken for the grandmother? She's heard of mothers in parks playing a game called 'gran or mum?' where they have to guess whether the carer of a child is the mother or the grandmother.

Really she ought to get pregnant sooner though, like now. But it just seems such a big thing to do without really wanting to. Maybe she has a gene missing, maybe she has no maternal gene and she just has to get over that physical shortcoming and dive in?

Or maybe as Ulrika says she just doesn't love Mark

enough to want to have children with him?

And if that's the case, she asks herself as she climbs onto the number 19 bus to Clapham, should she leave now and let him find someone who does?

*"Drugs may be the road to nowhere, but at least
they're the scenic route."*
Anonymous

Ollie Jordan is sure he will never be comfortable again.
He has been in the clinic for two weeks now. He is either
too hot, too cold, shaking or sweating. He can't sleep,
doesn't want to eat. He doesn't want to do anything,
except get hold of some drugs, any drugs, or even
alcohol – just something to make him feel normal again,
to ease the pain and what seems to be incessant itching.
There are times when it is so much more than
discomfort, when it literally feels as if his limbs are
being ripped apart. He imagines he is on the rack, the
torture instrument he remembers reading about at
school while studying Guy Fawkes. Then they come and
give him painkillers and the agony subsides.

His family comes in and out to see him. He has

nothing to say to them yet, but apparently this anger will pass, and he will start to feel gratitude. Right now he can't imagine feeling anything but the desire to punch whoever walks into his room.

The nurse comes in and opens the curtains, waking him up. This is what it must be like to be in an old people's home, he thinks. He remembers his grandfather complaining about it. "You have bugger all to do all day," he used to say, "but they insist on waking you up at the crack of dawn."

The nurse walks over to him. "Morning Ollie, how are we today?"

"I was asleep," he growls, refusing to open his eyes.

"I know, I know, but the doctor is coming in half an hour and we need you to be awake for his visit. It's your two-week anniversary today."

"Great, how do I celebrate? A cup of coffee? Am I allowed caffeine?"

"Oh, you are a one," she laughs. "Anyway, you had some post this morning, feels very important. Here." She pokes his arm with what feels like a piece of card. Reluctantly he opens his eyes; she is holding a stiff white envelope.

"Well, go on. Take it," she urges.

"Just put it on the table," he snaps. He still hasn't

forgiven her for disturbing the only peace he gets in a day – the few hours he manages to sleep.

"Oh suit yourself," she snaps back, and puts it down before leaving the room.

As soon as she has gone he pushes himself up in bed and picks up the envelope. It really does feel special. The paper is a very pale cream colour and extremely thick, his name and address are written on the front of it in beautiful calligraphy with blue ink.

Ollie Jordan Esq. it reads. Evergreen Clinic, 15 Forthway Lane, Hayfield, Sussex TN20 6DD.

He can't think of anyone who knows he's there. For a split second he hopes it is some kind dealer offering him drugs. He tears open the envelope.

More beautiful calligraphy, this time printed in raised grey type:

To Ollie

Katie Tomlinson invites you to relive our mutual past on December 31st for two nights at her villa in St Tropez. All costs and travel arrangements taken care of. Please email cherry@KT.com or call 0207 558 6464 for more details and to RSVP.

For a moment he has no idea who Katie Tomlinson is,

or why on earth she would be inviting him to St Tropez. Then from somewhere in the depth of his rather addled brain it all starts coming back to him – the shooting, Tom fleeing the country, his friends coming to see him in hospital, Katie and Mark bringing him grapes one time, the first thing he was able to eat since the accident, his stomach wound slowly healing but his dependence on painkillers staying with him even after he was pronounced "cured". The rapid descent into drugs – how long can it have taken? Only a matter of weeks, he thinks. Then fleeing to Italy where he had an old school friend who was a bit of a hippy, to be somewhere he could nurse his addiction away from prying eyes. Tom joining him shortly afterwards, the two of them getting high, then drifting apart as Tom got more work and sorted his life out.

"You're the bastard who shot me," Ollie used to joke. "You should be in prison, not taking pictures of scantily clad women."

But prison was the last place he wanted Tom to be – after all, he was his best friend, and it was an accident. Even so, it would be nice to finally get closure, as those dreary Americans call it. And it gives him something to stay clean for. Another three weeks to go – he will just have to make sure they let him out on time. For the first time since he arrived he feels there is a reason to live. He has an important date.

9

"I restore myself when I'm alone."
Marilyn Monroe

"Do you think we should go?" Mark asks. They are both staring at the invitation, which is propped up against the Dorset Organic cereal packet on the breakfast table.

It hasn't occurred to Marina that they won't, but of course the reason she wants to go is probably the reason Mark is less keen.

"I think we should," she says carefully. "An all-expenses trip to St Tropez is not something to turn down. Especially in December when the weather here is so horrible."

He looks at her questioningly. "And with a first love thrown in…?"

Marina smiles. "Really Mark, that was all so long ago, don't be ridiculous."

He sighs. "I suppose you're right. It'll be the first time

we've all been together since that night. Does Tom even know what happened?"

"I'm not sure. Maybe Katie kept in touch. I know as much as you do."

"Won't it just bring back a lot of painful memories? I mean of that night, and Ollie…" Mark trails off.

"I think it will be good to see them, and at least Ollie made it. It would have been a lot more painful if he hadn't. And that's thanks to you – you were the one who stopped the bleeding."

Mark smiles. "My first ever emergency." He pauses. "OK, well, let's go for it. Will you reply?"

Marina smiles back. "Sure, after yoga, have to dash now."

It's one of those perfect, energising winter mornings that makes you vow not to complain about the weather next time it rains for weeks on end and you feel you might just have to get on a plane somewhere to see a bit of blue sky. Marina stuffs her hands far down into her pockets in an effort to keep warm as she walks to her yoga class. In less than a month's time she's going to see Tom again. She can't believe it. What will she feel?

Crazy as it seems, she sometimes wonders whether it is the shadow of Tom that is stopping her from totally throwing herself into her marriage to Mark. She is not proud of the fact, and actually feels quite pathetic about it, but she's never really stopped thinking about him. Of course she doesn't think about him daily, but there have been times over the past fifteen years when she has wondered what would have happened if Ollie hadn't been shot and Tom had stayed in England and magically realised she was more than just a last resort. Not that there was any evidence that this revelation would ever have hit him. But it helps her self-esteem to fantasise that it might.

What does she expect? That she will see him, realise he's a twat, finally get over him and then get on with the rest of her life. Is that all? If she's really honest with herself, is that really all? Maybe not, but anything else would be disastrous. She is married. Maybe he's married too? Maybe he'll bring his wife? Or maybe he won't come at all?

The thought makes her catch her breath even more than the cold air. Maybe he's living on the other side of the world and is busy looking after his five perfect children and supermodel wife? Maybe he just couldn't be less interested in seeing them all? Perhaps he hasn't spent the last fifteen years wondering what on earth happened to her, or even Katie. Mind you, unless he was living in an igloo in northern Lapland with no internet access he would know what had happened to Katie.

Katie with her millions and her flat stomach. If Tom isn't married they will probably end up together, like they would have done that night if Ollie hadn't been shot. Maybe he will be the one to rescue poor Katie from her desperately lonely state. "Don't believe everything you read in the papers," Marina's mother would have told her. Of course now that she writes for the papers, she knows just how good that advice is.

Her BlackBerry beeps. It's a bbm from Ulrika. "Don't you want to know what happened?"

Marina laughs and types. "Yes, am desperate to hear, tell me all."

"I have two words to describe him; good, and big."

"Your ideal man," Marina responds, feeling faintly jealous. "So it was fun?"

"Heaven, I haven't been thrown round a room like that since fuck a fresher week. Only slightly irritating thing was he kept telling me what a marvellous writer you are. As if I don't know that."

Marina smiles. "Will call you later, yoga now, have some news too."

"Pregnant?"

"Noooooo. Over and out."

She switches off her BlackBerry and walks into the Clapham Community Centre.

Her yoga teacher, Ria, is warming up when Marina walks into the classroom. There is mellow music playing in the background and the room smells lightly of incense. Along the edge of the platform where Ria sits with her legs apart and her upper body miraculously flat on the floor in between them, small candles flicker. Marina spreads out her mat and inhales the zen atmosphere. This is about as far away as you can get from a newspaper office and she loves it. It's her favourite time of the week – an hour and a half of focusing on nothing but Ria's voice, her own breathing and her body moving.

She lies down on the mat and gently hugs her knees into her chest. The class starts to fill up.

"Good morning, yogis," says Ria after a few minutes. "Sit in any cross-legged position, close your eyes and hold your hands in Namaste. Anyone who doesn't know what that is, raise their hand and I will come over and show you. Any injuries I don't already know about?" Silence. "Anyone pregnant?"

Marina flinches.

"Not as far as I know," says one of the blokes, which always gets a laugh.

"Good. Let's get started." She pauses for a moment

before going on. "Every one of us harbours an inner desire, a wish or a dream or ambition, call it what you will. I want you to focus your inner desire right now, and visualise it happening."

Marina smiles as she bets herself that most of the women harbour an inner desire to look like Ria, and the men all harbour an inner desire to sleep with Ria. That's 90 per cent of the room taken care of. There will be some women who want to get pregnant, one or two who want to fall in love, possibly some lunatic who yearns to write a book, and at least one swot whose deepest desire is to be able to touch her knees with her nose when she does a forward bend.

And what about her? Marina inhales and exhales slowly. She should really visualise a family with Mark, being a happy mother and wife. But instead she visualises a villa in St Tropez and a tall, handsome man telling her how good it is to see her, and how she has barely changed in fifteen years.

And across town at her private yoga session in her parquet-floored basement in Knightsbridge, Katie Tomlinson is visualising more or less the same thing.

❦ *10* ❦

*"The most important thing for a good marriage is to
learn how to argue peaceably."*
Anita Ekberg

"Noooo, Felix, don't do that."

While Ulrika is busy making some toast and chatting
to her old nanny Kitty on the phone, Felix has taken what
was left of her soggy cornflakes and is using them as a
face-pack. And now Archie wants some too, so is
screaming like an angry monkey. Ulrika says goodbye to
Kitty, gets up to find a cloth while at the same time
heaving Archie from his Tripp-Trapp chair onto her hip
to calm him down. He decides that if he can't have
cornflakes he will have hair and starts tugging at her long
blonde locks maniacally. Will she go to work with Farley's
rusks in her hair? It wouldn't be the first time.

"Argghhh, Archie stop, please," she says wiping the
table and pushing Felix in his chair away from the mess.

This sends him into a frenzy so now both boys are wailing.

"Christ, Ulrika, what did you do to them?" asks Ben, finally looking up from his newspaper.

"Oh, obviously I've been torturing them with lit cigarettes, didn't you notice as you sat there stuffing your face with breakfast and reading about people who are more interesting than you?" she snaps.

Ben stands up and looks at her. Felix and Archie carry on screaming. "Were you always such a bitch, and how come I never noticed?"

"No, I wasn't, this is what I've become, you turned me into this, you with your selfish, useless attitude and fucked-up idea of how to treat your wife." She picks up the boys and tries to console them, one on each hip.

"Don't use that language in front of the children," he shouts.

"Like they understand? They're eighteen months old for heaven's sake."

"It's a wonder their first word wasn't 'fuck', the amount you use it."

"Well, at least I can say it. You can't even do it any more."

"Not can't, don't want to – there's a big difference. I just don't fancy you Ulrika, I don't even like you."

Ulrika is speechless for a brief moment. The thought of someone not fancying her, least of all her useless husband, is utterly absurd.

"Well, at least we agree on something," she says flouncing out of the kitchen with the twins. "I don't fancy you either."

As she gets them dressed, she has a mini daydream about Archie and Felix when they're older, in school uniform, looking impossibly cute as she drops them off at whatever posh school they end up at. She needs to work out where that is going to be, as it doesn't seem likely that she and their father will stay together much longer. At the moment they are in nursery school in the mornings and then collected by Donia, a skinny nineteen-year-old who always wears ridiculously high heels but seems to have an extraordinary sense of balance, as well as huge affection for the boys or her "squidges" as she calls them. She hates that her life has turned out like this; she can't understand where it all went wrong. She had everything going for her, could have married just about anyone, but made the wrong choice, and would pay for it for the rest of her life.

Downstairs Ben tries to go back to reading his paper but he can't concentrate. He has never felt such hate as he feels towards Ulrika at the moment. It's hard to imagine how much he used to love her, how just the sight of her was enough to give him a hard-on, the laughs they used to have and how excited he was when she agreed to marry him. He doesn't think he's changed. OK, he may have put on a bit of weight – Ulrika used to joke that he was putting on all the pregnancy weight – and financially things are not as good as they used to be, but marriage is all about 'for better or for worse'. Ulrika only seems interested in the 'for better' bit.

They were the golden couple: blond, tall, gorgeous. Everyone loved them, They were going to have golden children and live to a ripe old age in a contented bordering on smug state. But now it looked like the whole edifice was crumbling. Just as he found it impossible to imagine how he used to feel about her, he couldn't image ever not hating her. Was it possible to go full circle? Would there ever be a time again when the sight of her didn't raise his heckles? Maybe for the boys it was worth fighting and trying to fix it? He really didn't want to be a weekend dad, and God knows what sort of tosser Ulrika would find to look after his children. Then what if she had more children with the tosser? Would she start to neglect Archie and Felix?

All these thoughts are whirring through Ben's normally

rather emptier mind as Ulrika stomps downstairs with the twins to take them to nursery. He stands up to give her a hand putting on their coats and getting them into the car. She is still fuming. He tries very hard to reboot his mental attitude towards his wife, to try to see what everyone else sees – a stunning blonde you'd give your right arm to fuck. But it's no use – all he sees is a bitter, angry, bitch.

"You going to work?" he asks her, in an effort to be civil.

"I am going to work Ben, because one of us has to," she snaps and gets into her Range Rover, slamming the door behind her.

Ben walks back into their house, a beautiful farmhouse in the Surrey countryside, overlooking fields and hedgerows. He wishes he had a dog to take for a walk, but Ulrika won't hear of it. Too much of a commitment, she says, and too much hard work. He feels too guilty to go for a walk for no reason; he really should try to get some work, although he could do with some exercise. His rugby-playing physique was all very well in the days when he actually played rugby, but it's not looking too toned now.

He walks into his office and switches on the computer. He checks his emails in the hope that someone somewhere wants him to do something that will earn him some cash. They are right up to their overdraft limit again and in a week's time the mortgage goes out. If it bounces they get fined £250, and so the vicious cycle goes on. He is fed up with having no money, and doesn't want to ask his parents again. Really they ought to have been able to live on the proceeds of the sale of the family firm for much longer than they have, but Ulrika has expensive tastes and won't be seen dead in anything that isn't designer. Upstairs is a whole wardrobe dedicated to her designer cashmere jumpers – she maintains she's allergic to wool, possibly in the same way someone might be allergic to non-vintage champagne, Ben always sneers.

No interesting emails. Just one from his mother asking them to lunch on Sunday with the boys. Maybe he should go alone; Ulrika hates his parents, calls them mundane little people, and it would be much more relaxing without her. In fact, he reflects as he clicks on to the *Daily Mail* website, his whole life would be much more relaxing without Ulrika.

11

*"The fact that a man is a newspaper reporter
is evidence of some flaw of character."*
Lyndon B Johnson

Hugo Willoughby had been sure today was going to be a crap day when he stumbled out of bed and tripped over his golf shoes, landing headfirst on a wooden chair in his sparsely furnished Fulham bedroom. Typical that of all the places to fall he picked the same spot as practically the only piece of furniture in there.

One of the reasons he loves his job so much is that he finds his flat totally depressing. It is a classic bachelor pad, with nothing in it but the bare necessities. His parents were diplomats and moved around until they retired to a small village in Oxfordshire two years ago. So he hasn't spent more than holidays in a proper home since he was a boy and really has no idea how to make a home, and has never had a girl-friend who was around long enough to show him. He just hasn't met a girl who can hold his interest for more than a few weeks. He had high hopes when Marina joined *The Chronicle*, he'd always loved her columns, her way of writing and her sense of humour. And of course the fact that she was a Chelsea fan. Then he found out she was married to some glamorous surgeon. But Ulrika might prove a welcome distraction. He smiles as he remembers their encounter; nothing like a bit of unadulterated lust to cheer a chap up.

But the focus now is on work. He is here with a black eye and the editor wants to see him. Probably to punch him in his other eye.

Cameron Knight has been even more stressed than usual of late – everyone is expecting him to start chewing people up and it looks like Hugo is first in line today. Oh well, it can't be worse than a sound thrashing during the Eton wall game.

He walks into Cameron Knight's office, trying to appear full of confidence, which is difficult when you look like a panda.

"For fuck's sake, what happened to you? Your wife beat you up?" shrieks Knight bouncing forward in his seat.

"I'm not married," says Hugo. "It was a chair."

"You must have really pissed it off, what did you do?

Try to shag its sister?" Knight roars with laughter and motions for him to sit down.

As soon as Hugo is seated he stops laughing and starts fiddling with his pen – always a bad sign.

"This, er, issue, is no laughing matter. We're in trouble, Willoughby, I mean deep trouble."

"What's going on?"

"Well, you know that story we ran about the MP having sex with the headmistress who was married to the vicar and their sordid little telephone chats about chalk and where to put it?"

Hugo smiles. That was a big scoop a couple of months ago. "Yes, the 'Rude School of Rutshire' – fabulous story."

"Yes, at the time it did seem like a great story, it had it all: sex, politics, religion, infidelity and even a smattering of deeply perverted behaviour. I mean chalk? Who'd have thought it was so versatile."

He leans back in his chair. "But it seems there was another vital ingredient that we weren't aware of."

Hugo looks perplexed. "Was there a chair involved?"

"Very amusing Willoughby. No, the vital ingredient was phone tapping,"

Hugo opens his mouth to speak but his editor cuts him off. "Phone tapping that was not authorized by anyone in management but that might get the whole paper closed down. Scotland Yard has been on to me over the past few days and they are not going away. They say they will prosecute us and take us down if they have to. Unless we can find who the culprit was and they take full responsibility."

Hugo nods slowly and wonders briefly if his boss thinks someone is tapping this conversation. He concludes that must be the case, because phone tapping has been going on at all levels for years and of course management knows about it. Who else would authorize the massive payments to dodgy characters all over town? Not the staff writers, that's for sure. They've barely got the authority to pay for lunch at the in-house café.

"So, Willoughby, what I need from you is a list of names of the people who worked on the story so I can question them and get to the bottom of this. And I especially need to hear of anyone who might have been involved with the phone tapping, er, if you knew it was going on, that is. Which I am assuming you don't. Because if you did," he raises his voice, "you're fucking fired!"

Hugo nods. "Right, fair enough. Well, it's easy to tell you who worked on the story. It was me, obviously, and Millie, along with Felicia and Marina. But I can't tell you who, if anyone, was tapping phones. I mean, clearly it's not something that was discussed."

Cameron Knight nods and starts playing with his pen again.

"How can they be so sure of this phone tapping?" asks Hugo.

"Apparently they arrested some scumbag phone tapper and his records show the tapping. He told them he was doing it for us and showed the payments into his bank account for services rendered. Well, you'd better send the girls in, I'll have a word with them."

"Marina's away in France."

"Well I suggest you talk to the other two c**ts today and call Marina too. I need to sort this mess out before more than a few heads roll."

The editor gives him a look that signals the conversation is over. Hugo stands up. "And Willoughby, this is very serious, it could mean the end of the newspaper. I'm relying on you to see to it that there is a fast and relatively painless outcome."

Hugo Willoughby nods and goes back out to the newsroom. Millie and Felicia are busily tapping away. This will be a disaster for them. He knows Millie helps her parents pay the school fees for her little brother, and Felicia is just starting out, this will ruin her career. But he has to do something. Knight doesn't want the truth – he wants a scapegoat, he wants to save his paper, and, more importantly, himself.

Knight's message was not subtle. Scotland Yard would be delighted to see *The Chronicle* shut down for breaking the law. Knight's plan is to make out the paper isn't in the wrong but that reporters acted without approval from management, thus exonerating management (and the paper) from any blame.

He decides not to say anything to either Millie or Felicia. He then realises with some horror that if there is going to be a scapegoat here it will have to be Marina. He can see her face in front of her now, those intelligent brown eyes disbelieving and hurt. This is not going to be easy. But it's the only way to handle this. Last in, first out – it's only fair.

❧ *12* ❧

*"To me, photography is the simultaneous recognition, in a
fraction of a second, of the significance of an event."*
Henri Cartier-Bresson

December 30th 2010

Marina hears him before she sees him. His voice is just
the same – a deep distinctive voice, with undertones of
humour and seduction. She had often thought that she
was the only one who found it seductive, but as she
listens to him say hello to Ollie and then Katie, she
concludes that it's all in the tone and that most women
would be hard pressed not to fall for the silky smooth
sound. When Tom speaks to a woman, his voice softens
– it's almost as if he's caressing her with it.

Whatever effect the voice is having on anyone else,
Marina is catapulted back fifteen years and shocked to
find there is very little difference between her as a teenage
girl and her as a grown woman.

Her heart is pumping fast, her palms are sweaty and

she feels something between anticipation and anxiety. She is also very angry with herself for feeling this way; she's not a character from a Mills & Boon, for heaven's sake. She's a married, hard-nosed journalist in her mid-thirties. Next thing her bosom will be heaving and her corset ripping.

"I think Tom's here," Mark says looking up from the newspaper he is reading. "Shall we go and say hi?"

Marina turns around from the view of the sea she has been admiring from the window.

"Sure," she says, trying to sound as casual as possible, hoping Mark doesn't notice the slightly higher pitch her voice tends to go to if she is nervous.

They walk from the sitting room to the hall where Tom, Ollie and Katie are all standing next to the big table in the middle of the room, which bears an oversized vase filled with exotic flowers. Marina noted when they arrived that the hall in Katie's holiday home is bigger than her whole first floor – a fact that she is trying hard not to let ruin her weekend.

"Marina!" Ollie has spotted them and is racing to hug her hello.

He's so thin, is Marina's first thought, and he looks old. But maybe they all look old.

"Hi Ollie, great to see you." She hugs him and kisses

him on both cheeks, concentrating on not watching Tom, who is walking towards her. "How are you?"

"Great, good," Ollie smiles. Then adds, "Better. I'm in rehab, you probably didn't know…?" He turns to Mark. "Hey Mark, really good to see you. It's so cool that you two are married now. Any kids?"

"Not yet," says Mark, hugging him. "Good to see you Ollie."

Tom is right in front of her, looking down at her with those brown eyes, half-flirty, half-questioning, the way they always were.

"An old married lady eh?" he smiles, kissing her on both cheeks. "It's good to see you, Marina.

"You too." She tries to keep the kisses as casual as possible; they are old chums after all. "And less of the old please," she adds laughing, making a conscious effort to talk in a baritone voice.

He stands back from her and takes both her hands in his. "How old are you now? Thirty-three?"

"Spot on. How old are you?"

"Thirty-five. Looking good for thirty-three, I mean you always did look good, but you've aged well."

"You too," says Marina, again trying to make it sound as casual as possible but noticing that her voice is ever so slightly squeaky. Damn it. "And you remember Mark don't you?" She lets go of Tom's hands and gestures towards her husband.

"Sure, of course. Hey, good to see you Mark." Tom smiles and they embrace.

"Look at us all," says Ollie. "It's like some kind of weird dream, I can't believe I'm seeing you all again, together like this. Great idea of yours Katie."

"Thanks," she smiles. "I'm so happy to have you all here, it really means a lot to me. Let me show you boys to your rooms and why don't we meet back in the sitting room in half an hour for some drinks? I'll get Antoine to light a nice big fire and we can chat about old times."

"Sounds great," says Ollie. "Like a Fellini film. But no drinks for me."

Katie smiles at the reference to the Fellini film. It's all working out just as she planned. She puts her arm around him. "I know, I've had some special sparkling apple juice delivered for us all, we are all going to detox tonight – it looks just like champagne and tastes even better. Added to which, it's very restorative."

"As long as it's not addictive," laughs Ollie, running his hand through his hair slightly nervously. "Thanks guys," he adds looking at them all.

Mark and Marina walk to their room, which is in the guest

cottage just across the garden, on the other side of a large swimming pool that is covered with a vast blue plastic sheet. A gardener is raking leaves off the lawn.

"It must be heavenly in the summer," says Marina stopping to look around.

"It's pretty heavenly now," says Mark. "I love the view of the sea between the cypress trees, the colours are just incredible."

Marina looks out towards the water. "Beautiful. The kind of view you want to breathe in and take with you."

"Easier to take a picture," laughs Mark, getting his BlackBerry out. "OK, smile."

Marina looks at him and tries to smile – something she always finds impossible to do on command.

"Think about something nice," says Mark encouragingly.

She looks at her husband. He is such a good man, the kind of person any mother would be happy for you to marry, the kind of boy you'd want your own daughter to bring home. So why is her mind filled with a restless cad from years ago? Is she a silly goose? Undoubtedly. Will she fight it? Probably not. She smiles.

"Very Mona Lisa," says Mark pressing the button. "Now, let's go inside before we freeze."

When they get back to the sitting room the others are already there. Katie is standing by the fire with her elbow leaning casually on the chimneypiece, making her waist look even thinner than it did earlier. She is wearing a beige cashmere dress with a thin brown belt and brown stilettos. Marina wonders if she is standing up in order to show off her petite figure. Tom and Ollie are both in armchairs and Tom stands up as they walk in. Ollie follows suit.

"Apple juice?" asks Katie.

"Yes, please," says Marina.

"Sounds good," adds Mark.

"We were just talking about Laila, – do you remember, that slightly whacky girl we used to hang around with that Ollie was quite keen on?" asks Tom.

Marina nods. "Yes, she lived with her parents in Sloane Square, took too many drugs. Whatever became of her, I wonder?"

"I'll tell you – she now works as a psychiatrist in the rehab place I was in – I saw her there, she looks just the same," says Ollie.

"What? She still has a red Mohican?" asks Marina.

They all laugh.

"No, but she really hasn't changed," says Ollie. "I think the drugs must have pickled her or something. Wish they'd done the same for me. I did some counselling sessions with her."

"You'll find the damage is reversed very quickly," says Mark.

Ollie puts his arm around him. "The doc, coming to my rescue as always. Cheers!"

They all drink their apple juice. Marina can't help thinking that if Mark hadn't rushed to protect her the gun might never have gone off.

"I don't want to dwell on that night…"

"No, let's not," Tom interrupts Ollie.

"No mate, we won't, but I would just like to say that at this particular stage in my life, it feels good to be with you all again. I sort of lost my way after the… er…. incident…. and I feel I am finally getting close to finding the right path again. If that doesn't sound too corny. I mean look at you all, you're all so successful, especially you Katie," he raises her glass towards her and she raises hers back, "and I feel like a total waster really, I need to make amends. As Marlon says in one of my favourite old films, 'I could have been a contender'. Now I need to do something with my life. I could have died that night and in some ways it seems like I did. But I'm back."

"Hear, hear!" says Katie and they all join in another toast. "I would also like to add that I am so very happy we're all together again. It's been too long – in fact that night feels like another life. Anyway, to honour the occasion I have commissioned our very own star photographer Tom here to take portraits of us all individually and one group shot for us to keep as a memento of these couple of days. And also so that in fifteen years' time when we meet again we can look back and reminisce about how actually we really weren't that old! Obviously I'm going to have mine heavily Photoshopped so that I look younger than I did fifteen years ago..."

"The camera is all set up in the hall," says Tom. "Ollie, why don't I start with you?"

"Suits me mate," says Ollie, following Tom out of the room.

Once they have gone Katie turns to Marina and Mark.

"We have to keep him off everything, even alcohol," she says urgently. "He seems to be pretty cooperative, but they warned me this could just be a front and that he will gain our trust and then either drink the whole contents of the house including the bleach or skip off into town to buy drugs, which would be disastrous. So if he asks for any money don't give it to him, and don't offer him so much as a beer. I thought we could make a punch tomorrow, one with alcohol and one without, that way he won't feel too left out."

"How bad is it? I mean, what was he on?" asks Mark.

"He was smoking heroin and taking anything else he could get his hands on too. He got addicted to the painkillers in hospital after the shooting and never recovered."

"Poor Ollie," says Marina. "All those years, just wasted. Almost like he served the sentence Tom would have been given."

Katie nods. "Finally Tom got Ollie's parents to come to Rome to take him home to rehab. He's been there for five weeks and he's doing really well. It has been utter hell for him. But they only let him out on the condition that I take full responsibility for him so I feel I need to make sure he gets back there safely."

The door opens and Ollie comes back in. "Well, that was pretty painless. Marina, you're next."

She walks out to the hall. Tom smiles at her and asks her to sit down on the stool opposite the camera. She focuses very hard on not tripping over any wires or falling flat on her face. There is a black backdrop behind the stool and a silver umbrella set up to the right of it.

"Very professional," smiles Marina. "Katie certainly doesn't do things by halves, or did you bring all this stuff?"

"No, she rented it from a local studio. Ready?"

"Yes."

"Let's get going... smile?"

Marina tries but can't.

"OK Marina, tell me what I can say to make you relax," says Tom from behind the camera.

Marina smiles and the flash goes off.

"Well, that was easy," he laughs. "If only I had that effect on all the models I work with."

"Oh I'm sure you do Tom," she says, looking straight at the lens of the camera. She feels as if their eyes are connecting, despite the lens, but the fact that she can't actually see his face makes her braver. He takes another picture of her.

"I don't," he says, which, Marina acknowledges to herself, is probably a truer statement than he knows.

"Nice job though, taking pictures of beautiful girls all day long."

"So is yours, writing about what you think, talking to all those people through your articles."

Marina looks puzzled.

"Ollie's mother gave me a copy of your article about..."

"First love," Marina interrupts.

"Yes, I thought it was good...."

She suddenly feels defensive. "It's a job, Tom. I write

things that I know will get a reaction."

"So you didn't mean any of it?"

She sighs, the flash goes off again. "It's just so…"

"Long ago?"

She nods decisively, even if that isn't what she means. The flash goes off again.

"I think you're really lucky, I mean to have experienced that feeling."

"What feeling?"

"To care so much about someone that you would do what you did for me."

Marina looks down. "It wasn't much…"

"It was to me."

She smiles at him through the lens. He takes another picture.

"That is what those in the trade call 'the decisive moment'," says Tom getting up from behind the camera and coming towards her.

She stands up from the stool and immediately trips over a wire, which sends her falling into Tom, who catches her and holds her by her shoulders for a moment. She looks up at him and continues the conversation in an effort to seem unaffected by his touch. "The what moment?"

"The decisive moment," he says, still looking into her

eyes. "It's a phrase that the French photographer Henri Cartier-Bresson coined. It means you have the shot you've been after, the perfect image."

"Glad to hear it," says Marina. She thinks about saying something but instead walks towards the door. "Shall I send in the next victim?"

"I hope it wasn't that painful," says Tom laughing.

Marina leaves the room and hopes that her heart will have calmed before she has to get too close to anyone. It's pounding like she's just done twenty-five sun salutations at high speed or watched Chelsea in a penalty shootout to win the Champions League.

Tom sits down behind the camera to prepare it for the next shot. He looks at the picture he just took of Marina. She seems to be staring straight at him, her eyes open wide and honest, her mouth just at the beginning of a smile, her curly brown hair hanging naturally around her face. He can't stop looking at it. He smiles as he remembers her falling towards him – she always was incredibly clumsy.

And as Marina's husband walks in the room, Tom Stamford registers with some surprise that the thought of her elicits a feeling of affection that he hasn't felt for a very long time, if ever.

13

"It's sad to grow old, but nice to ripen."
Brigitte Bardot

New Year's Eve 2010

'Yoga is not a competitive sport,' she keeps repeating in her head. But still she can't help but glance sideways at Katie as they do the bridge pose to see how high her hips are. Bridge is the one yoga move Marina excels at, mainly because it doesn't involve her hamstrings that are always so tight she finds it impossible to touch her toes, even after years of trying, which drives her into a very un-Zen-like state of utter frustration.

"Marina, don't move your head sideways during bridge," says the teacher, "you will hurt yourself."

Damn, rumbled.

She sighs and tries to relax. She is glad to get away from Mark. They had another terrible row last night before going to bed, and this morning they are barely speaking. It was about the usual subject, but it's stepped up a gear. Mark is now arguing that she obviously doesn't love him if she doesn't want to have children with him.

"Why do men always think it comes down to them?" she had shouted. "Not wanting to have children is MY decision, based on MY feelings. It has nothing to do with you."

It is New Year's Eve morning and Marina has been invited to Katie's yoga studio for a private lesson. It is predictably exquisite, with a pale wooden floor (no shoes allowed) and vast French doors that lead on to a terrace where, Katie told her earlier, she does yoga outside when it gets warmer. Their teacher is a lanky American who lives in St Tropez, called Candy. She could tell you how flexible Sharon Stone is or if Michael Douglas can stay in downward dog for more than two seconds, but of course she won't.

"I'll have to be careful what I say," she smiles smugly when Katie tells her Marina works for a newspaper. Marina doesn't even react.

The yoga lesson is good though. Candy radiates a calm atmosphere and takes them through the moves slowly and precisely, focusing on their breathing as well as their positions. She gently moves their bodies into the right place now and again – something you don't get the benefit of in a class of thirty people.

Maybe because there is nothing to bump into or knock over, a yoga mat is one place Marina doesn't feel clumsy. And she loves the utter relaxation afterwards, lying in shavasana, surrendering her body to the ground and clearing her mind.

Katie Tomlinson never feels clumsy anywhere, but she does find the spiritual side to yoga slightly tedious. It keeps your limbs young and slender, though, so she does some religiously every day. There is nothing old about her limbs and she intends to keep them that way.

Ageing is Katie Tomlinson's main fear. Some people are scared of flying, or getting into debt, or their children being kidnapped, but for Katie there is nothing as terrifying as a wrinkle. Her anti-ageing battle rages twenty-four hours a day. She even fights wrinkles in her sleep by, among other things, sleeping on her back (so as to avoid wrinkling her face and décolletage), using a silk pillowcase in the event that she should roll onto her side in the middle of the night, and of course covering her face with magical serums and anti-ageing creams that work on rejuvenating her skin throughout her sleeping hours.

The battle intensifies as soon as she wakes up; she won't even open the curtains without putting on sunscreen. She keeps laughing and smiling to a bare minimum. And there is not an anti-ageing laser invented that Katie hasn't been under, with more or less pleasing results. There are of course days when she has to hide from the world, when she has what her glamorous Brazilian born dermatologist calls "downtime" and she looks like a red tomato due to some laser or peel. She often plumps her lips with a bit of Restylene at the same time and wanders around her darkened house looking like a rather unattractive, pained goldfish, but no one, except for Cherry is allowed to see her in this state. They are what she refers to as her "Dorian Gray moments", but instead of a portrait hiding in the attic, it is her skulking around the house in a silk dressing gown.

Marina falls asleep immediately during the relaxation and has an anxiety dream of waking up in her class in London when everyone else has left, with Ria leaning over her saying "You must be very tired." Here Candy's voice saying "Slowly wiggle your fingers and toes" wakes her, and she feels like she's been asleep for hours. She often thinks a quick shavasana in the newsroom would do wonders for the mood at *The Chronicle*. She sometimes catches Flora or Jo napping on a chair in the kitchen, dribbling slightly, but that's as close as you get to power naps in the cutthroat world of Fleet Street journalism.

"Keep your eyes shut and sit up in a cross-legged

position," says Candy. "Think about your practice, what you have got out of it, and what you want to do with your day, this gift of a day. Think about the new year ahead and where you see yourself at the end of that year."

It is New Year's Eve, exactly fifteen years on from the accident, thinks Marina. A day to take stock and think about what she has done with her life so far, about what she wants to achieve and her priorities right now. She needs to make a decision about whether or not to have children. By this time next year she should either have a baby with Mark or not. Which scenario is the one she likes the most?

She wonders briefly what Katie is thinking, the woman who has fame and everything money can buy. What will she want to achieve next year?

After the yoga, Katie invites Marina to come to her dressing room. "I have a few samples that are more your size," she tells her. "No offence."

"None taken," says Marina. It's true that she is larger than Katie, but then so are most 12 year olds.

They go to Katie's rooms, which consists of a bedroom, a vast bathroom, two dressing rooms and a sitting room. Marina feels like she's walked into a *Hello!* magazine shoot: 'Katie Tomlinson welcomes you into her intimate suite where nothing bad ever happens, everyone is beautiful and no one ever raises their voice'. The décor is minimalist, the stone walls whitewashed, the sofas all white, and the wooden four-poster bed has white mosquito nets neatly folded ready for the summer. There are huge wooden fans in the beamed ceiling.

"One of the dressing rooms is for casual stuff and the other for evening wear," explains Katie, showing Marina into the 'casual' dressing room. There are boxes and bags piled up on the floor, all bearing designer names.

"What size are your feet?"

"Five and a half."

"Shame. I have lots of shoes I don't wear any more but they're all size four."

Of course they are, thinks Marina. Perfect little feet to go with her perfect big suite. Then she feels guilty for being so mean. After all, Katie doesn't need to give her any clothes, she's just being kind. Maybe she's changed since the old days, matured a bit. Then Marina's cynical hackette voice comes back with 'She's only giving you clothes so she can show you how much she's got and how much thinner than you she is as you can only fit into the samples for fat people she happens to have left over'. There had always been competition between the girls. Marina was convinced Katie was vying for Tom's affection and with more success than she ever had. Katie was jealous of Marina for many reasons, not least her academic success and thick, curly hair.

"How about these?" asks Katie holding up a pair of beige trousers. "They're Ralph Lauren, last season, but still very nice."

"Oh I'm not sure I can wear last season," says Marina.

"You're so right," says Katie.

"Katie, I was joking, I have clothes from the 1980s."

"Oh, that's fine, that's vintage," laughs Katie. It occurs to Marina that Katie rarely laughs, which is a shame, because she looks much younger when she does.

14

"Diamonds are a girl's best friend."
Marilyn Monroe

After seeing him another couple of times, Ulrika decides that Hugo Willoughby is a starter rather than a main course. As a man he is not able to give her what she needs, and rather like a book without pictures, Ulrika reasons, what is the point of a man who cannot give you what you need?

"Morning Joseph," she says walking into her family's Bond Street shop, looking stunning in a trench-coat that could pass for Burberry but is in fact Zara; needs must. Happily Ulrika is one of those women who doesn't actually have to wear designer kit to look gorgeous; she would just prefer to.

Savage & Sons, Est. 1811 reads the carved sign above the door. Joseph Crabbe looks like he's been there since then.

"Morning Miss Ulrika," he smiles. "How are you?"

"Fine thanks Joseph, how are you?"

"Mustn't grumble, Miss," he replies, continuing his work assessing a rare ruby. Savage & Sons is a business that has made high-end jewellery for the royals and the elite for almost exactly 200 years. Nowadays of course, much to Joseph's disgust, the majority of its clients are TV personalities or football stars, people for whom taste is not a matter of education or breeding but rather something that can be bought as easily as a hamburger. But he is loyal to the family, having worked for both Ulrika's grandfather and father, and he will stay at the wooden counter he has stood behind for the past fifty years and knows every single scratch on until they carry him out in a coffin. He has already ordered the cuff-links for his burial suit, pure gold – extravagant perhaps, but you can't take it with you. The rest of his savings he will leave to the children of the only woman he ever kissed, a certain Joyce Etherinton who used to work at Savage & Sons until she got fed up of waiting for Joseph to propose and married someone else. They kept in touch over the years, rather more like siblings than lovers, and he is godfather to one of her daughters, a plump girl now in her thirties who works in a post office in Taunton.

When Miss Ulrika first came to work for her father

Joseph had been sceptical. A spoilt public schoolgirl whose only other job had been as a model – what on earth would she know about marketing a traditional business like Savage & Sons? But he had to hand it to her. Much as Joseph hated all that new-fangled internet stuff, even he could see it was the future, and Miss Ulrika had succeeded in launching the online business for the prêt-à-porter range so effectively that it now made four times as much money as the bespoke side of the business. She was what his mother would have called a "firecracker", and funny with it. He didn't want to get too familiar, it wasn't right, but she did make him chuckle at times.

Ulrika walks up the stairs to her office and switches on her computer. She loves this room, no one can bother her here; it is her sanctuary. When Marina describes how she feels about her Saturday morning yoga classes with Ria, Ulrika can totally relate to it and is reminded of her office. Much as she resents being forced to work, once she is there, she really loves it.

Here she is in control; no one can bother her. There's just her father and Joseph in the building – no screaming twins, no useless husband. The thought of Ben makes her head hurt. She needs to do something drastic – she can't bear to stay with him until he slowly bleeds her dry and she's too old to be remotely attractive to anyone, and has to start shopping at Asda. Even she would have trouble making their hideous clothes look good.

She sits down at her desk and calls Kitty. Most days she looks forward to talking to her old nanny, but today everything feels like a chore, like she has nothing to look forward to. Like nothing is going to make her feel any better. This is not a state Ulrika finds herself in often, and Kitty picks up on it immediately.

"You sound down darling, what is it?" she asks.

"Nothing beyond the usual, just the daily grind, and I'm so fed up with being penniless I could scream."

"I wish I could help you, you know I would if I could."

Ulrika smiles. "Of course I do, keep buying the lottery tickets, you never know, we might both end our days in some fabulous luxury hotel."

"I had tea at the Dorchester once, I liked that."

"I will book us a suite. Must dash, time to work, love you, Kitty."

They say goodbye and Ulrika opens her Outlook Express. Most of the emails have been dealt with on the BlackBerry on the train coming to town. There's nothing from Ben apologizing or explaining exactly how he plans to pay the mortgage this month. *Quelle surprise*! Twat. She lights a cigarette and looks at her diary. Coffee with someone from *GQ*, followed by lunch with Hugo, which she will cancel, and then a VIP customer coming in at 4pm for a consultation.

She calls downstairs on the shop phone. "Joseph, who is the VIP we have this afternoon?" she asks, hoping it's not that ghastly Simon Cowell again.

"It's Lord Mycroft, Miss," he replies. "You know, the one with the estate in Yorkshire, usually buys seven cuff-links a year, one for each day of the week and seems to spoil his friends with rare gems on a regular basis. His Lordship is coming in today to buy a diamond ring for his mother's birthday."

"Thanks Joseph," she says smiling and hanging up. She suddenly feels rather more optimistic about the day ahead. The main course is about to arrive.

❧ *15* ❧

"It is easier to forgive an enemy than to forgive a friend."
William Blake

By the time it is a quarter to midnight (London time – they already celebrated midnight French time almost an hour ago), they are all quite merry. The double punch idea has worked, there are two bowls on the table and Katie has put herself in charge of administering drinks, making sure Ollie only gets the virgin punch. They are sitting on the sofas and armchairs in the sitting room. There is a log fire burning, they have not drawn the curtains on the glass wall facing the sea so they can see the fireworks from town.

Katie has just put some opera on. "I need to educate you all," she laughs. "This is…"

"Dreary," interrupts Ollie.

"I used to agree," says Tom. "Until I lived in Rome, I learnt about the magic of opera there and am hooked now."

"As I was saying," continues Katie, "this is an opera written by the Russian composer Tchaikovsky, based on a poem by the Russian writer Pushkin. It is called *Yevgeny Onegin* and is the story of a hopeless first love."

Marina feels herself blush, even though she really has no reason to. Most people's first loves were hopeless. She is hardly in a minority.

"Tell us the story," says Mark, leaning back on the sofa, putting his arm around Marina.

Katie hopes she can remember; she studied it feverishly when she met the Russian opera singer and decided to seduce him. Before her plans turned to another man, sitting only two feet away from her. "Well, Onegin, our hero, or rather our anti-hero because he is a bit of a cad, visits a friend in the countryside and there meets the young and naïve Tatyana who falls hopelessly in love with him at first sight. After a few days and much deliberation, she writes him a letter telling him of her feelings."

Katie takes a deep breath, rather pleased with that last phrase – it has a certain intellectual ring to it. Really, she sometimes wonders if she's wasted in fashion.

"The next time he sees her, he has the letter with him, which he proceeds to tear up, right in front of her eyes. He tells her to forget him, that he is way out of her league basically."

"God, that's so cruel," exclaims Marina.

"See how nice I was?" grins Tom at her. She smiles and catches his eye, for a split second she forgets everything in the room. But then she remembers that her husband is sitting next to her.

"Go on," Mark urges Katie, smiling encouragingly.

"Of course the lovely Tatyana is utterly devastated. Fast forward maybe ten years or so and our hero is in St Petersburg, he has been roaming the world unsuccessfully looking for love, and is invited to a very smart event hosted by some incredibly important ambassador. Who should he see on said ambassador's arm but Tatyana, who has grown from a fumbling, shy girl into a sophisticated, rich and powerful woman. He immediately realises his grave error and falls into a terrible depression, following her around for weeks and desperately trying to catch her alone. Eventually he does, and this time it is he who confesses his undying love to her." Katie pauses for dramatic effect, as the opera plays on in the background.

"So what happens?" asks Ollie, who has seized the moment to replenish his glass without anyone noticing.

"Well, Tatyana listens to Onegin's declaration of love and then reminds him that all those years ago, her words were greeted with nothing but "fierce rejection" as she puts it. And she tells him that it is too late. 'I love you,' she says, 'why should I deceive you? But I am given to another now, and I will eternally keep my vow.'"

There is silence for a moment. "What a sad story," says Marina. "But I suppose operas aren't really supposed to be jolly."

"Nor is first love really," adds Ollie. "I mean who can remember their first love? Was it fun? Mine certainly wasn't. We went out for a bit and then she dumped me for my brother."

"Was that Laila?" asks Katie.

"Yes, she said sorry though when I saw her at the rehab place…"

Everyone laughs.

"Well, that's all right then," says Tom.

"Who knows, you might even end up with Laila in the end. Fate has thrown you together again," says Mark, waving his arms in a dramatic gesture, which seems oddly incongruent with his character. "Just like Onegin and Tatyana."

"Amazing how it does that," says Ollie.

"Just think that fifteen years ago we were all together…" says Marina. She trails off. She can't remember if it was before or after midnight that Ollie got shot. After, she guesses.

"Let's try not to leave it another fifteen years before

we meet again," says Mark, raising his glass.

"Hear, hear," says Katie, raising hers to touch his and smiling. Marina has the sensation of catapulted back to Notting Hill Gate and everything in front of her happening in slow motion. That smile of Katie's, it contained a lot more feeling than just your normal smile. Suddenly things seem incredibly clear. How could she have been so dim? Yet another reason Katie used to loathe her.

"Guys, it's almost midnight," shouts Tom. "Quick, raise your glasses, here's some more punch. Everyone stand up, can you believe it, fifteen years ago we were all high on some unspeakable substance laced with nutmeg. Now here we are drinking the most delicious punch in a luxury villa in St Tropez – that's what's I call progress."

They all laugh. Katie turns the opera down so they can hear the chimes on the television from Big Ben in London.

"Who knows the words to *Auld Lang Syne*?" says Mark.

"No one ever does," laughs Marina, "but we can sing it anyway."

Two hours later the opera has been substituted for a 1990s compilation album, songs that take them back to the era they met in. *Country House* by Blur proves the final frontier for Ollie, whose body can't handle the alcohol he has been furtively downing, having worked out pretty much immediately that he was being given virgin punch. He passes out on the sofa, smiling. Katie suspects that he is drunk and promises herself to call the clinic first thing. She feels a little like an errant parent does when their child trips over something they have left on the floor and ends up with grazed knees. But it is party time and the atmosphere is great. They dance in a four, singing at the tops of their voices, laughing and drinking champagne. Now that Ollie is asleep the bottles can come out. And the hits keep coming, each one better than the last. Now it's Oasis *Wonderwall*. Katie struts around like a model, Mark mimicking a one of the Gallagher brothers, it's tough to tell which one. Katie is having real fun for the first time in years, and also exercising, she tells herself while sipping some more champagne – this dancing is all good cardio.

Marina feels invincible. Dancing is one of her favourite things – it's another time, along with yoga, where she can let herself go without fear of knocking something over. She moves well in time to the music; these songs are all so familiar she can anticipate the next beat, even in her slightly inebriated state.

An old saying goes through Tom's head as he watches

her, about dancing being a vertical manifestation of a physical desire. He wonders how she feels about him now. He's sure she feels something, he can sense it. But she is married, and seemingly happy. So why no children? Maybe they can't have them.

Katie runs out and comes back with a bottle of tequila and some limes. "In the old days we had nutmeg, now we have tequila slammers!" she shouts. Everyone cheers. Ollie remains resolutely passed out.

The shot acts like an injection of adrenalin – the dancing becomes more frenetic, the mood even more energetic.

"Let's have a dancing competition," suggests Tom. "You can pick a song and you have one minute to dance its socks off."

"Good idea," says Katie grabbing her iPod. "Who's first?"

"More tequilas first," laughs Mark. "If I have to be publicly humiliated, I need more alcohol."

Katie lines up another slammer while Marina scrolls through the iPod. She has to squint slightly to see what is written. It's time to stop drinking, probably, she thinks fleetingly.

"I'll go first. I'll take Shakira's world cup song."

"OK," says Tom, downing his slammer and putting on

the iPod, "you're on."

Marina does a perfect impression of Shakira, hair-waving and African bum wiggle included – something she learnt from a Masai Mara girl while on a family holiday in Kenya aged sixteen, and very useful it has proved too.

"Excellent!" says Mark. "I certainly can't top that. Can I just sit it out?"

"Oh no," says Katie handing him the iPod. "Choose your poison."

He opts for *Satisfaction* by the Stones and more or less does an impression of a man playing air guitar while jumping around. He looks very sweet with his floppy blond hair flying around, but the judges are not convinced.

"I would say five out of ten," says Katie, "although much better looking than Mick. But don't give up the day job. Tom?"

Tom takes the iPod and flicks through. "I can't believe this is here," he smiles. "Might bring back some memories."

Harry Nilsson comes on and Tom does a Tom Jones crooning impression, serenading them all. Marina is catapulted back to the night fifteen years ago when he sang it in the basement in Ladbroke Grove. Just like then, she can't keep her eyes off him, however hard she tries. Mark and Katie are both watching, rolling around with laughter. Marina tries to look casual when he stares at her intensely. It might be mock intensity, but she's not sure, and the uncertainty is partly exhilarating and partly uncomfortable.

"OK, that was crap too," laughs Katie. "My turn." She puts the iPod in the base and stands in the middle of the room. Debbie Harry's *I Want That Man* blares out. Katie does a perfect impression of the blonde rocker and wins an ovation from the judges.

"I think it's a draw for first for the girls and last for the boys," says Mark. "Let's dance some more."

"OK, I'm putting the iPod on shuffle, so you'll just have to take what comes up," says Katie.

Twist and Shout is first. They split into pairs, Tom with Marina and Mark with Katie, and twist up and down. Marina doesn't know where to look – Tom is watching her every move, and she suddenly feels incredibly shy. She focuses on the song and trying to look nonchalant. By now she had hoped that she would be drunk enough to be impervious, or at least more laidback about it. But as always she seems to have drunk herself sober while everyone else is off their heads.

She glances at Mark and Katie, their eyes are locked, their bodies twisting up and down until the end of the song.

'Iiiiiif I should go....' Whitney Houston laments. "Shall we?" asks Tom, opening his arms. Marina walks into them slowly. She puts her arms around his neck and he puts his around her waist. They start to move in time to the song. She leans her head against his chest.

'And Iiiiiii will always love you,' sings Whitney. Marina feels like a teenager, and wonders briefly if people always feel like teenagers, however old they get. It's quite a good feeling, she thinks.

Tom leans forward and kisses the top of her head. How can he do that, she wonders, with her husband dancing next to her?

She looks up at him. He smiles down at her and then, almost in slow motion, he leans down and kisses her quickly on the lips.

"Happy New Year," he says.

"Happy New Year," she whispers.

He smiles and holds her tighter. She responds and their bodies start to move to the rhythm of the song. It feels so good Marina doesn't want to stop. She just hopes Mark hasn't noticed.

In fact she has to stop – she's married and here she is schmoozing with another man on the same dance-floor as her husband – crazy. This is not some surreal French film.

She looks up at Tom, ready to break away, and out of the corner of her eye she sees Katie and Mark dancing closely. Shit, maybe this is some surreal French film after all. She catches her breath, unsure of how to react. There is nothing that she wants more than to melt into Tom's arms, but suddenly she is totally sober and realises what a bad idea it would be. When the song ends she eases herself out of his arms.

"It's late," she says. "I should go."

Tom looks at her and nods. Before he can say anything Mark is by her side.

"Shall we make our way back to our billet?" he asks.

Marina nods and smiles. "Yes, let's," she says. The atmosphere of the night, the dancing and closeness to Tom is suddenly gone. As she leaves the room she tries to look around subtly to see if Tom and Katie are talking, or getting closer. She doesn't think she can bear it if they are. Some things never change, she concludes as she follows her husband to their bedroom.

❧ *16* ❧

"Marriage is an alliance entered into by a man who can't sleep with the window shut, and a woman who can't sleep with the window open."
George Bernard Shaw

They walk across the garden towards their room in silence. Marina wonders how drunk Mark is, and if he is going to say anything about her dancing with Tom. Probably not, unless he wants her to shout at him about flirting with Katie. Not that she feels like shouting. She doesn't really know what she feels like, except escaping to Tom's bedroom.

"Did you have a good time?" Mark asks while they're getting ready for bed.

"Yes, and you?"

"Yes, it was great fun. You looked like you were enjoying yourself. I bet your pelvic floor is feeling neglected."

Marina is not sure whether he's being sarcastic or trying to be funny. She decides to go for the latter and laughs.

"Yes, not much time to focus on that between the vintage champagne, tequila slammers and dancing," she replies. "You seemed to be enjoying yourself too."

Mark gets into bed. "Yes," he says. "Katie is an extremely attentive hostess."

"She always was," says Marina.

"I wasn't flirting, if that's what you're insinuating. She was flirting with me, but I made a concerted effort not to flirt back."

"Oh, it was an effort, was it?"

"Well, Katie can be very persuasive. She hasn't got where she is without certain powers of seduction."

Marina is unsure of how to react. She should maybe be angry, but suddenly just feels so very tired. And the image of Tom keeps cropping up in her mind.

"Anyway," says Mark, rolling over to go to sleep. "Tom can deal with them now, he's got plenty of experience."

Marina says something non-committal and lies down too. The atmosphere between them is not good, she knows that, they're just pretending everything is fine to avoid having a conversation that might lead to them saying things they would regret in the morning.

People always say you should never fall asleep on a row; this will be two nights on the trot. After ten minutes or so he starts to breathe deeply. Marina feels her body relax now she knows there will be no more arguing. She hates fighting with him, but at the moment they seem to do little else. Why has it suddenly got so bad? They were always such good friends but now they seem to have lost focus on everything but the one thing they disagree about.

Her mind wanders back to the evening. Dancing with Tom already seems like it was hours ago, but in fact it was only about thirty minutes since she was in his arms wondering how she could possibly stay there. Does this mean her marriage is over? Or just that she's looking for a bit of side-salad, as Ulrika would call it.

She wonders if Tom is sleeping. There was definitely something between them this evening that hadn't been there before. But maybe he was just doing his normal trick of making sure she is still keen. Why is she still so keen? Surely that first love never dies thing is actually tosh? She's even written about the whole imprinting thing. And yet she hasn't felt this alive for years. Her whole body seems sensitised, almost electric. The thought of him lying in a bed somewhere in her close vicinity makes it impossible to sleep. She practically has to force herself not to tiptoe out of the bedroom to go and find him. It feels like she's just managed to fall asleep when she hears a voice.

"Quick, wake up," Katie is shaking her. "Ollie's gone."

She sits up, immediately wide awake.

"Shit, you're not serious? Did anyone see him go?"

"No, no one saw a thing, but he's stolen the house-keeping money I keep in a jar in the kitchen. I've called the clinic and I've called the police, but we need to go and look for him. I suggest we all drive into town and then split up but stay in constant contact, then meet again in the main square after an hour's search. What worries me is that he's managed to find the worst part of town and scored some drugs. St Tropez is quite a small place and he doesn't have a car, so my hope is he won't be hard to find."

Marina jumps out of bed to get some clothes on; Mark is already up, pulling on his jeans. They drive into town and search for two hours, then go to the police station to file a missing persons report. Once back at the house, they find the staff have cleaned up after the night's festivities and there is breakfast on the table: fresh orange juice, croissants and hot coffee. The four of them sit down, exhausted and worried about the one member of the group they should have been looking after, and that they have all now failed.

Katie has called the clinic and talked to Laila. It was one of the most difficult calls she has ever had to make. Normally Cherry handles anything remotely uncomfortable for her, from chucking a boyfriend to turning down hopeful job applicants. But this is something she needs to do herself. In fact just being with them all again makes her feel more grounded than she has in years, and she has actually enjoyed the feeling, until Ollie's disappearance.

They all travel to Nice airport later that day. All except Ollie, whom there is still no sign of. Tom will fly straight to Rome, while Marina, Katie and Mark will head back to London.

Apart from Ollie's disappearance, Marina is also worried she will never see Tom Stamford again. Every second with him seems so precious now, because he will soon be gone. They check in and walk through security together. Tom's plane is taking off in half an hour, theirs fifteen minutes later. They walk him to his gate and say goodbye.

"Thanks Katie, for an amazing time. I'll call you if I hear anything from Ollie," says Tom, hugging Katie. "And I'll try to get hold of Carla again to see if she's heard from him as soon as I land."

Tom turns to Marina and put his hands on her shoulders. She feels the warmth of his hands through Katie's generously donated Ralph Lauren polo-necked jumper and remembers the turbulent night she has just had, imagining the feeling of his hands on her. He probably slept like a log, oblivious. Or maybe with Katie, a victim of her seductive powers as her husband called them. He leans forward and kisses her forehead.

"Great to see you again Marina, great to see you both," he nods towards Mark. "Give me a call if you're ever in Rome," he adds, handing her his card. She swears he squeezes her hand as he hands it over, and she catches his eye. There is something there. Something she has never seen there before: interest, or even affection – she's not sure.

Marina focuses hard on remembering the exact look so she can dissect it better when she's feeling less haggard. Then she watches him walk through the gate onto the plane.

The remaining three go to their gate where the plane is ready to board. Marina is by now too exhausted and fraught to get excited about walking into first class. She sits alone while Katie and Mark sit next to each other chatting. She looks down at her BlackBerry and sees several missed calls from Hugo Willoughby. She hopes there isn't some crisis at work. Maybe he wants to talk about Ulrika. Or the latest Chelsea game. She had switched her phone off to save on roaming charges. The stewardess walks past offering them champagne. Marina takes a sip; she can't possibly feel any worse than she does now. She is asleep before they are in the air.

17

*"Well,' said Pooh, 'what I like best – ' and then he had to
stop and think. Because although Eating Honey was a
very good thing to do, there was a moment just before
you began to eat it which was better than when you
were, but he didn't know what it was called."*
Winnie the Pooh

"He's called Lord Mycroft," Ulrika tells Marina over
lunch in a small French bistro off High Street
Kensington a few days later. "But I prefer to call him
Lord Mycock."

Marina laughs and takes a sip of her mineral water,
almost dropping it as she puts it down.

"Married?"

"Divorced, praise the Lord! Was married to a rather
mousy county girl called Jane for years and years. They
have two grown-up children."

"How old is he?"

"Early fifties but in GREAT shape. He strides around his enormous Yorkshire estate constantly, making sure all his minions are behaving themselves. Reminds me of a real life Rupert Campbell-Black from that Jilly Cooper book *Riders*."

"When did it start?"

Ulrika smiles. "It only just has. I had to play a bit of a long seduction game; three days. It all began when he came in to buy a ring for his mother's birthday. I happened to be at work and rather conveniently when I heard he'd arrived flounced down to the shop floor looking ravishing, even if I say so myself, in killer heels, skinny jeans and a cashmere jumper. I had done some research on him beforehand and discovered that one of his dreary ancestors had fought in the Battle of Omdurman in the Sudan, which gave the family the title. So when Joseph introduced us I piped up with 'Oh, as in the Battle of Omdurman Mycroft? What an honour,' and shook his hand. He was of course utterly amazed and fell in love on the spot. So that evening we went out for drinks and I made him laugh and actually he made me laugh too. He's much more entertaining than I'd hoped for."

"Ulrika, please tell me you wouldn't just go for someone for financial security? Tell me you would have to like them too?"

"God Marina you're such a romantic. I tried that with Ben, remember? And now I hate him more than I hate Gordon Brown. Haven't you read that Edith Wharton book, *The House of Mirth*?"

Marina shakes her head.

"Well," continues Ulrika, "it's brilliant, Kitty lent it to me. The heroine, Lily, is broke and desperately needs to get married. She fixates on a certain eligible young man called Percy Gryce. This is what she says about him, makes me howl with laughter every time I hear it." Ulrika clears her throat and puts on a fake serious face. "'She had been bored all the afternoon by Percy Gryce, but she must submit to more boredom, all on the bare chance that he might ultimately decide to do her the honour of boring her for life.' You see, it's our destiny as women to marry dreary fuckers, but really as far as I'm concerned, as long as we're stinking rich he can be as dull as he likes. To me there's nothing on earth as dreary as being broke. Even living in Yorkshire is better than that."

"But he's not dull? And how about the sex?"

"No, he's not. I'm getting to like him more and more, and the sex, well it's only happened once, at his club in Mayfair. Oh my GOD the poor man did not know what hit him. I think Jane must have kept him on a starvation diet. He was like a schoolboy in a sweet shop, his eyes literally popping out of his head. These county girls are all very well, but they can't fuck for toffee. He has all the right instruments and is extremely adept at kissing and in fact anything to do with his tongue, so I'm happy. And he's really very sweet, such a gentleman, and overwhelmingly charming, you know that kind of old school charming that older men do so well. I'm smitten."

Their food arrives; both have opted for the day's special, an omelette with chips and salad.

"Anyway, enough about *moi* and my lovely lord; tell me ALL about you and the cad. So you ended up in a clinch?"

Marina sighs. "Well, almost, yes. I stopped myself just in time and have thought of little else. Mark and I are now barely speaking. We argued the whole weekend and I just don't know what to do."

"So the cad still has the same effect on you? Incredible after all these years."

Marina smiles. "Yes, he is still drop-dead gorgeous, and the strange thing is he still makes me feel like that teenager, all excited and on edge and desperate to rip his clothes off. Something I haven't felt with Mark for years."

Ulrika tucks into her omelette.

"That's the difference between husbands and lovers; just like the difference between new shoes and old ones.

New ones will fill you with a delicious sense of anticipation just before you slip them on, you feel like you're the sexiest woman on earth, about to go and do something extraordinary. Old ones just leave you feeling cold. So what's next, what's going to happen with Mark?"

Marina sighs, she can barely face eating. "I just don't know. We seem to have lost the ability to talk to each other. It's like there's a wall between us. I just feel awful the whole time. I can't even face going to work, I've called in sick since we got back. Hugo called me and said he needed to see me, so I had to tell him Mark and I were going through a bad patch. He very sweetly said it could wait. Have you seen him at all?"

"No, he's forgotten now, thanks to the lusty lord. Poor you. Do you think it's best to maybe split for a bit?"

"Who knows? Yes, probably, but I can't see either of us suggesting it – it seems so final, so scary. And like we've failed. Poor Hugo as well. He joins the ranks of the 'chewed up and spat out by Ulrika'".

"Oh well he's in good company. Any news from the cad at all?"

"No, apart from a friend request on Facebook. But he hasn't got my email, or phone number. He gave me his card."

"Fucking Facebook? Why Facebook? We're not

sixteen for God's sake."

Marina laughs. "Although I read somewhere that Facebook is used more by women our age than sixteen years olds. Apparently only one in five women in their mid-thirties prefer sex to Facebook."

"I'm amazed it's that many," says Ulrika. "So did you respond to his little friend request?"

"I think part of the reason he did it was the article I wrote, and yes, I did respond. But not for two days. I've learnt from bitter experience with Tom that the best way to get him interested is to feign disinterest."

"Marina! That was fifteen years ago."

"I know, but I just don't think people change."

"So you're Facebook friends. What next?"

Marina picks at her lunch. "I don't know, he's in Rome, I'm here. I was hoping he might message me on Facebook once he got my response, but nothing so far."

"Not even a poke?" Ulrika interrupts.

"Very amusing. I'm desperate to see him again, to sort out in my head whether this is all real or whether it's just some fantasy that is not going to last. I want to spend some time with him, maybe even get to know him again."

"Ew, perish the thought," says Ulrika pushing the remains of her lunch away and laughing. "Sounds far too grown up. Next you'll be having sober sex. Although I did have a rather satisfying sober encounter with an old flame of mine who works in the City about six months ago during his lunch break. Such an advantage to fuck a man who has to go back to work – means he doesn't hang around too long. I suppose Lord Mycock has his estate to roam around. Ben of course does nothing but sit around getting fatter and poorer, hideous creature. Tom's a photographer isn't he?"

"Yes, fashion. So takes pictures of beautiful models all day long."

"How deeply irritating of him. So what's the plan Marina? Come on, you must have one, I know you too well to believe you're just sitting around waiting for your husband to bugger off and Tom to drop by carrying an enormous lens."

Marina sighs and finishes off her wine. She really can't eat a thing. "Plan is to wait another day. If he hasn't messaged me by then, I will send him an email saying how are things, asking if there's any news on Ollie, who by the way went awol in St Tropez and has yet to be found. If that little exchange goes well, we'll take it from there. But remember I am still married."

"Not for long by the sounds of it."

Marina sighs. "This baby thing has really wrecked things for us. It's funny, I didn't think it would. Maybe I should have been more flexible. But if you don't want a baby, there's not much you can do to convince yourself to have one. It just all feels wrong."

Ulrika orders another two glasses of wine. "I think it's time for decisive action. You and Mark are over in my view. Let's just send the cad a message now and see what happens. Don't you think you're a bit too old for games? You have known each other for more than half your lives."

"An email, text or Facebook message?" asks Marina, suddenly also convinced this is the best idea since the second glass of wine.

"Forget Facebook – deeply unsexy. And if he's stuck behind a camera all day he's unlikely to be checking emails, unless he has a BlackBerry or an iPhone. Did you happen to check as you were eyeing up his general crotch area?"

Marina laughs. "He has an iPhone."

The wine arrives.

"Good health," smiles Ulrika. "Right, an email it is then. How to strike the perfect balance between casually interested, devastatingly sexy and utterly fabulous?"

By the time they have finished their wine, a message has been sent to Tom that they're both happy with. Ulrika possibly more so than Marina, but Marina reasons, if anyone knows how to get her way with the opposite sex, Ulrika does.

Mark's pager goes as soon as he gets out of surgery. It's the duty nurse at the main reception.

"Dr, there's someone here to see you," she begins.

"Yes?"

"Well, she's that lady, you know, the fashion lady, Katie Tomlinson." She whispers the name as if it's a secret of some kind.

"Thank you nurse, please tell her I'll be right there," he says quickening his step.

He spots Katie immediately in the waiting room among the usual crowd of Londoners in their grey coats and thick jumpers. She is clutching a cream fur coat around her slim frame. Her long blonde hair is perfectly straight and glossy; it looks like it has been bathed in milk and honey. He can imagine it smelling divine. She looks slightly lost, vulnerable in the stark surroundings, scanning the horizon for the only familiar face she is likely to see there.

"Katie," says Mark as he approaches her. She skips towards him, her face filled with relief. He can't remember the last time someone who wasn't directly related to a patient he had just saved looked so happy to see him.

"Hello," she says. "It's so good to see you." She pauses.

"Green suits you."

Mark laughs. "That's lucky, I don't really have much choice in the matter. It's good to see you too. How have you been?"

Katie looks at the ground and bites her lip, reminding him of a recalcitrant schoolgirl. "Can we go somewhere and talk?"

"Sure, let's go to the canteen, it's not very glamorous, but the coffee is good and we can chat."

On the walk there Mark is astounded by the attention she attracts. Is it because she's famous? How famous is she anyway? Or is it because she looks impossibly glamorous, all golden and gorgeous, in this most unglamorous of environments.

He picks a table close to the window and goes to get them some coffee. He sees colleagues milling about, obviously desperate to ask him what he's doing with this woman but far too polite to ask. He only has one close friend at the hospital, his boss, and he still hasn't told him about the troubles he and Marina are having. What is there to tell really? Lots of couples have problems.

Katie sits at the window trying to focus on the view. There will be no easy way to tell him. Should she just come out with it, or should they make small talk beforehand. Will either of them mention their dance together, which was bordering on the not so innocent?

Mark sits down with the coffees. Katie is playing with her hair nervously. She waits for him to sit down.

"There's no easy way to say this," she begins. "They found Ollie. He's dead."

"Oh no. Where? What happened?"

"In the pool at the house. They think he must have slipped in the dark and fallen in, got stuck under the cover and drowned."

Mark rubs his forehead. "Shit. What a waste, I can't believe it. Just as he was getting back on track."

Katie shakes her head. "I feel terrible, it was all my idea, the reunion, and then we drank too much and..."

"Don't," he interrupts her, putting his hand on hers. "It's not your fault, it was an accident. Ollie was an adult, he made the choices he made, we didn't exactly ply him with alcohol."

Katie is slightly ashamed when she remembers that she did however ply the rest of them with alcohol. To achieve what? To seduce Mark? To repeat the one night they had together all those years when she had managed to prise him away from Marina for once? What was her plan really? She had to admit that she didn't really have one, but she wanted change of some kind. It was a bit like when she started a dress design and wasn't sure where it would end: would it have long or short sleeves, be cut on the bias or empire – she wouldn't know until she started drawing and the whole thing began to take on its final form.

"Have you told Tom?"

"No, I only just found out. I came straight here. I'll call him afterwards. Will you tell Marina?"

Mark nods. "Poor Ollie, I can't believe it."

Katie nods and sips her latte. It tastes good; it must be full-fat milk – she can't remember the last time she had that. "I know, I keep remembering his speech about how he wanted to make something of his life, quoting that Marlon Brando film. And now his life is over like the opening scene from *Sunset Boulevard.*"

"Tom will take it badly, and what about his girlfriend?"

"Carla, yes, I guess it's best if Tom tells her. I will talk to Laila at the clinic. I feel so awful about it, I just wish I could rewind the clock and make none of it happen."

"None of it?" says Mark watching her.

Katie feels herself blushing, something else she hasn't done for years. For heaven's sake, she's not eighteen any more. And it was only a dance.

"Mark, there's something else."

"What?"

She closes her eyes for a moment. This is not easy.

Honesty does not come naturally to Katie.

"OK, here goes." She takes a deep breath. "Mark, I don't know if you remember when we were all kids?"

He nods and smiles. "Yes, of course, you haven't changed that much."

"Very charming. Anyway, I was…." Katie stops to take another sip of her latte. Her heart is beating so fast she can barely speak.

She looks out towards the car park, Mark follows her gaze. People coming and going, some about to receive good news, some very bad. Some will arrive with the person they love and leave without them, their lives changed forever.

"Go on," he says leaning towards her.

She turns back to him and smiles. "Well, of course I was keen to see everyone, to get everyone together, but most of all I wanted to…"

Suddenly there is a sound like the incessant beeping of a car coming from Mark's pager. He looks at it as if he wants to hurl it across the room.

"Shit, an emergency, I've got to go." He gets up. She does the same. She can't get over how tall he is – he must be at least six foot four – and she feels minute in his presence, minute and rather protected.

"I'll call you straight after this emergency," he says,

leaning over and kissing her gently on the cheek. "Let's have dinner tonight, if you're free that is," he adds.

"I'm free," she smiles, watching him run towards the emergency room before picking up her taupe Birkin bag and going back outside where her chauffeur is waiting to take her home.

❦ *18* ❦

"When the gods want to punish you, they answer your prayers."
Karen Blixen.

Most mornings, reflects Marina, you wake up and nothing much has changed overnight. You look through your emails and there are the usual offerings from Groupon you don't want, along with press releases from dreary PRs. A quick look at Twitter confirms that no one important has died and that black is still in.

This morning is not one of those mornings. Among the flood of dreary emails is one from Tom. Just the sight of his name takes Marina from her half-slumber to upright in bed, BlackBerry in hand, panicking in case she accidentally deletes it by flicking the touch-screen in the wrong place.

'Ciao Bella' it reads. Good start. 'Thanks for your message, was on location all day just got back. How about a visit to Rome?! I would love to see you. Cheers – Tom.'

OK, so stay calm, she tells herself. Slightly dodgy use of exclamation mark, and she hates the word cheers, but he is after all, an images man, not a word man. And he would LOVE to see her. But does he mean her, or her and Mark? Talking of Mark, where the hell is he? He didn't come home last night. Maybe there was a late emergency and he slept at the hospital.

Marina bbms Ulrika to tell her the news. She leaves out her slight disappointment at his use of language, after all that's her hang-up and would not bother anyone else. It's just something she's going to have to get over.

Her phone rings as soon as the message has been sent. It's Ulrika.

"Shall I read it to you?" gasps Marina.

"Have you seen *The Sun* this morning?"

"It's raining."

"No, you moron, the newspaper."

"No, why? Do you want to hear what he wrote or not?"

"Go downstairs. You get all the papers, don't you?"

"Yes, OK, I'm on my way, what's the big deal? There's nothing on Twitter about any news. Frank Lampard hasn't suddenly died, has he?"

Marina grabs her dressing gown and goes downstairs to the front door. On the mat is at least three kilos of newspaper print, waiting for her to browse through, assess, be inspired and infuriated by. She picks up the pile and puts it down on the kitchen table with a thud.

"Get *The Sun* out," yells Ulrika.

"Right, *The Sun*, where is that scummy rag?"

She picks up the broadsheets in her search. "Typical, right at the bottom of the…." She stops mid-sentence. She even drops her precious BlackBerry. There under the headline 'Who is Katie's handsome date?' is a picture of her husband getting out of a black limo.

"Maaarriiiiinaaaaa." Ulrika sounds like she's underwater. Marina picks up her BlackBerry.

"Blimey."

"Yes, well now you know how those millions of victims of the tabloid press feel," says Ulrika.

"Thanks for your sympathy."

"Oh pull yourself together. You didn't want him, did you? Or his pesky offspring. But just because someone else does…"

"It's not that," snaps Marina. "He's still my husband, and I still love him, and frankly it's a bit of a shock to see him on the front page of *The Sun*."

"Yes, obviously he should have been on *The Chronicle*'s front page."

"Ha, very amusing. Well, he didn't waste much time, did he?"

"About as much as you did. Don't forget two minutes ago you were all full of your message from lover boy."

Marina sighs. Ulrika has a point. As usual. Maybe it is time to move on. But all the same. Mark is the last person she would expect to see on the front page of *The Sun*. What is he doing with Katie? Maybe they are an item already and he just never told her? Of course Katie has been out to get him for years, she realises that now. Maybe they have been together ever since the trip to France. She can't imagine that he would just deceive her and not mention it at all; he's too nice for that kind of behaviour. Clearly Katie engineered this, she's a brilliant manipulator of the media, but there is no doubt that he is there, in full colour, so her husband is at the very least to blame for that.

She drags herself upstairs to get ready for work, her column is due in today and she can't defer any longer.

Walking through the newsroom an hour later Marina has the impression that she has two heads. Of course no news spreads as fast as bad news about a member of staff. Last time someone was sacked, the whole place was buzzing with the scoop before the poor man had even walked into Cameron Knight's office.

She knows what awaits her as she goes up in the glass

lift; she hasn't spent every working day of her life in a newsroom not to know how they work. They are ruthless places, where you make friends and enemies for life, where you're only as good as your last story, and personal charm and good looks count for little. What counts is the column inches you get on the page. Women rarely have cat-fights over the men in a newspaper office, but if one of them feels her story has been pushed further down the order to make way for someone else's, then retribution will be severe and immediate. Grudges are held for years, sources are never shared and there is no such thing as teamwork.

Marina always found it a cutthroat and scary environment, but it is one she had never considered leaving. Ever since she was small she wanted to be a writer, and journalism seemed the natural way to achieve that. At school her friends would tell her who they were in love with and she would make up stories with them as stars and their crushes in the leading man role, a bit like AA Milne did for Christopher Robin. Only Winnie the Pooh was more amusing than most of the boys at St Bartholomew's Comprehensive School in Newbury, and slightly brighter.

During her mother's four divorces she was always being shunted from one long-suffering relation to another. They would look at her sympathetically and say 'One day you'll write a book about all this, dear' as if that made it all OK. She would look up at them with her big brown eyes and think 'Yes, I will, and you might even be in it'.

Like most journalists, Marina has several unfinished novels on her computer. In fact most of them are barely begun. She has found it more and more difficult to get into a writing rhythm and also is now totally undecided what to write about. The misery memoir has been done to death, so to speak, and anyway her memories are not nearly as miserable as those of most people who plunder their past for a living. A father missing in action after her birth (and as a consequence of her birth her mother never tired of telling her), a sequence of irritating stepfathers and a vain and selfish mother who never wanted children in the first place and was obsessed with ageing (or rather not ageing) – to the point that she went through a phase of introducing Marina as her younger sister to acquaintances – is not really much in comparison with people who spent their entire childhoods locked up in a cupboard and were taken out only to be beaten, or eaten.

So Marina has moved on from the misery memoir to chick-lit. Except that every time she sits down to write something she wonders if anyone will be interested and then can't really get that interested herself so gives up and reads a chick-lit instead for inspiration. Which takes up all the time she has set aside for writing it.

She had promised herself that the job at *The Chronicle* would be a good excuse to write a novel. How long can it take to write one column a week for heaven's sake? She'd have plenty of spare time. But it hasn't turned out that way. The column takes up a couple of days' research and writing and she is often asked to help out on features or news. Newspapers are hardly a growth industry; the days of the prima donna columnist are over, unless you're Jeremy Clarkson.

So the unfinished novel sits in her drawer, or rather on her desktop, as with so many other hapless hacks all over London. In fact, Marina would be willing to bet that the only people who didn't harbour book-writing ambitions at *The Chronicle* were Flora and Jo, although their memoirs as tea-ladies to the almost-in-the-gutter press would probably make fascinating reading.

Jo is the first person she sees when she steps out of the lift. She knows that she knows and Jo knows that she knows she knows but doesn't say anything, just smirks under her rather badly cut fringe. Marina sighs. If Jo knows, even the non-*Sun* readers will have heard about it by now.

The Sun helpfully reveals the identity of Katie's mystery date on page five, just for those in the office who didn't know who Marina was married to. 'Dr Mark Chadwick, aged 35, consultant cardiologist at St Thomas's hospital in London, married to *Chronicle* columnist Marina Shaw,' it reads. And then goes on to say that the couple enjoyed a romantic dinner at Lorenzo's Restaurant in Knightsbridge before leaving together in Katie's chauffeur-driven Mercedes.

Clearly her husband found somewhere more comfortable to sleep than the hospital staff quarters where he told her he would be spending the night.

She gets to her desk and puts on her computer.

"Morning," says Felicia.

"Morning," says Millie.

"Morning," says Marina. Silence. She takes a deep breath. "OK, I know you've all seen it. The fact is Mark and I are having a trial separation," she lies, "and if he wants to hang out with Katie Tomlinson then of course there is nothing I can do about it."

Both girls start saying how sorry they are. Marina is touched by their sympathy. Hugo arrives mid-conversation and joins in.

"What on earth is he thinking of?" he says. "Why would he want to trade you in for that scrawny self-obsessed creature. Really, he needs his head examining. I'm going to buy you something good from M & S to cheer you up, what do you want? You can have anything at all; mini-trifle? Blueberry muffin?"

Marina smiles. "Now you're talking. Muffin please. Low-fat."

"Oh no you don't, we love you just the way you are around here. Full-fat or nothing." Hugo swans off to M & S, and Marina settles down to do some work.

"It will make a great column," says a voice behind her after a few minutes. Cameron Knight, on his way to make Les Misérables' day even more miserable, has stopped at her desk. "The hackette who reads about her own husband moving on in the gutter press. The revelation of how it feels to be on the other side of the newspaper. Could be very moving?"

Marina nods slowly.

"Think about it, Marina," he adds before moving on.

Marina puts her head in her hands. He has a point – of course it will make a great read. And of course he doesn't mean think about it. He means do it.

But even though she has always lived by the adage that everything is copy, she is suddenly feeling extremely squeamish about sharing the demise of her own marriage with two million readers.

19

"My one regret in life is that I'm not someone else."
Woody Allen

"I should have done more to stop him taking drugs," Carla says to Tom, crying inconsolably, "I just thought he would stop of his own accord. He was too clever to stay a junkie."

Tom hugs her and strokes her hair. Her whole body is convulsed with grief; he wishes he could make her feel better. "Look, we both tried, I feel terrible about it too, but I know what it was like when I was taking drugs you don't really take any notice of anyone, your priority becomes the drug. What hurts so much though is that we finally had him on the road to recovery."

When Katie had called to tell him, Tom had walked around Rome for hours remembering his friend and reflecting on the fact that if he hadn't been so taken with Marina he might have noticed that Ollie was drinking and stopped him.

For the first time in years he also went back to the painful memory of the night that was the beginning of the end, when he shot Ollie in the stomach. The girls had protected him then, telling the police that Ollie had been larking about and shot himself by accident. But this time no one could protect him; he would live with the guilt forever, even if he was trying to make Carla feel better by telling her it was no one's fault.

The last time he was in her flat he was there to save Ollie from himself, to hand him over to his mother and try to change his destiny. It seemed like a different life, even if it was only a few short weeks ago.

"Have they had the funeral?"

"No, it's next week. I'm going over for it. Come with me if you'd like to."

Carla nods. "Yes, I would like to. I want to say goodbye."

She gets up and walks to the window. "I had plans for us, you know. I thought he would get himself together and we would have a normal life; even have children together one day. I really loved him, you know. I can't believe I spend all day controlling thirty or so kids in a classroom but I couldn't control the one person in my life who really mattered."

"Carla it's not your fault. The problem was he couldn't

control himself. You can't blame yourself for this."

"I know, but I will," she replies. "As the eldest of seven children, I will always blame myself for anything that goes wrong. It's genetically impossible for me to do otherwise." She sighs. "I have to go and meet my mother for tea at the Café Byron. Let's walk out together. Anyway, how are you? "

Tom pauses. "Not sure, devastated of course about Ollie, but also full of hope, or some feeling I don't really recognise. There was this girl there over New Year I used to know…."

"Oh," Carla looks surprised. "That sounds like good news. Tell me more."

"Not good news. She's married."

"Even better," says Carla, putting on her light pink duffel coat and grabbing her handbag. "You might stay interested for more than five minutes."

*

Mark wakes up before Katie and looks around the room. He feels like he's woken up in a *Hello!* magazine article. There is nothing out of place. Marina would hate it. In theory, he should love it. Marina always teases him about how anal he is – everything in its place and so forth. He finds it tough not to crave the order of the operating theatre at home as well.

The walls are white, the ceiling is white. The floors are polished wood – but not the sort of thing you see in IKEA, but parquet made of oak that wouldn't look out of place in a ballroom. There are woolen rugs on the floor, off-white in colour, just deep enough to sink your feet into. The curtains are off-white, probably around three metres high; they hang down over the windows in a purely decorative role as the windows have blinds.

It's lucky they're both blond, he thinks smiling to himself, or they would be terribly out of sync with the décor.

He sneaks out of bed and goes downstairs to put the kettle on; he remembers where it is from the night before. He also remembers having wild sex, fun sex, exciting sex. How is he going to explain all this to Marina? Maybe she doesn't need to know. No, he has to be honest with her.

"Morning Mark." Katie is standing at the door in a cream silk dressing gown, smiling at him. "Is the kettle on?"

"Yes," he looks up at her and smiles. "I'll make some tea. We should talk, Katie."

"I agree," she says, moving towards him, glancing briefly at the papers strewn out in front of him. She sees *The Sun* at the bottom of the pile and wonders if Mark has spotted it. He would be furious if he knew she tipped the papps off. She pulls up a stool and sits down opposite him.

"This has all happened so quickly," he begins. "I'm not sure it's what I really want. Not that last night wasn't great," he smiles, "it really was, you know that, but Marina and I have been an item for so long, it just seems too sudden to let it all go."

Katie nods slowly. She remembers a friend of hers once telling her that life is a bit like a game of football. You trundle along at nil – nil until the ninetieth minute and then you suddenly score, finding the man of your dreams and getting pregnant, all in a matter of weeks. She listened, but didn't really believe it, until it happened to her. In fact it didn't even take her weeks.

Katie is convinced she is pregnant from her encounter with Mark just a few hours ago. She knew it the instant it happened, it was as if something clicked inside her. She cannot afford to lose him now. She almost has her dream. How would she deal with this if it were a management buyout?

"I agree," she says. "I've been thinking the same thing. I would never forgive myself if you hadn't done everything you could to save your marriage. After all, Marina is a good friend of mine." She stands up and walks over to him. She has never seen anything more beautiful in her life; the way the morning sun catches his blond hair gives him an ethereal feel. He is wearing just his white boxer shorts; his tall lean body is propped up against the island in her kitchen. She puts her arms on his shoulders and places her face against his chest. She loves the clean smell of him. He folds his arms around her.

"I love you Mark," she whispers, "but you need to do what's right." She looks up at him and smiles. "But there's no reason we can't say goodbye in style," she says before sinking her hand into his white boxer shorts.

❦ 20 ❧

"Ashes to ashes, funk to funky, we know Major Tom's a junkie."
David Bowie

As they lower Ollie's body into the soft Devon ground, Carla lets out a sob. Ollie's mother consoles her, but she is weeping too. The remaining members of the congregation stand staring at the grave.

Marina is horrified by the finality of it all. This is the first funeral she has ever been to and until you see that coffin being lowered, she realises, you have hope. Irrational hope, of course, but still, hope. Now it is dawning on her that Ollie will never be back, that they have failed to save him this time.

Tom and Mark are standing either side of her, staring at the ground. Mark is remembering the night he stopped Ollie bleeding to death. Tom is thinking about all the good times they had and wondering what life will be like without him. Katie is at the back of the gathering; she flew in from New York this morning and arrived just as the funeral cortege walked slowly up the path to the church.

"Ashes to ashes," says the vicar, as earth is thrown on to the coffin. "Dust to dust; in sure and certain hope of the Resurrection to eternal life, through our Lord Jesus Christ; who shall change our vile body, that it may be like unto his glorious body, according to the mighty working, whereby he is able to subdue all things to himself."

It is a grey, freezing-cold January day. Katie wishes she had opted for the black-wool trouser suit instead of the dress. It's the kind of cold that penetrates her bones and makes her neck and shoulders hurt they tense up so much. She is already tense – when she flew to New York four days ago, Mark went home to talk to Marina and try to work out what to do. She suggested they not speak until she got back, to give him the space he needed to make the right decision.

"You don't need to worry about me," she told him. "I'll be fine."

She still hasn't told him she thinks she's pregnant, something she becomes more convinced of day by day. She feels sick almost the whole time. And the sight of them standing next to each other by Ollie's grave is not helping, however picturesque the surroundings are.

The village of Bampton is surrounded by undulating hills and quiet countryside. The 13th-century stone church sits on a hill, overlooking the high street with its teashop, pubs, hairdresser and bakery. It is the kind of place people come to spend their summers eating scones and clotted cream, not watch friends being buried.

They all follow Ollie's parents home to their thatched cottage on the High Street. His parents are tiny, and grief makes them seem even smaller. They hunch up around each other and their relations, seeking comfort. Marina, Tom, Carla and Mark feel like giants in their sitting room; only Katie blends in without being too noticeable. She and Marina have exchanged a curt 'hello', Marina relieved that the focus is on Ollie's tragic death. How do you react to a woman who seduced your husband? Even if you are actually lusting after someone else? Katie wasn't to know that, for all she knows Marina could have been utterly devastated. But these are all things she pushes into the back of her mind as she and the others focus on trying to make Ollie's parents feel better. This is the place they raised Ollie, his bedroom is upstairs, and now he will never sleep in there again.

"I can't believe I will never hear his voice, or kiss him good night," weeps his mother. "My little Ollie, he was such a lovely boy." Her husband puts his arm around her.

"Come out to Italy for a break," says Tom. "There's a cottage you can borrow. You know you're welcome any time."

"Thanks Tom," says Ollie's mother. "I'd like to see where he lived, where he spent his last years. He never wanted us to come out of course…"

Her voice trails off and Tom hugs her.

"I'll show you everything," says Carla. "Just tell me when."

Ollie's mother is crying again and his father embraces her, making a sign for them to leave behind her back. He smiles and nods as they wave goodbye in silence.

"Shall we go to the pub?" suggests Tom when they get outside. "I know it's only five o'clock but I could really do with a drink."

The others agree and they traipse into the White Horse. They spot Laila, who is sitting alone nursing a Coke.

"Can we join you," asks Katie, "or would you rather be alone?"

"Please do," she says, adding, "Wow, what a blast from the past. So you two ended up together then after all?" she asks motioning at Tom and Marina who are standing next to each other.

Marina blushes.

"Er, no, Marina actually married Mark," says Tom.

"Oh sorry," says Laila, "I always thought Marina was sweet on you, and Katie was sweet on Mark."

"Things change," laughs Tom sitting down. "Marina obviously came to her senses."

"What would you all like to drink?" asks Katie.

They all order a drink and Mark offers to help her.

"Sorry about that," says Laila when they've gone. "I'm always putting my foot in it. Mark didn't look too happy, I guess it's not much fun having the first love pitch up again. Mind you, looks like Katie's still sweet on him, the way she's gazing up at him."

Marina turns to look. Katie is looking at Mark, smiling; he is smiling back. He looks more relaxed than he has during the past few days at home. They have talked, a lot, but come to no real conclusion. They agree there is nothing really terribly wrong with their relationship, bar the fact that he wants children and she doesn't. They also touched on the fact that Marina has feelings for Tom, but Marina wasn't willing to give them much credence. "I'm not a dizzy teenager," she had told him. "The Tom thing is not really relevant, it might just be a manifestation of the fact that things are not right between us."

Neither of them seemed willing to take the first step towards actually splitting up, although both of them had voiced the thought silently. The closest they got to it was Marina suggesting a trial separation. Mark said he thought they should wait until after the funeral to decide. So now they were still in limbo, not together, but not apart. And seeing Tom has made Marina more convinced she wants to be apart, despite what she told Mark the other night.

Katie and Mark are still ordering drinks. Mark asks her how she is. Katie wonders for a split second whether she should tell him her news. No, that would be below the belt so to speak. And what if she's wrong? Instead she decides to go for the 'independent but deeply devoted' woman.

"I'm fine Mark, really fine, just very happy to see you," she says.

Mark smiles down at her. "I'm very happy to see you too."

Katie bites her lip. "I've thought a lot about what happened," she stops.

"And…?" Mark encourages her. He is so confused about his own feelings that he would love to know hers.

"Well," she smiles brightly. "It was a great night…"

"And morning," adds Mark.

She laughs. "Indeed. Want to do it again?" she laughs. He laughs too.

"God I feel guilty laughing," she adds. "This is such

a sad occasion. Look, I love you Mark, I always have done, you know that, and if you decide to, well, if you decide that's what you want, then I'm here. That's all. No pressure."

Mark nods and smiles. The drinks have arrived. "Thanks Katie," he says.

Meanwhile Laila and Carla go into a deep conversation about Ollie. Tom turns to Marina.

"It's good to see you," he says quietly. "I thought about you, a lot."

"Me too," she says.

"What did you think?" he grins.

She shakes her head, half-smiling. "I thought I was being stupid and immature and acting like a schoolgirl. And that I ought to snap out of it and get a grip on reality."

She is interrupted by Mark putting a glass of white wine in front of her. Katie joins them carrying a Perrier.

"I'd like to make a toast," she says. "To Ollie."

"To Ollie," they all repeat, raising their glasses.

By eight o'clock they have relaxed. Laila tells them about being an addict, how serious it is, and how hard to extricate yourself. "I still call myself recovering after all these years," she explains, "which is why no alcohol.

And I want to tell you all something. You can't possibly blame yourselves for Ollie's death; the desire to get high and the addiction is stronger than all of you put together."

"I suppose we all underestimated it," says Mark.

They drink and chat. The pub starts to fill up.

"Shall we go and get something to eat?" suggests Katie at some stage.

"Good idea," says Mark. "I saw a fish and chip shop earlier. I haven't had fish and chips for years."

"Do you think they'd let us eat them here?" says Marina.

"I can ask," says Katie, heading to the bar.

"She certainly gets things done, doesn't she?" says Laila. "What a whirlwind."

Katie comes back smiling. "I had to give them a corkage fee, but we can bring our dinner here."

Tom stands up. "I'll go," he says. "Marina will give me a hand," he adds matter of factly. "What does everyone want?"

They walk down the high street towards the fish and chip shop.

"So, tell me why you were feeling so immature?" he asks.

Marina feels slightly relaxed from the wine. She looks

at her feet, willing them not to trip over anything as she explains.

"I just feel that, well, I'm a woman in my mid-thirties, a married woman in my mid-thirties, and that it seems ridiculous to be thinking about someone I was in love with years ago…"

Tom looks at her and smiles. "Were you having impure thoughts?"

Marina blushes.

"Glad to hear it," he laughs.

"Yes, but the point is, it might not be real. I mean my feelings for you might just be some silly schoolgirl fantasy that actually has nothing to do with reality and what I really ought to do is utterly ignore them and get on with my life. My married life."

"Is that what you want?" he asks as they walk into the fish and chip shop. The neon lights are glaringly bright and Marina feels exposed in more ways than one.

Tom orders the food, and then repeats the question. "Is that what you want?"

Marina sighs. "What I want is to be sure of my feelings for you before I even think about wrecking my marriage." She blushes and adds quietly. "That is, assuming you have any feelings for me."

"And how do you propose you decide that?"

His face is close to hers; she longs to kiss him, to touch him. She wishes someone would turn the lights out.

"Maybe," she suggests, "we could kiss, we could have just ONE kiss, and then I could exorcise you from my mind forever."

He takes a step closer to her, and for a moment she thinks he is going to kiss her. But then he shakes his head slowly. "Much as I would love to kiss you," he says, "I don't think that would work. Because as you well know, it all starts with a kiss."

Marina is now so desperate to kiss him she will stop at nothing. She loves the warm feeling of him being close to her; she imagines what his hands would feel like all over her body. "It might not. We might hate it, and decide we were better off before and not to see each other for another fifteen years."

"Your order's ready," says the man behind the counter.

Tom smiles and kisses her softly on the cheek before whispering in her ear, "and just how likely do you think that would be?"

Marina picks up three packets of fish and chips and shakes her head in defeat. "You're probably right."

"Look, you're the one who's married," he says once they're outside. "You've got the big decision to make. If you decide to split from Mark, then, well…"

"Well, what?" she asks.

"Well, then maybe I'll kiss you," he laughs.

After their fish and chip supper and a couple more drinks they head back to the little bed & breakfast they are staying in, which is tucked away behind the High Street a short walk from the church where Ollie now lies buried. It's been an exhausting day, but Marina knows as she and Mark walk into their twin room that it is going to get worse. They get ready for bed in silence, Marina thinking all the time that this might be the last time they get ready for bed together. Is Mark aware of how she's feeling? How is he feeling? Did he like seeing Katie again? What effect did it have on him? These are all questions buzzing around her brain. She can't go another day without more clarity.

"Marina, we need to talk," says Mark, sitting down on his bed. Marina sits down on hers. Why does she feel like a naughty schoolgirl? He's the one who's been unfaithful, at least if she believes what she read in *The Sun*.

"We need to make a big decision," he begins. "We need to decide whether or not we want to stay together."

Marina nods. "What do you want?"

Mark stands up and starts pacing the room. "I just don't know any more. I love you, Mina, but I'm not happy. You don't make me happy, no that's unfair; our relationship doesn't make me happy any more. I don't think there's anything terribly wrong with it, it's just that I think there has to be more to life than just sticking with someone because you're comfortable?"

He looks at her questioningly.

"I agree," she says. "I still love you, and I love hanging out with you, and I'm sure we could hang out happily for another ten years, but is that enough? It's like the difference between living and partly living. I'm too young to settle down into a relationship that is only right because there's nothing terribly wrong."

Mark nods, while Marina decides she must remember that line for a column. Then berates herself for being so insensitive, this is her marriage breaking up. Then again...

"Well, there is the baby thing too," he says. "We're never going to agree on that."

"I agree," smiles Marina.

"I can't believe even when we're splitting up we don't argue," says Mark. "Are we crazy to be separating? Most people don't get on as well as we do."

Marina starts to cry. And once she's started, she just can't stop. It's as if something has been released and it needs to come out, her grief over Ollie, along with the break-up of their marriage. Mark sits next to her and puts his arm around her.

"Sorry," she says between the tears. "It's just so sad. But then I can't see any other way round it, and in a way I want to split up, but it doesn't make it any easier."

Mark hugs her. "Same here." He stands up. "Look, shall we not make it so final? I mean could we agree on a trial separation? For say three months?"

Marina grabs a tissue and blows her nose. She looks around the room. It's a typical little English B&B. The matching bedspreads and curtains have roses on them, the carpet is thick and cream. She nods. "I guess that doesn't make it seem so drastic."

Mark is pacing again. "You stay in the house," he says. "I can go and stay with Charles. Let's keep the disruption as minimal as possible."

Marina looks up. "Or you could just stay with Katie? You seem to be getting along well."

He looks angry for a moment. "About as well as you and Tom?"

Marina looks down. "Mark, let's not fight, we're both being distracted right now, and maybe it's better that way. But I'm sure Katie is keen to know how you're feeling, just by the way she looks at you."

He smiles. "She is. But can we just agree to sleep on it

tonight. I don't like the idea of us both going off down the corridor into other relationships before we've even really finished ours?"

Marina nods in agreement, even if part of her is longing to join Tom, Mark is right, it would seem disrespectful, even a little sordid. "You're right. We can go to sleep in our twin beds like an old married couple."

And in two rooms just down the hall, Tom and Katie are both pacing, wondering what is happening, waiting like vultures to pounce if the outcome is right.

Marina sleeps fitfully and when she wakes up the next morning, the first thing she thinks is: "I'm single."

Mark is sleeping in the twin bed next to her, but he is no longer hers. She needs to tell Tom, and he and Carla are leaving first thing for the airport. It's already eight o'clock. She gets up and jumps in the shower. There isn't much time for make-up, but she quickly brushes on some bronzer and puts some clear lip-gloss on. She ties her hair back and throws on a jumper and some jeans before rushing to the breakfast room. It's empty and her heart sinks – she must have missed them already. She goes out of the front door into the freezing winter morning. Carla and Tom are there, just about to get into a taxi.

"Tom," she calls, and runs over to him.

"Marina, wow, you're up early." He smiles and hugs her.

"We split up," she says breathlessly. "Mark and I split up last night."

Tom hugs her close to him and whispers those three magic words into her ear. "Come to Rome."

21

"Everything in the world is about sex except sex.
Sex is about power."
Oscar Wilde.

The whip is probably slightly unnecessary, but she reasons: Why not? If you are going to be someone's ultimate fantasy, there's no point in going into it half-heartedly. And it's a well-known fact that anyone who has endured the English public school system secretly yearns for a good flogging to remind him of the good old days. If that flogging is given by a woman wearing nothing but riding boots and kinky red underwear, then so much the better.

This, thought Ulrika as she waited for Lord Mycroft in a suite at his Mayfair club, is why the aristocracy are so much more fun to seduce than the middle classes. Nothing shocks them. They are not bound by hideously bourgeois rules and mundane expectations of what a woman should and shouldn't be. A woman can be a slut and a wife all at the same time, both pleasing at the dinner table and erotic underneath it. There are no boundaries. They are simply light years ahead when it comes to equal rights.

As soon as he walks into the room she comes out from her hiding place (no point in giving the staff a free thrill) and grabs him, kissing him and ripping his coat off. As soon as he tries to touch her she brings the whip down on his arm.

"Hands off," she growls.

Lord Mycroft is used to formidable women. His mother was one, Matron at school was another. In fact he is rather fond of them. But never has he met one who combines the grit of a gurkha with the lasciviousness of a character from a French erotic novel. And he knows better than to argue with her, instead surrendering completely as she removes all his clothes, licking him all over as she undresses him. When he is naked she pushes him onto the bed and ties his arms above his head with his Hermès tie, a Christmas present from his former mother-in-law he had little imagined would come in so useful.

Still wearing riding boots and underwear she straddles him, teasing him by touching herself and gyrating sexily just above the level of his cock.

"Please," he moans, watching her.

"Please what?" smiles Ulrika.

"Please fuck me," he gasps.

She brings the whip down across his chest. The pain hovers between exquisite and too sharp for an instant, and then she moves down and takes his cock into her mouth.

Some women spend hours at secretarial college, learning how to type, or at cooking classes perfecting their béchamel sauce. Ulrika has spent more hours than most of her friends put together with cocks in her mouth, learning how to give the perfect blowjob. If she had to describe her technique (although why would she – no need to create competition, is there?) she would say the key to a good blowjob is to worship the cock you are sucking. Really admire it: kiss it, lick it, caress it, roll it between your tits, love it, use everything in your power to show how much you want it. Most men will have had blowjobs from women who would rather be anywhere than stuck with their heads in some bloke's crotch, so you need to really show them how much you enjoy it. One of the keys to great sex is watching the other person enjoy it, and if it's your cock that is sending them into a frenzy, how sexy is that?

Ulrika slowly moves her mouth up and down on his cock, and at the same time she caresses his balls. She feels his whole scrotum tighten with pleasure and increases the speed of her movements, bringing one hand to the base of the penis and using that to move it in and out of her mouth. He lifts his hips to push himself further into her mouth, groaning. Slowly she lifts her body up and straddles him again. She starts kissing his neck, letting go of the whip and resting her hips on his, ready to let him inside her.

"Please," he groans once more.

"Please what?" she asks, gently.

"Marry me," says Lord Mycroft.

Marina gets to the office early. She has a flight to catch at 3pm and wants to finish the column and sort out the content of the next one before then. Her column this week is obviously about finding out about her husband's new girlfriend via the press. She wonders what Mark will think of it. Maybe he won't even read it. Too late now, she thinks as she presses the 'send' button.

After a coffee break she moves on to next week's idea: equality in the workplace. She loves to get ahead on columns, the more time the idea has to mull around, the better the end product. She finds she even comes up with incisive opinions in her sleep sometimes.

"Excuse me," says a voice behind her. "Marina Shaw?"

"Yes," she turns around, irritated at being disturbed in mid-flow. She had her outro in her head and now it's gone.

"I'm Martin, from HR," says a man wearing a nylon suit.

"I'd never have known," she's tempted to say, but actually he might be quite useful. "Perfect, what do you think about equal rights in the workplace? Do you think women will ever have them?"

Martin looks perplexed. "Er, that's not really my area. I need you to come with me please, Miss."

"Why? What for? I need to finish my column."

"No Miss, you need to come with me. Now please."

Marina doesn't much like his tone but gets up from her chair. She sees Flora and Jo watching her, which is not a good sign – those two witches are only ever interested if there's trouble brewing.

Marina is in the queue for the loo on the plane. She knows the 'fasten your seatbelts' sign is about to come on but simply has to get in to put some make-up on before they land. Ulrika had read somewhere that the key to looking fresh when you land is to keep your skin moisturized during the flight. And of course you can't keep slapping moisturizer on with a face full of make-up.

The night before she left they had been for a drink together. Ulrika was terribly over-excited about Lord Mycroft, who she sees as a kind of escape clause from her current life.

"He's really into me," she told Marina. "He asked me to marry him."

"But you're already married."

"Don't be so old-fashioned," she had snapped. "Anyway, Ben will be much happier without me. He hates me being around nagging him about getting a job and irritating him. With me off the scene he can just live happily ever after with his sofa, slippers and dreary mother."

Then they talked about what Marina should do when she arrived in Rome.

"Should I try to play it cool? Maybe be slightly aloof?"

"Bit late for that, isn't it?" said Ulrika.

"Why?"

"Look, you've been in love with the man for more than fifteen years. I think the time to play it cool has passed. If he doesn't want you this time, then just fucking live with it. There's no point in wasting time on him. OK so you didn't want to have children with Mark, but who's to say you might not want to have them with someone else?"

She called her on the way to the airport to tell her the news from the office.

"Where is that fucker Hugo? Why didn't he warn you?" shrieked Ulrika.

"He called, he did sound devastated, but I hung up on him."

"Good, I should never have shagged him, the toad. But at least I chucked him."

'Bing.'

Damn, the seatbelt sign is on. There's only one more person in front of her; she hopes the stewardesses are too busy to notice.

She is about to walk into the loo when a stewardess called Claire approaches her and says "Can you make your way back to your seat please Madam?".

She looks like the kind of woman who was a prefect at school and will not take no for an answer. There's only one solution. Lie.

"I'm so sorry, but I'm pregnant and about to throw up," says Marina, trying her best to look green, which is quite easy with all the gunk she's got on her face.

Claire suddenly looks vaguely sympathetic – a rarity

for an EasyJet hostess. "Oh I see, well go on then, be as quick as you can," she says in a tone of voice that implies, 'If you must get pregnant please make sure you're able to cope with the consequences'.

Marina locks the door behind her and congratulates herself on her ingenuity, while inadvertently clutching her stomach to appear sick, even behind the closed door. She never was much good at lying. She puts on her make-up and brushes her hair. She smiles at her reflection in the mirror; her eyes are sparkling with anticipation. She wonders how Tom is feeling. Is he as excited as she is? Maybe boys don't get excited about things in the same way as girls. But why not? – they're human too. At least some of them are.

Her thoughts are interrupted by bossy Claire banging on the door. "Please take your seat, landing is imminent."

Marina unlocks it and smiles as she squeezes past her and goes to sit down. They descend through the clouds and she can see the Umbrian countryside spread out beneath her. She is determined not to let the news that she is being suspended from the paper ruin her time with Tom. The whole thing is utterly ridiculous. They all knew phone tapping was going on, and she is furious that she is being made a scapegoat. Cameron Knight must be desperate to hang on to his job and save his paper. The orders have obviously come from him. As soon as she gets back she will get a lawyer and fight to clear her name.

She wonders what they will do about her column. The scoundrels will undoubtedly publish tomorrow's, they probably waited to suspend her in order to get that one in the bag, as it was a particularly juicy one. But what happens after that? Will any of her readers miss her? No doubt the charming HR employees who escorted her out of the building, much to Flora and Jo's delight, will issue some bland statement. All she could think as she was being frog-marched towards the door was Clint Eastwood's line about how "personnel's for arseholes".

Marina walks out into Fiumicino Airport wondering how she will ever find Tom among the hundreds of faces all gazing expectantly at the door she walks through. She doesn't want to stand there for too long looking like 'the one they forgot to pick up'.

"Marina!" She hears his voice and then sees him pushing his way towards her. She waves and walks to meet him. They stop in front of each other.

"It's great to see you," he grins. His mouth is close to hers, and she hopes he will kiss her; she doesn't care about anything or anyone else. His presence is utterly intoxicating; she can't believe how happy she is.

"You too," she replies, moving closer.

"Good luck with the pregnancy," says an irritating voice behind her. It's bossy Claire, walking past wheeling a little red suitcase.

22

"But these backwaters of existence sometimes breed, in their sluggish depths, strange acuities of emotion."
Edith Wharton.

It is the kind of house you imagine that people would be happy in. Perfectly proportioned, on top of a hill, with wooden shutters and an olive tree to the left of the front door. A gravel path leads from a gate to the steps in front of a wooden door.

"It belongs to a friend. He's gone to south America for six months so I'm looking after it for him," Tom told her on the drive from the airport once Marina had explained the fact that she wasn't actually pregnant, or even thinking of getting pregnant.

"It's in Umbria, in a hilltop village called Borgheria. I thought we could stay there for two nights and then come back to Rome for the last night before flying to London. I'm coming over to meet my publisher about a book."

Every phrase gave Marina hope. They would go to Umbria together, then to Rome, then they would fly to London. There was a future for them, even if it was short-term. She didn't have to worry about what would happen after the London trip, because she was right at the beginning, like the beginning of a holiday, with it all to come.

They arrive just before 5 o'clock. It is a bright afternoon, crisp and cold. The winding road leading up to the house takes them higher and higher until they reach the walled village of Borgheria.

"This place is like stepping back in time fifty years," says Tom. "The inhabitants all work the land and I don't think they'd ever seen a foreigner before I came along. They all call me *l'Inglese*, and I expect they always will, even if I speak Italian and come here every weekend for the next fifty years."

Marina breathes deeply. The air is cold and clean. She thinks of the yoga class she will be missing on Saturday morning and promises herself to at least do some yoga breathing while she is here, to clean out her London lungs.

They park the car and walk down the drive to the front door. There are olive trees in the garden either side of the path and a beautiful view down the winding road they have just come up towards the valley below. Tom takes out a massive metal key, which he puts into the lock. The door opens.

"Follow me," he says, walking down the narrow hall in front of her until they reach the kitchen. He puts down a box of groceries he had in the car, taking out a bottle of Italian red and opening it to let it breathe. Marina looks around. The kitchen is basic, to say the least, with a sink, a draining board, a round table in the middle with six chairs, and a dresser that looks like it's been there for more than a hundred years, with various cups and plates on it in no particular order. In fact, there isn't much order anywhere; it's all a bit messy, notes Marina. But then she chides herself and tells herself she's been living with Mark for too long and he likes everything to be as organised as a surgical unit.

"It's a bit of a mess," says Tom. "I meant to clean up last time I was here but I got distracted on a walk photographing trees so didn't end up with enough time."

"Oh, I can help you," says Marina, wondering if there are any rubber gloves.

Tom walks over to her and strokes her hair. "Come on," he says gently, "let's go upstairs." He grabs her Mulberry hold-all in one hand and tells her to follow him.

Marina is barely able to breathe as she walks up the

stairs behind Tom, and her mind is racing with anticipation. Suddenly they are in his bedroom. Tom leans forward and kisses her. She kisses him back; fifteen years of frustration go into that kiss and she will never forget it.

He presses her up against the door and kisses her with such ferocity she is somewhere between pain and pleasure. 'Story of our relationship' she tells herself, half laughing. She starts pulling his shirt out of his trousers to be able to get her hands on his torso. She feels him press up against her, his hard-on more and more obvious. He groans and kisses her neck. She runs her fingers through his hair, almost pulling at it.

Suddenly she can't think of anything at all apart from how much she wants to rip his clothes off and have sex with him. Which is how sex should be, she briefly concludes before she loses all grip on reality; if you're not into it, then you may as well be doing something useful.

Still kissing her, Tom unbuttons her black shirt and slides it off her shoulders and down her arms. Then he unbuckles her belt and undoes her trousers. They fall to the floor. Marina is caressing his back and kissing him when he tells her to wait and pulls his jumper over his head, along with his T-shirt. She looks at his torso. He is broader than Mark, maybe with a bit more flesh on him, as well as muscle. She moves towards him and forgets the fact that her trousers are round her ankles, so ends up falling instead of seductively gliding into his naked arms. She is mortified but Tom laughs; "Why is it the most attractive women are always so clumsy?"

She doesn't answer but starts caressing the bulge in his jeans, then unbuttons them and pulls them down over his hips. He is wearing boxer shorts; the front of them stands up like a tent. She takes them down and falls to her knees in front of him. She takes him into her mouth and enjoys the first feeling of his cock probing her mouth. He gasps and puts his hands on her head, gently moving it back and forth over himself. She puts her hands on either of his hips and pulls him even closer. He sighs again and then gently kneels down to join her on the floor. He puts his arms around her and undoes her bra. Her full breasts fall out and he takes one nipple in his mouth while caressing her buttocks with his hands. He moves on to the other breast, licking and sucking the nipple. Marina grabs his buttocks and pulls him towards her, then eases herself gently onto the floor, guiding him down on top of her. There's no time to take off her knickers. She pulls them to one side and steers him in.

Tom suddenly stops kissing her when he is on top of her.

"Are we finally going to do this properly?" he asks, edging closer.

Marina smiles. "I hope so."

Nothing has ever felt so good. Words like 'complete' and 'full' float through her mind as they make love. She knows she can have an orgasm and it's just a question of when, not if – something that makes her smile and move up to meet him with even more vigour.

She opens her eyes to find him staring at her, a strange look in his eyes. "I want you to come first," he says.

"Fine with me," she says, closing her eyes and releasing herself to the movement of their love-making and the rhythm of the building orgasm. The feeling is between exquisite and painful, so pure and powerful that for a moment she forgets where she is and whom she is with.

As soon as she has come, Tom does the same. She feels an incredible release of emotion as he does so, along with the physical release.

He kisses her gently on the forehead afterwards and lies down next to her. "You came right?" he asks her, sounding vaguely insecure.

"Yes," she laughs. "Couldn't you tell?"

"Well, I thought you had, but you know, it is trickier with women." He leans on one elbow so he can see her. "That was amazing, really, just, well, incredible. I can't believe we're here, together, after all this time."

Marina smiles and realises that for the first time in all the years she has known him they are approaching a level footing.

She wakes early, despite her promise to herself not to, fretting over her suspension. There is no traffic outside, just the sound of birds singing and the wind. She lies in Tom's bed, his purple sheets wrapped around her naked body, and listens to his breath like one listens to the tide going in and out. She wonders what Mark is doing, whether or not he's with Katie. Does she mind? They split up three days ago and here she is in bed after a night of wine and love-making with the man she always dreamed of. And so far he is turning out to be everything she imagined he would be in terms of a lover and someone to hang out with. And he even seems to like her this time around.

They'd cooked pasta together, drunk, laughed, made love in the kitchen, and then taken a bottle of red wine upstairs and sat around in the bath together, drinking and chatting before tumbling into bed again.

Marina's body is aching like it does after a tough yoga class; she stretches out and enjoys the feeling of having exercised. She feels very sexy. Tom has that effect on her

– he seems to eat her up with his eyes, to adore every inch of her, even the bits she finds too flabby and tries to rub away with slimming cream. "Voluptuous" he calls her. "A prettier Nigella Lawson." He says he wants to photograph her naked, in black and white, that he can't think of a sexier subject.

Last night he showed her the pictures he had taken that weekend at Katie's. She thought she would cry when she saw Ollie's smiling, hopeful face. It is hard to imagine how different their lives were when those pictures were taken. How much has changed in such a short space of time.

She wonders if he takes her picture this weekend how much will have changed when she looks back on her own portrait in a few weeks' time.

Back in London Mark has left the white tranquility of Katie's bedroom and gone downstairs to make a cup of tea. He picks up the papers from the mat, throws them onto the island and puts the kettle on. While he's waiting for it to boil he flicks through them. It's Friday today, and Marina's column will be in; he pulls *The Chronicle* out from the bottom of the pile and turns to her page. He's taken aback by the headline:

A Taste of My Own Medicine – how I discovered my

marriage is over via the tabloid press.

He sits down and reads on.

'Here's the thing,' Marina begins. 'I know most of you won't have any sympathy for me at all. 'Serves her right' I hear you say. Or 'You live by the sword, you die by the sword'.

"Having worked for a tabloid newspaper for most of my career, I know how a lot of you feel about them, and about us journalists who spend their lives writing about the 'news' readers pretend not to care about but read all the same. The amount of times I've had to stop myself biting someone's head off at a social event when they've found out where I work. "Ooooooh, I'd better watch what I say," they crow. "I might end up in the newspaper." Well, let me let you all in on a little secret. We do not go around waiting for people to come out with things, especially if we happen to be at a dinner party with our husbands, just trying to have a nice evening. We're not programmed to pounce on innocent nobodies who would not be of any interest to anyone reading the newspaper anyway.

"Yes, I did say 'my husband'. Incredibly, I found someone willing to marry me, despite being in this sordid profession. A decent, kind and successful man, who – I just found out from the front page of *The Sun* – is dating another woman.

"OK so I admit it, I probably drove him away. We wanted different things from life; let's just leave it at that. But still, seeing him there, in full colour, with a minor celebrity, looking handsome and happy, was a bit of a shock to me.

"And it did get me wondering, as I have done in the past, if the press doesn't overstep the mark at times. How could details of my husband's date at some plush restaurant possibly be in the public interest? Who would possibly really care where he ate dinner except for me, the lady he was with and possibly his mother?

"The other thing that struck me was the effect it had on me, not as a journalist, but personally. I suddenly felt like our marriage was no longer between us – it had become the business of snooping journalists. And slowly I began to understand how violated a person can feel when their private life is publicized. Especially someone who, like me, is not a celebrity, so doesn't bring the attention upon themselves.

But most of all it made me understand that our marriage will probably never recover from this. That he has moved on. And that made me very sad, even if the separation was (mostly) my fault and I wanted it.

No one can be happy when their marriage fails. It is the end of a dream, an ambition, a love story that you shared. Suddenly you two are no longer an entity and you never will be again. That is the brutal truth about a break-up that I hadn't really understood until I saw that picture. So maybe it was just as well that I did."

23

"If you must break the law, do it to seize power:
in all other cases observe it."
Julius Caesar

The courtroom is packed. The magistrate has yet to arrive. Marina sits next to her lawyer, squeezing her toes to contain her nerves. She turns around to make sure her supporters are still there. Tom and her mother are sitting with Ulrika a few rows behind her. Mark said he would come, which was really kind of him, but she can't see him yet so maybe he decided against it. They have been oh-so-mature about the split; no tantrums, no arguments about who has what. So far not a single argument. Ridiculous really.

"Makes you wonder why you split up at all," Ulrika joked this morning in an effort to make Marina relax — something she has found hard to do since she got back from Italy to the summons.

The visit from the HR department just before her trip to Italy was the beginning of the nightmare. A week or so later the court summons arrived.

She was already suspended from her job, which gave her plenty of time to prepare her defence. What shocks her most is that her colleagues just dropped her in it. Especially Hugo, a fellow Chelsea fan, whom she'd always got on so well with. She thought they were good friends. And Millie and Felicia – they worked on the story with her, they knew as well as she did that none of them had the budget or the authority to sign off on phone-tapping bills, that had to come from Hugo or even possibly Cameron Knight. But journalists are a fickle bunch. She has always known that.

If the judge decides that the case warrants a trial, he is likely to refer it to the Crown Court – a process that will take months and will mean much more stress and anxiety. As it is, she has had four weeks of it, and she doesn't think she can stand much more. It's like a bad dream, like someone has just put a curse on her and suddenly she is no longer free. Her every waking moment is taken up with worrying about the court case. She falls asleep and when she wakes up it is the first thing she thinks about. There are mornings when for a split second she thinks it *was* all a bad dream and is flooded with relief. But then her consciousness reminds her: no, it is all true, she is in terrible trouble.

Marina is accused of authorising phone tapping and then using material acquired through phone-tapping in an article about a teacher, some chalk and a vicar. At the time it seemed like such a stupid story that they all laughed as they wrote it, trying to come up with as many silly expressions involving chalk as possible. Now it seems a lot less amusing. It is about to cost Marina her career. And she could go to prison.

The thought of it is risible. She has never broken the law – well, not since the night Ollie was shot anyway, when she told the police that Ollie had shot himself by accident. That he'd been fooling around with the gun and it had gone off. That was technically breaking the law, but it wasn't harming anyone, it was just keeping Tom out of jail, which Ollie would have wanted anyway.

What was the worst that could happen? They weren't sure. It would depend on so many things; a case of this kind had never been heard before. The technical charge was 'obtaining information by illegal means'.

Marina sighs and looks towards the door the judge is due to appear through any minute. Maybe if she ends up in prison she will finally write her book. Look on the bright side, eh?

A few miles away from the City of London Magistrates Court, in rather plusher surroundings, a drama of another kind is unfolding. Katie Tomlinson is trying to work out the best place to tell Mark that he is going to be a father. Should she be serene in her bedroom, wearing just a dressing gown, some lace knickers and her not-yet-discernible bump? Or maybe she should go for a more business-like approach in the sitting room, wearing her suit? Or how about the domestic goddess look in the kitchen, in casual kit and a Cath Kidston apron? Did she even own a Cath Kidston apron?

The doorbell rings. Damn it, she should have remembered he's always on time. She will have to go for a mixture of domestic goddess and Zen master in her designer lilac and black yoga kit.

"Mark, come in," she coos, opening the door. "How are you?"

"Fine thanks," he kisses her on the lips. "How are you?"

"That's exactly what I want to talk to you about," she replies. "Let's have a cup of tea."

Mark sits down. Katie puts the kettle on.

"I just want to tell you a bit about myself, will you bear with me?"

"Of course."

"I grew up in a large apartment in Sloane Street and a country house in Wiltshire," she begins. "At an early age I was sent away to boarding school. On the surface I had a perfect childhood. My parents didn't get divorced, there were rarely any arguments and my governesses were all fairly benign. And yet there was something fundamental missing: warmth and tenderness, and some kind of involvement and interest from my parents in my life. I often felt like we were three people all living together leading totally separate lives. There was no sense of family or belonging."

She pauses to get them some tea. Mark notices her hand is shaking as she pours.

"I wanted for nothing in material terms," she goes on. "People looking at me might even say I was spoilt. My room was redecorated every year, my clothes were the latest fashions, my hair was cut by the best hairdresser in London."

"So no change there," smiles Mark.

Katie laughs for a moment and then looks at the ground. Mark senses the next sentence is a difficult one for her to say out loud.

"But I was lonely for a lot of the time, and longed to be closer to my parents, who were so wrapped up in their lives they barely noticed me. More than clothes or posh schools I wanted a hug, and some of their time." Katie is silent; she bites her bottom lip. Mark strokes her face. "What is it?"

"I had their presents, but not their presence," she says. "And for any children I have, I want it to be the other way around."

Mark gives her a hug and strokes her face. She looks so vulnerable and small; he has an overwhelming desire to protect her. "Why are you telling me this now?"

"All rise, all rise," says the clerk of the court.

Marina has almost squeezed her toes numb by now and stumbles slightly as she tries to stand. Her heart is beating so fast she can hardly breathe. The judge walks slowly along to his imposing leather seat in the middle, behind the bench. Marina wonders if he instinctively hates her already because she is from the press. It's amazing, she thinks, how low down on the list of popular professions journalism is – it's right at the bottom, along with traffic wardens and lawyers.

The judge coughs and starts reading from a piece of paper in front of him. "We are gathered today to hear the case of the Crown versus Marina Claudia Shaw."

He looks at her.

"Are you Miss Marina Claudia Shaw of 91 Holland Park Road, London SW4?"

Marina's lawyer nudges her.

"Yes."

"How do you plead?"

"Not guilty," she squeaks.

"Speak up, Miss," says the judge sternly.

"Not guilty," she says again.

The judge looks mildly irritated. Maybe he was hoping to get to Sweeting's before the lunchtime rush.

"Well, can we hear the case for the prosecution please?"

A man wearing a blue suit that is two sizes too small for him stands up. He outlines the case against Marina. There are phone records of her talking to a number they suspect belongs to the phone-tapper. And there's the piece in the paper, which carries her byline.

"The prosecution holds, my lord, that the defendant did use this improperly acquired information to write an article in *The Chronicle* newspaper on November 15th 2010."

The judge nods slowly. Marina feels like jumping up and protesting, but her lawyer advised her against it. "A courtroom is no place for emotional outbursts," he warned. So she sits quietly and hopes he can defend her adequately.

"And has anyone spoken to the person accused of

carrying out the phone-tapping?" demands the judge. "Surely the answer to the whole case lies with him. Or her."

"My lord, we have tried our best but so far no contact has been possible."

"Right. Case for the defence please?"

Marina's lawyer stands up and tells the judge that she does not deny using improperly acquired evidence for her story but that this practice is endemic in Fleet Street and that she is not the guilty party here.

"Those who authorized the phone-tapping are the ones who should be prosecuted, not the reporters, who were just following company policy – a policy dictated by the ever-more competitive environment in journalism, which means papers are forced to use underhand methods to get information in order to stay ahead of the game. My client is merely another victim in this situation, a young woman at the peak of her career who is being used as a scapegoat to save the jobs and livelihoods of those more powerful than her."

The judge looks at his notes and then surveys the room again.

"In the circumstances I have no option but to refer this case to Crown Court," he says. "The prosecution and the defence have eight weeks from today to prepare their case. I would suggest you make all possible efforts to contact the man accused of carrying out the phone-tapping. It seems the answer will lie with him."

He stands up. "All rise," says the clerk.

"Court dismissed," says the judge.

At the back of the room Ulrika catches sight of an unusually tall figure wearing full abaya and burqa sneaking out. She wonders briefly why a woman would be wearing the most enormous black loafers. "A strange bunch, those Arabs," she mumbles to Tom nodding in the direction of the figure in black. But, she reasons, if you're dressed like Darth Vader, who on earth is going to care what you've got on your feet?

❦ *24* ❦

"I sincerely believe that if I had been born with bigger breasts,
I would have been an entirely different person."
Nora Ephron.

Ulrika is in tears. Marina is in shock. In the fifteen or so years she has known Ulrika, she has never known her to cry. Not even when she tripped over her Jimmy Choos rushing to get into Harvey Nichols before it closed and one of the heels snapped off.

Marina was at home trying to come up with yet another excuse not to start writing her book, such as cleaning out the airing cupboard, or painting her toe-nails blue, when there was a prolonged ring on the doorbell. She opened it, ready to start yelling at the culprit, and Ulrika fell into her arms sobbing.

Now they are in the kitchen, Marina has put the kettle on, and Ulrika has calmed down enough to speak.

"He wants me to have a boob-job," she says.

"Who?"

"Lord Mycock."

"But I thought he proposed?"

Ulrika starts weeping again. "He did, he did, and I thought that FINALLY all my worries were over, that I could relax and start looking forward to a life of security and comfort and no overdraft, and now, well apparently my tits just aren't big enough for him."

"Don't be ridiculous," says Marina. "There's nothing wrong with your tits. What an insane request, he sounds deeply perverted."

Ulrika sighs and takes a sip of her tea. She looks around Marina's kitchen. "It's not as tidy as it was when Mark lived here," she comments.

"Thanks. Can we get back to your tits now?"

"Or lack of them."

"I was about to crack that joke and didn't because I thought it was insensitive," Marina wails.

"Big mistake; never let sensitivity get in the way of a cheap laugh."

"So what have you said to him?"

"I told him to go fuck himself, obviously."

"Obviously."

Ulrika is silent for a moment.

"And then…?" asks Marina.

"Then I started thinking, well, I am only a B-cup, and he is going to pay to get it…"

"No, no, you insane woman, just STOP," Marina interrupts her. "You are NOT going to have a boob job to satisfy the pervy needs of some aristocratic wanker who still misses his fat matron from prep school."

Ulrika looks down at her chest. "Up until today I was quite happy with my boobs, Now they suddenly seem… well, inadequate."

Marina puts her arm around her. "Ulrika, you're the most stunning girl I know. There is NOTHING wrong with your body. This guy is clearly deranged."

Ulrika leans into her and starts crying again. "I can't believe I married a total loser. I always thought that I, of all people, would end up with a decent man for God's sake. All I know is how to treat a man well, and now I have one who is a no-hoper and another who's an utter perv and won't marry me unless I'm a C-cup. It's not fair. "

Marina strokes her blonde hair, it feels strange to be consoling Ulrika; she's always so strong, so confident and happy. It seems like nothing can ever faze her, she just takes it all in her stride. This is a side to her she's never seen, and she hates Lord Mycroft even though she only met him twice and he actually seemed like a decent bloke.

Ulrika pulls away to grab some kitchen paper to blow her nose on.

"So, it's a C-cup or bust?" asks Marina, putting the kettle on again.

"Very droll. He's too aristocratic to go really enormous, I suppose. You'd be all right," she adds, nodding at Marina's chest. "What's it like anyway, having big boobs? Do you think men treat you differently?"

"I wouldn't know, I've had them since I was a teenager. But I do find it quite annoying when I meet someone and they say hello to my chest instead of my face."

"I don't think that would bother me. I sometimes find myself saying hello to men's crotches. They just jump out at me."

"But at least you haven't demanded he have a penis extension."

Ulrika looks glum. "He doesn't need one, the bastard. That what's so fucking annoying, he doesn't need anything. He's got money, looks, charm, a stately home and an enormous cock. And the only thing standing between me and all that glory is a pair of silicone implants. Maybe I'm being a tad churlish?"

Marina sighs. She wishes she still had a column to write; she could really go to town on this one. She wouldn't describe herself as rabidly feminist by any stretch, but this kind of thing makes her furious.

"Listen, this man is trying to change you to suit his taste. He's basically saying that in order to be good enough for him, you need to change. Have you demanded that he change?"

Ulrika shakes her head slowly.

"Precisely, so what the hell gives him the right to demand that you do? And what kind of an idiot would want to change you anyway, you're perfect. And another thing…" Her speech is interrupted by the doorbell. She glances at her watch.

"Shit, that'll be Tom, he's still in town, talking to a publisher about a book. Sorry, I'll tell him to come back later, hang on…"

"No, don't." Ulrika grabs her arm, "There's nothing like a good-looking man to cheer me up," she smiles. "Bring him in."

Marina goes to let Tom in. Ulrika fills up her teacup. She wipes the mascara she is certain will be under her eyes and digs out a lip-gloss. No need to let the side down, even if she is only a B-cup.

✒ 25 ✒

*"I cannot think of any need in childhood as strong as
the need for a father's protection."*
Sigmund Freud

By midday he has already saved two lives. A good day in
the office by anyone's standards, he reflects as he cleans
up after the open-heart surgery. And as well as saving
lives, he has now created a life. Katie's news has had a
profound effect on him. He hovers between elation and
confusion. Elation because he is finally going to be a
father, confusion because he is not entirely sure that
Katie is the woman for him, the ideal mother of his baby.
He wishes he could be more relaxed about it all. Most
men would be delighted. She is rich, beautiful, graceful,
and pregnant. What's not to like? as Marina would write
in one of her columns. A good question.

"Nice work, Doc," his boss and friend Charles is
standing next to him, washing his arms and hands.

"You're on a roll today. I thought the old lady was a goner, I was already composing my 'we did everything we could' speech in my head. I hate that speech, I must have said it a hundred times. I'm eternally grateful to anyone who saves me from having to roll it out."

Mark smiles and rubs the lather up and down his arms, removing all traces of the morning's work. "Well I've had some good news," he says, straightening up and looking at his friend.

"Has your ghastly football team won some trophy or other?"

Mark laughs. "No, even better than that: I'm going to be a father."

Charles smiles and throws his wet arms around him. "That's fabulous news! Wonderful, you and Marina must be thrilled. Wait till I tell Victoria, she'll be so happy."

Mark hugs him in return, patting him on the back. He's never quite sure what to do when a man hugs him, so patting him seems like a good option – not unfriendly but not too intimate.

"We were a bit worried about you," he continues. "Apparently there was some story about you and another woman…"

"Yes, well, there's something I need to tell you," Mark interrupts him.

"Such as…?"

"Well, the thing is, I'm not having the baby with Marina."

"What? So there is another woman? My, times have changed," Charles pauses. "All the same, it's a bit unusual. I say, won't Marina mind?"

Mark laughs. "I haven't been having an affair, well I suppose technically I have, but then so has she. We, er, we're in the midst of a trial separation. She was reunited with the first love of her life, and at the same time I met another woman and apparently I was the first love of *her* life. We had a one-night stand many years ago, which I thought was just a bit of fun, but apparently I meant a lot more to her than I reaslised. And well, there we are." He always finds talking about emotions with men a little embarrassing.

"There we are? That's it? No, no, no, you don't get away with that young man. I need details. How did this young lady get pregnant?"

"Well, Doctor, apparently the male sperm inseminates the egg of the female…"

"Very amusing," Charles interrupts him. "May I remind you that I am your boss and could have you sacked for taking the piss out of me."

"Ah, yes, good point. Well, I suppose the beginning of

the end was on New Year's Eve. Marina and I had a terrible row about the one subject we always row about, that is my desire to have children and her desire not to. Then we all drank far too much and I ended up dancing with this Katie girl while Marina was dancing with her first love, a bloke called Tom. Then we got back to London and everything seemed broken really, and I couldn't see how we would get it back together, not with the first love on the scene anyway. Then Katie declared that I was and am the big love of her life. And she's quite hard to resist."

Charles nods his head. "It sounds like something from *EastEnders*, not that I've ever watched *EastEnders*. But I suppose you have at least got what you wanted in one sense, that is a child? Where's Marina now?"

"She's er, at our home, with Tom. Tom lives in Italy, but he's here working on a book deal apparently."

"This is first love of her life? The subject of her column she talked about when you came for dinner?"

"The same."

"Right. So are you happy with the way things have worked out?"

Mark thinks for a moment. "Can anyone really ever be happy about splitting up?" he asks. "But I suppose if it had to happen at least there isn't an injured party this way.

Marina has the man she always loved, and I have the child I always longed for. As well as a beautiful, extremely talented and successful mother of said child."

"What does she do, this *Fecunditas*?"

"This what?"

"Fertility goddess."

Mark laughs. "She's a clothes and accessories designer. She owns and runs a multi-million-pound business with shops all over the world. The brand is called KT, it's very well known."

Charles shrugs. "Never heard of it, though I dare say Victoria will have done." His sentence is interrupted by his pager. He looks at it briefly. "The scalpel beckons," he says walking off. "Let's get together soon, you and *Fecunditas*."

"Good idea," says Mark, watching him go. He thinks about the last time he had dinner with Charles and Victoria. Marina and he had argued again about having children in the cab on the way home. Would they ever have reached an agreement if they had stayed together? To be fair on her, she had always said she never wanted children. He always used to say he thought she would want to when the time was right. But it never was. And probably never would have been. So maybe this really was the best thing that could have happened. He couldn't have coped with a long and painful separation. He will call her as soon as he can to tell her the news. He doesn't want her to hear it from anyone else.

Marina is experiencing a disturbing sensation for the first time in her life. She is angry with Tom. She didn't think it was possible. She always had him on such a pedestal. But maybe that's a good sign; you can't have a mature relationship with a man you worship beyond all reason.

"I think you're over-reacting," her true love is saying. "It's a pair of breast implants, not face-changing surgery or even like he's told her there is something he doesn't like about her personality."

"The point is, it is just wrong to demand that a woman change in that way. I mean it's wrong to demand that she have surgery to become more attractive to you."

"So if you got fat, or even I got fat, it would be wrong of either of us to demand the other lose weight?"

Marina sighs. "Can't you see how much more of an imposition this is? The difference between 'I think you should go under the knife' and 'please don't eat another bag of crisps'?"

Tom rolls his eyes. "That's so typical of a journalist; simplify and exaggerate. Of course there's a difference. But what I'm saying is the underlying sentiment behind both is the same, and I don't see why Lord doo-dah should be vilified for wanting Ulrika to have bigger breasts. He's perfectly willing and able to pay for them, so good luck to him. And, the other things you keep forgetting is that it's Ulrika's choice, not yours."

"I can't believe you can't see how WRONG it is," says Marina, "but I need to go, I have a meeting with my lawyer in half an hour."

She storms out of her house and looks for a taxi. It is cold and windy outside, a typical February day in London, with the kind of grey sky that makes you forget what the city can look like when the sun shines.

She finds a cab after a few minutes and turns the heating on full blast before sinking into the back seat. Tom has been living with her these past weeks, while he is working on a deal to collate his best work into a coffee-table book. It's been amazing having him there; she has to keep pinching herself to believe it's real. But now for the first time she is questioning his judgement.

Her phone rings. It's Mark.

"Hi," she says. "Can you believe Lord Mycroft is making Ulrika have a boob job before he marries her. Isn't that outrageous?"

"Whoa," laughs Mark. "I have missed *The Chronicle*. But who is Lord Mycroft, and what does he have to do with Ulrika's breasts?"

Marina laughs too. "Sorry, I forgot you're no longer privy to my daily news flashes. Well, briefly, Lord Mycroft is the man who is going to save Ulrika from a life of penury and change her destiny. But only if she agrees to upgrade to a C-cup."

"What does Ben think of all this?"

"Ben probably doesn't care what cup size she is. They barely speak. They only communicate via bbm to make arrangements for the boys. But I don't think she's told him anything yet. I think she wants the deal secured first."

"And that will only happen if she has her boobs done?"

"Yep."

"What does Ulrika think of it? Not much I can imagine."

"That's the amazing thing. She went from utter fury and indignation to thinking it might be a good idea. She just bbmd me to tell me she's definitely going to think about it. I can't believe it."

"Seems unlike her, she's one of the most confident women I know. In fact *the* most confident woman I know. But maybe she's worrying about getting older, and poorer."

"Very possibly, yes. She's so fed up with being broke. And she saw Lord Mycroft as an escape. But there must be other options that don't involve plastic surgery?"

"You'd have thought so. What a prat he sounds."

"I agree! I think it's outrageous. Tom and I had a huge argument about it just now…" She stops herself mid-sentence. She's still not sure how Mark will react to her talking about Tom.

"Mina, don't worry," he says softly. "I think it's great it's all worked out for you two. Really. In fact I was calling you with some news."

"Oh Mark, I'm so sorry, typical me, I just launched into the Ulrika boob thing without even asking how you are."

Mark laughs again. "Don't mention it. With you the news is always first. By the way, how's it all going on that front?"

Marina sighs. She can hardly bear to think about it all, let alone talk about it. The whole thing has gone round and round in her mind so much that the track it has travelled on is rubbed raw. As a journalist on *The Chronicle* she did what they all did, used the information made available to write stories. How that information was acquired was not really her concern, or her job. They had been tipped off by the wife of the vicar, who was naturally furious that her husband was visiting the head-mistress's office more often than was strictly necessary.

The vicar's wife gave them the mobile phone numbers of the lovers and they were then passed on to phone hackers the paper used on a regular basis. This was normal practice.

And in a culture where you're only as good as your last headline, Marina was hardly going to ignore the fact that the vicar told the headmistress that he used to fantasize about where to put her chalk. Apart from anything else, it was amazing that anyone still used chalk.

"What gets me," she said to Mark, "is that we all worked on that story together, we even shared the byline."

"So if you're guilty, then so is everyone else?"

"Exactly. Why me? Why haven't they hauled Hugo and the whole gang up in front of the judge?"

Mark sighs. "Well, remember when we were all in that police cell after Ollie got stabbed?"

"Yes, of course, what's that got to do with it?"

"You and Katie decided someone had to take the rap. As it turned out, you cleverly decided the victim should be the one to do it, so no one got into trouble. You can hardly go to jail for shooting yourself. But my point is, this is just the same, but this time you're taking the rap for the greater good of the group, which this time is not a group of mates in Notting Hill Gate but a whole newspaper. It's like a football player taking one for the team."

"Yes, but I'm not taking my red card willingly."

"No, but then I suppose one could argue that Ollie didn't take the rap willingly either. You and Katie decided it for him."

Marina shakes her head. "No, he would have done anything for Tom. The last thing he wanted was to see Tom go to jail."

"And I'm sure Cameron Knight feels the same way about himself," says Mark. "Look Mina, if you're going to stand a chance here, you're going to have to change your plea."

"What? But I'm not guilty," she shrieks.

"Technically you are. You are guilty of using illegally acquired material."

Marina feels like weeping.

"Mina?"

"Here."

"Look, I don't mean give up and go to jail. I mean fight them, admit your guilt, but bring them all down with you. Get the paper closed if you have to, but prove it wasn't just you involved, that this is a bigger thing."

"How on earth do I do that?"

Mark laughs. "That I don't know. But I have a feeling

that if you go for it, you could change the way newspapers work forever. If they're all breaking the law then it's time to stop them."

"I love your faith in me, how can one person change a mighty institution like Fleet Street? My lawyer made a speech to this effect the other day, the judge didn't even blink. I'm sure everyone knows I'm not the only guilty one, but they don't really care. The police just want a conviction and the paper just wants to get rid of the case hanging over their heads. I'm a useful pawn to both of them."

"Yes, but that doesn't mean you have to play along, does it? Listen, Charles's brother is a top QC, let's get him on the case. He'll know what to do. Do I have your permission to call him?"

"I can't afford a top QC," says Marina, "I've been suspended on half salary pending my 'investigation' as those charmers from HR call it."

"Don't worry about the money, we can work something out…."

"Oh, I forgot you're now Mr Moneybags," laughs Marina. "Are you sure Katie will agree to you spending her hard-earned millions on your ex-wife?"

"Don't worry, she'll be delighted," he laughs. "And anyway, you're not my ex-wife. Yet. Damn, must dash, my pager is going, speak soon." He hangs up.

Marina looks down at her phone. For the first time in weeks she feels more optimistic about her court case. What a star he's being. And she didn't even find out why he called.

⁓ *26* ⁓

*"I definitely believe in plastic surgery. I don't want to be
an old hag. There's no fun in that."*
Scarlett Johansson

They are in the doctor's Harley Street consultation room.
The doctor is examining her breasts as Lord Mycroft looks
on. Ulrika Crawford rarely feels vulnerable, but right now,
standing half-naked in front of this stranger with cold
hands, she does.

"What do you think, Doctor?" her future husband asks.

Doctor Maurizio Veil looks at Ulrika's chest, says
"Excuse me once more" and lifts up the skin on the upper
part of her breast between his thumb and forefinger. Then
he squeezes her breasts diagonally from top to bottom.
Finally he cups them in his hands and lifts them up, all the
while staring at them intently.

Ulrika is embarrassed by her nipples, which are standing
on end, not because of the effect of the man touching her

but because of the chill in the room. Although he is rather handsome, as are most men in a white doctor's coat, she has never felt less erotic in her life. In fact this must be the first time a man has seen her half-naked and not been overcome with lust. Clearly time to get a boob job. Maybe old Mycock is right.

"She is a perfect candidate for a small augmentation, I would say 220 grams in each breast," says the doctor to Lord Mycroft. "You see when a woman has had children and breastfed, the skin is much looser, so really it is like me going in and filling up a space that is already there. Added to which there is," he prods her breasts again, "a certain amount of fat tissue here, which makes an implant over the muscle possible – a much less serious operation with a quicker recovery period."

"But still a natural result?" asks Lord Mycroft.

"Er, hello?" Ulrika butts in. "Could you possibly include me in your little chat about my breasts?"

Dr. Viel smiles at her. "Of course my dear, now put your bra back on and I will show you what a difference 440 grams will make to your life."

Ulrika does as she is told and the doctor takes out two see-through rubbery things from a drawer in his desk. Imagine, thinks Ulrika, having tits in your office drawer. Beats paperclips.

"Now, if you will excuse me, Mrs Crawford, I will just ease them in here," he says, tucking one and then the other implant into her bra. "Take a look now without your shirt, and then with. I think you will be pleased."

Ulrika looks at herself in the full-length mirror on the wall. She looks like a woman with silicone implants stuffed down her bra. She puts her shirt on.

"Oh, well, that's better," she says. She looks thinner, and sexier, her breasts just a little more obvious than they normally are. "But I guess I could just wear a padded bra?"

Dr. Viel grimaces slightly. "You could, but the effect is not very good when you take it off. False advertising some might even call it."

Ulrika nods. "Tell me about the risks of the operation, the scarring and the pain afterwards. How long before I can exercise again? Not that I really ever do any exercise."

"The operation is very simple, and relatively risk free. You are not fully sedated and it is a very small incision. The scar will not be visible, it will be just under your breast, and as for recovery, well it is four to six weeks. For the first four weeks you will not be able to lift your arms above your head and you will need to wear a support bra at all times, even at night. There really shouldn't be much pain. As I said I will place the implant over the muscle.

We will prescribe Voltaren but if you need more pain relief we have a stronger one. But to be honest, none of my ladies have ever asked for it."

"And how natural will they be? I mean I don't want to look like Lara Croft."

Dr Viel grimaces again and emits something between a cough and a laugh. "They will take two to three months to settle completely, but no, you will not look like Lara Croft. They will follow the natural shape of your breasts."

Ulrika looks at herself in the mirror again. When she walked into this consulting room, she was convinced there was no way she was going to go through with this ridiculous scheme, even if she had told Marina she would, just to see her reaction. She was coming along to humour Mycroft and then talk him out of it by showing him how perfectly adequate her breasts are already. But looking at her reflection, there is no denying she looks good with the added boost.

"I just don't like the idea of being cut open though," she says. "And for no reason, really, except that I will end up with bigger boobs."

"There is another option," says Dr Viel, "of harvesting some of your fat and injecting it into your breasts. It is known as the organic breast operation, and is a little less invasive."

"An organic boob job? I love the sound of that," says Ulrika. "Can we do that instead?"

"Please undo your trousers," says the doctor.

She does as he tells her and he slides them over her buttocks, then starts pinching her thighs and bum.

"Hmmmm, there's not enough fat here to harvest," he says.

"Can I bring a fat friend?"

"I'm afraid that won't work," says Dr Viel. "No, for you, if you do want an augmentation, the implant is the best solution. I think you would get a very good result."

She looks at her silhouette in the mirror again. She is resolutely against this, isn't she? Insulted by the very thought of it. But actually, she looks great. How bigger breasts can make a person look thinner she can't fathom, but she does look thinner, and also more, well, feminine, not to mention sexier.

"What do you think, darling?" asks Lord Mycroft.

She turns to face him. "I think I look great. What do you think?"

He smiles warmly. "You always do, but yes, even greater."

Ulrika faces the mirror again. The old phrase about diamonds being forever goes through her head. Diamonds and breast implants – whatever else happens, once she has them, these babies are hers to do whatever she wants with. And when were a pair of big boobs not useful to a girl?

"Right," she says turning back to the surgeon. "Let's go for it. Book me in, Doc."

"Excellent," says Dr Viel. "I will have Sarah prepare the paperwork. On your account as usual, Sir?"

"Your account?" laughs Ulrika. "What the hell have you had done? A penis extension?"

"No, nothing," laughs Lord Mycroft. "I just pay for my mother's treatments here."

⸙ 27 ⸙

"Getting divorced just because you don't love a man is almost
as silly as getting married just because you do."
Zsa Zsa Gabor

Ben can't believe he is sticking up for her. The words are
coming out of his mouth, and as he says them, his brain
rebels.

"She's my wife and the mother of my children," he
hears himself telling his mother, who has launched into a
tirade about Ulrika. "You have no right to talk about her
like that."

"She's a total bitch," his brain is complaining at the
same time. "God knows who she's fucking, but it's not
you, she hates you. And what's more, you hate her."

His mother and his brain are in total agreement.

"Ben, calm down, all I'm saying is I hate to see you
stuck in a loveless relationship," says his mother. The
twins are lying in the dog-basket, poking Sam the

Labrador on her nose. Ben knows she is harmless; he spent his childhood poking her mother's nose. Sam looks on mournfully, wondering when her bed will be free again.

"You're too young to be living like this. You could find a lovely girl who would love you, and the twins, and have a happy home life. Like your father and I did."

Ben raises an eyebrow. Happy as long as his mother does as she is told, that is. Maybe one of the reasons he picked someone as strong and feisty as Ulrika was that he didn't want a repeat of his parents' relationship. Isn't that what everyone tries to do? Avoid the mistakes of their parents? Well, he had certainly done that so far. Ulrika wouldn't pass him the sugar, let alone dedicate her whole life to making sure he was comfortable and in a good mood.

How did it go so wrong? The Ulrika of before the children has vanished; that sex-crazed, funny, gorgeous woman has gone, only to be replaced by a howling harridan. Or more likely she is out being funny for someone else. Was it the children that changed her? The twins are one year-and-a-half now. She was happy to begin with – tired and quite ratty at times, but not on the cataclysmic levels she is now. Maybe it wasn't the twins but rather the money running out. The timing seems to work better. Is it really that simple? Can she be so superficial?

"Ben, are you listening to me?" His mother's voice penetrates his thoughts.

"Yes, yes, I am. It's just not that easy, Mother. As I keep telling you."

"Marriage isn't that easy darling, but you have to ask yourself whether this one is worth working for."

Ben looks at the twins giggling at Sam. Lots of kids grow up with divorced parents nowadays. It is not ideal, but they manage. But because he had a secure and stable background, he feels obliged to provide the same for his children. He will feel like a failure if he doesn't. But how to go from a situation where they hate each other to one where they want to stay together? Talk about Mission Impossible.

"I've got to go, Mum," he says, scooping the twins back into their double buggy. "I've got work to do."

Sam slinks gratefully back into her bed and Ben's mother sighs as she watches her son walk down the lane towards his car, looking at his BlackBerry.

Ben reads the message from Ulrika twice. The tone is different, almost friendly. And it's not his birthday until May. It's asking if he can possibly mind everything at home for a couple of days as she has to go away on urgent business for work. She has even ended it with an x.

"Of course," he responds. Then adds a kiss. That's the first time he's done that for months. It feels good. This is a good start; maybe things are salvageable after all.

Marina is in the London Library close to Piccadilly Circus at the behest of her new lawyer, Mark's QC contact Rodney Edwards, who has galvanized her into action to prepare for the court case. He is a tall, dark thirty-something man with a vague resemblance to George Clooney. He is also incredibly bright and amusing. Just the kind of man any sane girl would fall in love with, were she not already in love. Marina wondered whether to introduce him to Ulrika and save her B-cup, but then he told her his wife was expecting their first child, so in the interest of the innocent unborn babe she decided against it.

Rodney has told her to go through back-issues of *The Chronicle* and note down stories that she knows, or suspects, are the result of phone-tapping. She can only go back to June last year, when she joined, but just from that one month she has pinpointed fifteen stories already.

It is tough work, going through each issue. She also re-reads some of her old columns; they're not bad.

Newspapers are such a transitory thing – you can write something it's taken you a lifetime to come up with and get to grips with yet the day after you come out, it's already forgotten. Maybe that's why so many journalists write books – in an effort to give their words some permanent meaning.

She has started her book. It is a novel about a journalist. Write about what you know, the self-help books for frustrated authors always tell you. Her heroine is a foreign correspondent based in an African country, fighting to stop the building of a dam – a white elephant project that is doing nothing but ruining the lives of the people in the region concerned and lining the pockets of the government ministers. It is based on the true story of the Turkana dam in Kenya, which Marina reported on when she first started out in journalism. Unfortunately there was no journalist hero to stop the real project, or if there was, they were soon silenced by corrupt politicians.

So far, Marina has written two chapters. She is finding writing fiction a real challenge. In reporting there are the facts dictating what you have to write; with fiction you have the freedom to do what you want. Although some, she thought, might argue that tabloid journalism is closer to fiction than fact.

She starts on the month of July. The front page is all

about new evidence to come out relating to the death of Dr David Kelly. She scrolls to the home news pages, scanning headlines for any that she remembers working on. One catches her eye:

'Serial Boob Job Merchant – the man who makes plastic surgeons smile.'

Marina feels her heart jump as she reads on:

'A former City trader is being sued for breach of contract by a woman who claims he forced her into having a breast augmentation.

'Caroline Cross claims that Edward Sullivan promised her he would marry her once she had her breasts enlarged from a C cup to a D cup. After the surgery, he split up with her, citing irreconcilable differences.

' "I left my husband, my children and a comfortable life to marry him," Ms Cross told the judge at Harrogate Magistrates Court. "In addition I went through a lot of pain and suffering as a result of the implants." The implants have been removed due to a reaction when the body's fibres tighten and grow around them, called Capsule Contracture.

The case continues.'

She grabs her bag and leaves the room to call Ulrika. There's no reply. Damn. She can't be at the clinic already. She last spoke to her two days ago, after the consultation, and Ulrika had told her she had decided to go ahead with it. What if Lord Mycroft is another Edward Sullivan?

"The way I see it," she had said, "I can't lose once he's married me, I have my insurance policy. Since when were bigger boobs a disadvantage?"

At the time Marina had asked her what happened if he didn't marry her, an idea that Ulrika had dismissed as preposterous.

"Why on earth would he want to spend all this money on getting my boobs done if he has no intention of enjoying them?"

Marina walks back into the library, bbming Ulrika as she goes. 'Call me urgently, your Lord might not be the marrying kind – boobs or no boobs.'

By the time Ben gets home, both boys are sound asleep in the car. Teasing Sam has obviously taken it out of them. He carries the first one and then the other into the house in their car seats and puts them down in the kitchen. They don't stir. Ben can't remember the last time he slept so soundly, at least not without a few beers inside him. He has spent the past few months trying to work out what to do when all the money finally runs out – something that will happen very soon if he doesn't start generating some income. He looks down at his boys.

They're asleep without a care in the world. They trust him, are relying on him, and what is he doing at the moment? Heading for divorce and poverty, probably in that order. What a great dad.

He puts the baby alarm on and then walks into his office. He checks his emails but there's nothing of any interest. He opens up Word and searches for his CV; he must have one somewhere. But he finds nothing at all. So he opens a blank document and begins: Benjamin Nicholas Crawford, born May 1st 1976.

By the time Archie stirs he has finished. He prints it out and reads it over a cup of tea while he feeds the boys. He doesn't sound like half the loser Ulrika maintains he is. Now he just has to prove to her, and himself, that he's not. Underneath bitch-Ulrika he's convinced the woman he fell in love with is lurking, the woman who used to make him laugh and who loved him back. The woman who gave the best blow-jobs in the world. And most importantly the mother of his children. For the sake of their boys he has to make one last effort to find her and the first step is to earn some money with which to lure her back to him.

28

"Every man is guilty of all the good he did not do."
Voltaire

The last thing on Ulrika's mind when she wakes up is her husband. She struggles to remember where she is, and what she is doing. She tries to open her eyes, but it feels as if something is pushing down on her eyelids. When she eventually manages to force them open she can't see anything beyond two pyramid-like structures on her chest. Then she remembers. She is in a Harley street clinic having a boob job in the hope that some aristo will marry her. How idiotic. But this moment of brutal honesty is quickly replaced with happiness that soon she will out of her loveless, poverty-stricken marriage and admiring diamonds nestled between her new boobs in a stately home in Yorkshire.

The nurse sitting at her side stands up when she sees that she's awake.

"Are you feeling all right?" she asks. Ulrika tries to speak but her mouth is too dry. She remembers the charming anesthetist chatting to her about his skiing holiday in Megève, and then nothing bar a brief moment of pushing and the handsome surgeon telling her she was going to have the most beautiful breasts in London. She hopes he is right.

"Would you like some water?" asks the nurse. Ulrika nods. The nurse lifts her head up to an angle and puts a plastic cup to her lips. Never has water tasted so good. She drinks the whole glass and manages to ask for another.

"We just need to wait a minute or two to see if you hold it down," says the nurse. Ulrika lies back and tries to relax, but suddenly she is utterly desperate for a pee. She tries to sit up and immediately the nurse is at her side again.

"Don't strain dear, I'll move the back of the bed so you can get up. Do you need to be sick?"

"No, pee," says Ulrika, the effort of saying the two words totally exhausting her.

The nurse nods and presses a button, which moves the back of the bed up until Ulrika is sitting upright. She swings her legs on to the floor. For a moment she feels like she's treading water, until she touches the ground.

The nurse helps her to stand up. She feels giddier than after six glasses of wine as they walk slowly to the bathroom.

"Ugh," says Ulrika as she catches sight of herself in the mirror. Green never was her colour, and this surgical gown is hideous. She looks at her profile. Her boobs are taped into pyramid-like shapes and she looks utterly ridiculous. She was warned about this. The tape stays on for a week and then you start to look a little less Lara Croft like. She has still not decided how she is going to explain it to Ben, but she will stay with Marina for the next couple of days – something she forgot to arrange in all the rush of getting organized.

Once back in the room, Ulrika asks if she can have her handbag, as well as some more water. At least she's not throwing up, and every minute her head is feeling clearer.

She looks at her BlackBerry. Ben has sent her a picture of the boys playing with Sam the dog. She feels guilty for a moment before moving swiftly on. Marina has sent her a bbm asking her to call her. She dials her number.

"Where have you been?" shrieks Marina. "I've been desperate to talk to you."

"Under the knife," replies Ulrika.

There is silence for a moment. "You lunatic. I've been reading a story about some bloke who made women have boob jobs for fun, what if he's the same?"

"Who? What are you on about?"

"Put women through breast implants. There was even a court case last year. Some woman sued some bloke for breach of contract because he made her have her tits done and then refused to marry her."

"Oh for God's sake Marina calm down. Anyway it's too late now."

"I can't believe you've gone through with it. You didn't even tell me it was today. Shall I come and get you? Where are you?"

"51 Harley Street. Yes, please. I'll find out when they're going to release me and my torpedoes and let you know."

Ulrika hangs up. Marina has a point. How does she know that he will marry her just because of her enlarged bust? Maybe that was just an excuse and he's as amazed as Marina that she actually went ahead with it. Why did she go ahead with it? She glances at herself in the mirror. She looks like she's been in a major car crash. Which actually is where she feels she has been headed over the past few months.

Marina goes back upstairs to find Tom. She knows where he is and what he's been up to all day. He leaves a trail of clues around him – a book here, a discarded glass there, a bit like a child would. She walks into the bathroom. He is in the shower; she can see the frame of his body through the glass door. She never tires of looking at his body, touching his body. She tries to remember back to a time when she felt like that about Mark. She knows she did, once. Is it the inevitable outcome of all marriages that you start to lose interest? And if so, why does anyone bother to get married? To have children is the obvious answer. But maybe that's where it normally starts to go wrong, as it did for her parents. So what happened with Mark and her? Did they just fall out of love? Will she ever fall out of love with Tom? Or is the reason that she didn't feel too excited about her husband any more because she never fell out of love with Tom in the first place?

"Hey gorgeous, a penny for your thoughts," says Tom, smiling, walking out of the shower, wrapping a towel around his waist. "That would have made a beautiful photograph."

"You should invest in an underwater camera." Marina giggles as he puts his wet arms around her. He kisses her neck and she runs her fingers through his wet hair and pulls him closer to her.

They tumble towards the bedroom; Tom taking her clothes off, his towel falling to the floor. She loves this moment, the anticipation just before they make love, knowing the feeling that is about to come. She wonders if he feels the same. He gives so little away. She pulls him down on top of her and guides him inside her. For a few minutes she forgets her court case, her ponderings on life, her yet barely written novel and her surgically enhanced best friend. All that counts is the sensation of Tom inside her, how complete it makes her feel, and how happy she is to have him there.

*

Three hours later she is back on her bed, with Ulrika sitting next to her, leaning against some pillows, pyramids in the air.

"So how long do you need to wander around looking like Madonna?"

"A week, then the straps come off, then I have to wear a support bra for another three weeks, day and night."

"And when does Lord Mycroft get to see his new assets?"

Ulrika sighs. "I've been thinking about that," she says. "I can't decide whether to tell him they're a no-go area until I have that ring on my finger and access to the joint bank account."

"You still want to marry him? After all this?"

"Are you referring to my pyramids, or the fact that he might just be leading you on?"

"Well, a bit of both really."

Ulrika interrupts her. "Look, he didn't lead me to the surgeon's table like a lamb to slaughter. I'm a grown woman, I can make my own decisions about my body. Granted it had never occurred to me to have a boob job before, but it's useful to have somewhere to hang your smalls if you run out of room on the washing line." She laughs and hangs one of Tom's stray socks on her strapped up boob.

"Ow, actually, it hurts to laugh," she adds, removing the sock. "And it smells."

"Poor you," says Marina, throwing the sock towards the laundry bin. "And what about Ben and the boys? You're welcome to stay here as long as you like but when you go home, eventually, what are you going to tell him?"

"Yes, I've been pondering that too. I could pretend I was in a car crash, or I could tell him the truth."

"What, that you hate him so much that you went through surgery in the hope that another man might marry you?"

"God, you journos are always so to the point. No, silly."

"Just don't tell him what Italians call *la verità vera*," says Tom, who is standing at the door watching them.

"Hello sexy. So what do you think?" says Ulrika laughing.

"An interesting look," laughs Tom. "I feel a *Vogue* cover coming on…"

They all laugh.

"What was that about the Italians?" asks Marina.

Tom walks into the room and perches on the edge of the bed. "The Italians have two truths, la *verità*, the truth, and la *verità vera*, the real truth. I think with Ben, the kindest thing would be tell him the truth, and to leave out the real truth. Say that you had a boob job, that you inherited some money and decided to spend it on yourself."

"So just lie?" asks Marina.

"Oh come on, call yourself a journalist?" says Ulrika. "And anyway, it's only half a lie. I like your thinking Tom. Marina, you need to spend more time in Italy and stop being so po-faced. You'll never make a proper hack."

"Maybe when you've fully recovered, we can all go to Italy, you with whoever you and your breasts end up with and me with Marina," Tom smiles. "We could all go and stay in the little cottage Marina and I stayed in close to Rome."

"Yes, it's heavenly," says Marina, "really gorgeous, all old stone and surrounded by olive groves. I love it there."

Tom smiles. "Cup of tea anyone?"

"Please," say Ulrika and Marina together. Tom goes off downstairs.

"Well, your taste in tea-ladies has improved since the days of *The Chronicle*. And you've got him well trained," says Ulrika sinking back into her pillow.

'Not really, he's quite messy."

Ulrika sits bolt upright. "What? Mark was too tidy and this one is too messy? Get a grip, woman!"

Marina laughs. "No, I'm not complaining, I'm…"

"Just saying," interrupts Ulrika. "Yes, I know, I know."

"I'm loving having him here," Marina smiles.

"I bet you are, he's a scorcher. Never mind all this first love bollocks, I might have to shag him myself."

"Happily, I know you well enough to know you wouldn't stoop to such depths."

"You hope," laughs Ulrika. "So what's happening? I mean long term? Any news since I lost consciousness?"

Marina looks towards the door. "No," she half-whispers. "Nothing's been said, but it's been almost three months now. He comes and goes from Rome to work on his book here and basically it's just like we're living together when he's here, and when he's not, we talk on the phone and email and stuff. But neither of us has said anything about the future. I suppose I'm too scared to in case he looks horrified and runs away for another ten years, and also I need to get the court case over and done with."

"Oh God Marina, me and my boobs, I haven't even asked. What's going on with it?"

"Mark put me on to a top QC and we're busy preparing my defence. That's why I was in the library researching when I came across the Mycroft article. I was looking for other stories that I know phone-tapping was used to get info on for the paper. Basically our defence is that although I may have used evidence secured through phone-tapping, the whole paper was at it, as I'm sure every other paper on Fleet Street is."

"Tea's up ladies." Tom walks in with a tray. "Don't spill it." He hands a mug to Marina and another to Ulrika.

"The case is in four weeks' time," continues Marina. "I'm so nervous about it, but at least it will be over."

"Same time as my breasts will be back to their fighting fittest," says Ulrika. "We must all celebrate somehow, Maybe that rich new bird of Mark's can throw a party."

"Good idea," says Tom. "But without the disasters this time."

"Yes, sorry, I'd forgotten about poor Ollie."

Marina sighs and finishes her tea. "Must be terrible for you Tom, going back to Rome without him, seeing all those places you used to go to and your old friends. And how's Carla?"

"She's OK, bearing up, but still blames herself."

"We all do," says Marina.

Tom looks up and for the first time ever in all the years she's known him Marina sees him looking vulnerable. "Not as much as I do," he says quietly.

❧ *29* ❧

"All British people have plain names, and that
works pretty well over there."
Paris Hilton

Katie Tomlinson has had what most people would regard as a pretty miraculous life. Granted she has worked hard, but she has also dined with the Queen and slept with some of Hollywood's leading men, and all the while running a multi-million-pound retail empire. But perhaps her most enviable asset is the apartment next door to her house in Knightsbridge, accessible from her bedroom that she uses as a dressing room.

Her clothes are ordered into day and eveningwear, haute couture and designer. Her many bags are divided into clutches, totes and Birkins, stacked neatly on perfectly polished wooden shelves. Her 300 or so pairs of shoes are similarly organized. It is an apartment that most women would be happy to spend the rest of their lives in, and it still makes Katie happy every time she walks into it. Yet the feeling is nothing like the feeling she is experiencing right now, as she lies on a bed with some cold slimy substance rubbed over her tummy and watches her unborn baby move on a small black screen.

"It is still too early to determine the sex," says the doctor.

"Doesn't matter, I don't want to know," says Katie, surprising herself with her lack of desire to be in total control.

The father of the child nods. "No, I don't want to know either," he says. "Just want to know that everything is OK so far."

The doctor moves the scanner around. "Yes, all looks good. The nuchal fluids are fine, and the foetus has two arms, two legs, ten fingers and ten toes. All in order."

Katie gazes at the screen like a love-struck teenager. Mark is not much better.

"This is your first, I take it?"

Both of them nod.

"Yes, I thought so. Well, the miracle of life still manages to charm even the most scientific of us, doesn't it Dr Chadwick?" he says, wiping the excess slime from Katie's stomach with a bit of paper. Katie wonders for a brief moment whether it will help with stretch-marks –

not that she intends to have any.

"It certainly does," says Mark. "Thank you Dr Graham. See you in a few weeks' time."

After the examination they go to the hospital café.

"Remember last time we were here?" says Katie. "It seems like a different life."

"It is a different life," smiles Mark, patting her tummy. "What would you like?"

"Skinny latte please, decaf."

"Of course."

Mark goes off to get the coffees. She wants to talk to him about the future but doesn't want to come across as a demanding, insecure type. Of course Mark and Marina need to get divorced before they can get married. Not that they've discussed marriage; they've just slipped into a comfortable life, sharing her home, living like an old married couple. Not that she's so old fashioned (heaven forbid) to want to be married just because she's pregnant, but she would like to know where she stands.

"Here you are." Mark puts the coffees down.

"Thanks," Katie yawns. "God, I've never been so tired in my life. All I want to do is sleep."

"Then you should sleep. Can't you get someone else to run the empire for a few months? Actually the tiredness is probably at its worst now, because this is where everything starts to be formed, where all the hard work happens."

"And when it least shows, so everyone just thinks you're being lazy. OK doc, I will go straight home after this coffee and work on my bed with my laptop."

"I envy the laptop, but try not to fall asleep with it on your face this time."

Mark had come home a few days before to find her splayed on the bed with her MacBook Air on her head.

"No, must be terribly ageing, all those rays," says Katie. To Mark's slight consternation, she is only half-smiling.

"I think in sleep mode, the rays are diminished," he laughs.

"Have you thought at all about names?" asks Katie.

"No," says Mark, rather surprised. "It's quite early days isn't it? Why? Have you?"

"Of course; Amelia for a girl and Salvador for a boy."

"Oh. Right."

"I figured that if his or her surname is Tomlinson, it needs something rather floral to go with it, rather like a plain blazer can be beautifully offset by a floral skirt."

"And if his or her surname is Chadwick?"

Katie blushes slightly. "Well, it's more or less the same thing, isn't it? Quite a down-to-earth, robust sort of name that could benefit from something a bit frilly to go with it."

"Yes, fine, but Salvador? Isn't that just a bit, well, out there?"

"It worked for Dalí," says Katie, finishing her coffee and standing up. "Anyway, as you say, it's early days, we don't need to discuss it now."

"Quite," says Mark. "Go home and get some rest, I'll see you later on."

He kisses her on the lips and as always is struck by how good she smells and tastes. It's like hanging out with the perfumery floor at Harvey Nichols.

"OK, will do. See you at home." She picks up her bag and leaves, turning after a few paces. "But please at least THINK about Salvador," she smiles.

Mark promises he will and smiles back, and hopes fervently that his first-born child is a girl, whatever her surname turns out to be.

"Christ almighty, Ulrika, what the fuck happened to you?" Ben is at the train station to meet her with the boys. Happily they are too busy fighting over a blanket in their double buggy to pay any attention to their father.

"OK, OK, calm down, I'm fine. I just had a boob job."

"What? Why? There was nothing wrong with your boobs."

"Can we go home, please?" she leans over the buggy and kisses Archie and Felix. "Hello boys."

"That's what Eva Herzigova said," says Ben.

Ulrika glares at him.

"Oh, so you go and have a boob job unannounced and I get an old-fashioned look?"

"I know it's a bit of a surprise, but, well, I inherited some money."

"Who on earth from?"

"A godparent, no one you know. Anyway, I thought I would spend it on myself."

"Very selfless of you."

She glares at him again. "Yes, well, before it got eaten up in the debt situation that I'm sure we're in now that I've been away for two days and…"

Ben interrupts her. "OK, let's not start fighting the minute you get home."

"We're not even home yet."

"Precisely. Let's just get home, have a drink and you can tell me all about it. Er, them," he adds, looking at her pyramids.

She smiles at him and realizes it's the first time she's done so in about a year. The boys start laughing and the sun even comes out. In April, in Surrey. Talk about a scene you seldom see.

Mark and Marina are having coffee at Picasso in the King's Road. It is a café that Marina's mother used to take her to as a child for a treat, and she likes it partly because of that but also because she hates the fact that Starbucks and Costa and Prets now seem to have taken over the world and there are only a few places left that haven't been swallowed up by them.

To Marina it feels odd to be meeting Mark as a friend, almost like she is doing something wrong or clandestine. But why shouldn't they be friends? Just because their marriage didn't work doesn't mean they can't be friends. They don't exactly hate each other. Maybe it's just that for most people it's all or nothing – you don't normally stay in touch with people you've been married to unless there are children involved.

"You look great Mina," he smiles as they sit down.

"You too," she says. "She must be feeding you well."

"Are you suggesting I've put on weight?" He looks down at his body.

"No, no," laughs Marina. "You just look, well, glowing."

Mark raises an eyebrow. "Glowing eh? Well, that might have something to do with my news."

"News?"

"Yes, your favourite word!" He leans back in his seat.

"You're gloating now, just waiting for me to beg you to tell. Well, I'm not going to."

She waits for him to weaken. Nothing. "All right then. Please, please dearest Mark, tell me your news."

"That's more like it. With pleasure. Katie is pregnant, I'm going to be a dad."

Marina almost knocks her coffee over, which is not unusual per se, but she wasn't even anywhere near the cup.

"Wow! That's amazing." The words are coming out of her mouth because she knows they are what is expected of her, but she is still not really sure how she feels about the news that her husband – he still is her husband on paper – is going to have a baby with another woman. This must mean the trial separation is no longer a trial.

"You must be thrilled. I mean, it's what you always wanted." Marina collects herself and puts her hand on his. "Mark, it's great, really great, I'm so pleased for you."

"Thank you," he says, looking genuinely happy. "I'm really excited."

"Any ideas on names? Do you know what sex it is?"

"No, neither of us wants to know beforehand, but if it's a girl, the name Amelia has been mooted."

"Lovely name, very classic. And if it's a boy? How

about Frank? Or Gianfranco, given that he'll grow up as a bit of a Eurotrash with all Katie's jet-setting."

Mark looks slightly shifty. "Well, we haven't really discussed it in detail, but, er, Katie quite likes the idea of Salvador." He almost whispers it.

"Salvador!" shrieks Marina, and now she does knock her coffee cup over. "What, as in the place? The Brazilian city?"

"The very same," says Mark, mopping up her coffee.

"And how do you feel about that?"

"Well, it has to be said that I think it is among the sillier names I have ever heard, but I guess he could be Sal for short."

"Look on the bright side, eh? Can't you just say 'no way Jose'. Actually, maybe you should mention Jose, she might quite like that. But can't you just say no? I mean it's your child too."

"The thing is I don't see the point in arguing about it before it's happened. If it's a girl then we have Amelia which we both love, and if it's a boy, then we need to start negotiations."

"Negotiations? You make it sound like a boardroom coup!"

"I think for Katie most of life has been like a boardroom coup. She is endlessly plotting and politicking.

I am only just getting her to relax and think about the really important things in life, like our baby."

"And how is she responding to that?"

"A bit better. She has even taken a few days off recently for the first time in living memory. She's been very tired. But she can't seem to let go – she's a bit of a, what you would call in one of your columns, control freak."

"She was always like that, even as a teenager. But I think when she actually relaxes she changes and becomes more, well, human really, not so perfect, if that doesn't sound rude."

"Not rude at all, spot on. She is always so concerned with keeping up with the ridiculous world she lives and works in that I think finding me has been a bit of light relief."

Marina laughs. "Yes, until you put your foot down over Salvador that is."

Mark smiles in a non-committed manner.

"Mark, you ARE going to put your foot down over Salvador, aren't you?"

"It might grow on me," he laughs.

"Yeah, like fungus." Marina looks around. "Well, here's to a girl." She raises her empty coffee cup. "I suppose we ought to talk about practical things, such as the house, and getting divorced and all that."

"I guess we should. Do we need to get lawyers involved or can one just get divorced on the internet these days?"

"I can't see why not, you can do everything else on the internet. Are you keen to get married again?"

"I don't know if keen is the word," says Mark. "But I feel I ought to do the right thing and marry Katie. Not that I'm not keen on marrying her of course, but all I'm saying, in a rather clumsy manner, is that I'm not desperate to divorce you."

"Same here," says Marina, who is feeling quite saddened by the whole conversation, even if it has all worked out so well for them all. "I don't know what Tom's plans are long term, and I just want to get the court case over with really before I move on to the next stage of my life."

"I can understand that. What's going on now?"

"Just waiting for a firm date for the court case, it will be about three weeks from now. Thanks again for your pal, he's been great. But it's been really stressful."

"I can imagine. Shall we meet again when it's over? Let me know the exact date. I want to come and support you. Are you working at the moment?"

"Writing, and freelancing. I have a book review to write this afternoon."

"Good book?"

"Dreadful, all about love on a Greek island. I thought I would begin; 'Makes me want to run away to a Greek island, without this book.' But that might be a bit harsh. After all, I'm a struggling author now."

"Let me know if you need any help, and I mean it about the court case."

"Thanks Mark, I will. And you can catch up with Ulrika and her new assets in court."

"She went ahead? The mad woman. And has he married her?"

"Not yet, I bet he doesn't you know, I just have a feeling this boob-job thing was a stalling tactic. Or tactit."

"Very droll. I think she'd be well rid of him, sounds like a thoroughly nasty piece of work. How are things going with Ben and her?"

"Haven't heard. She went back today with the pyramids. She isn't going to tell him the whole truth, but of course she'll have to tell him about them, they're pretty obvious."

Mark shakes his head. "What a pickle she's got herself into, poor girl."

Marina nods. "Yes, but knowing Ulrika, she'll find the most comfortable way out of it."

Ulrika is leaning over the bath while Ben rubs shampoo

into her long blonde hair. He is not doing a bad job; in fact, it's quite relaxing.

"Conditioner, madam?" he asks once he has rinsed out the shampoo.

"Please, and a head massage too," she replies.

Ben obliges by covering her head in creamy conditioner and then massaging her scalp in small circular motions, systematically from the front to the back and then up again across the middle of her head. For the first time in days, Ulrika totally relaxes.

"You're wasted in marketing, I think you've found your true calling," she tells him.

Ben laughs. "Not much money in head massages."

She's about to say 'there's not much money in your kind of marketing either', but she stops herself and goes back to enjoying the massage.

"Actually talking of work, are you around to pick up the boys tomorrow?"

"Sure, I wasn't planning on taking the pyramids to the office. I can wear a large coat to the nursery. Why?"

"It's just that I've got a meeting, about doing some consultancy work. It's only 10 hours a week, for an IT firm in Guildford. They want someone to take over their internal and external communications."

"Sounds good," says Ulrika. "If slightly dull. "

"The pay's not dull," says Ben, increasing the pressure of the massage.

"How much?"

"They're offering 200 quid an hour. So it's 8000 quid a month, plus time to do other stuff."

Ulrika stiffens slightly. Is he under the utter delusion that if he tries to buck his ideas up she will go back to him and abandon her plans for escape?

"Rinse please," she says. "That was lovely."

"Any time Madam," laughs Ben. "But I may have to charge you my hourly rate in future."

❦ *30* ❧

"It is the spirit and not the form of law that keeps justice alive."
Earl Warren

Three weeks later; Crown Court, Ludgate Circus, City of London

Marina has been trying to assess the sympathetic predisposition of the jury from across the courtroom, but it's impossible. There's not much you can tell about people sitting motionless and silent, most of them probably wishing they were somewhere else and rather angry to have been caught up in this sordid little tale of Fleet Street skulduggery.

The defence and the prosecution have both made their cases. Marina feels it went as well as it could have done. She is of course guilty as charged, but she has done a good job of convincing the court that she was not aware of the legal implications and was simply following normal newspaper practice. All the research she did in the library has come in handy – she was able to cite 124 articles where she knows phone-tapping was used to get information.

"It is ridiculous," her lawyer concluded, "to convict this woman for this crime, because if we do, we need to convict the whole newspaper industry along with her. My suggestion is that you throw the case out and that a review into newspaper practice would be a more appropriate way forward. All the police are after is a conviction for their records, and it doesn't matter to them what happens to this young lady and her career. But, Ladies and Gentlemen of the jury, it would be the wrong thing to do, to send her down and ruin her life for something she was not even aware was illegal."

The judge is about to sum up when there is a scuffle at the entrance to the courtroom. Ulrika, who is in one of the back rows, turns around and sees the loafers she noticed at the last hearing marching towards the judge. They belong to Hugo Willoughby, who is followed by about forty people carrying placards saying 'We are all guilty', 'Marina Shaw is a scapegoat' and 'Stop this sham trial.'

"Order, order," shouts the clerk of the court.

"What is the meaning of this?" demands the judge.

Hugo and his gang stop just in front of him. "Your Honour," says Hugo. "We have collected a petition of

2483 names from various newspapers across the country to demand the crown drop any charges against Marina Shaw. We are here to represent the signatories and I am also here to add my own personal evidence in this case. I am the Features Editor of *The Chronicle* and I can confirm to you and the ladies and gentlemen of the jury that Marina Shaw is no more guilty than any other journalist in the country who has ever worked on a tabloid news or features desk. I can confirm that when the newspaper management was faced with this charge, they asked me to find a scapegoat and I picked Marina because she was the latest addition to the team. I know it was wrong, but this is how callous and cutthroat Fleet Street is. I am not proud of my actions, which is why I have worked tirelessly to put things right since that day. Marina is a talented and hard-working journalist who deserves better than this."

The judge leans back in his chair. There is silence throughout the courtroom. Marina can hardly breathe. Imagine, Hugo Willoughby turns out to be a hero. You couldn't make it up. And he actually looks a bit nervous – a rare sight. The whole newsroom is there – even Flora and Jo, all dressed up in their Sunday best, hoping for an execution no doubt. Jo has even got her knitting with her, making her look even more like a Tricoteuse during the

French Revolution. Felicia and Millie give her a clandestine wave and smile.

"And why have you waited until this moment, young man, to come forward?" the judge asks Hugo.

"Sir, because I agree with the defence that the system needs to change, but that will only happen with public awareness and pressure. I figured this was a way to get maximum publicity and exposure."

"I see, I see. And can you name the member of management who asked you to find a scapegoat?"

"I can Sir, it was Cameron Knight, the editor."

"And does this mean you are now unemployed?"

Hugo smiles; "Undoubtedly Sir."

"And was the defendant in any way aware of this, er, plan of yours?"

"Not in the slightest Sir. If we were to ask for them, taped phone records would show there has been no contact between myself and the defendant since she left the paper."

The judge nods slowly. "Ten minute recess please. Defence and Prosecution to my chambers immediately."

The courtroom rises as the judge walks out.

Hugo walks over to Marina. She's not sure whether to kick him or hug him.

"OK, I've been a total shit," he begins. "I know that,

but that was the culture there, you know that, and the way I was told it was either one person or the whole damned paper. I'm sorry Marina, I really am. The whole thing made me realise I don't really want to work in that kind of environment any more."

Marina stares at him. "I never thought I'd see the day when Hugo Willoughby showed a human side. What on earth happened? Did you fall in love or something?"

Hugo laughs and blushes slightly. Another first. "Good lord no! I haven't gone that soft. I guess I just realised there was more to life than dicking people over." He looks around the room. "I see Ulrika's here. How is she?"

"She's fine. About to bag some millionaire and finally leave her husband."

"Shame," grins Hugo. "She was such fun as a desperate housewife. I think the role rather suits her."

Marina nods. "Hugo, thanks for this. I mean, obviously not the dropping me in it, but all the stuff afterwards. Will you really lose your job?"

"Probably, but only until they arrest old Knighty," he laughs. "Look out, Uncle Rupert's back."

"Uncle Rupert?"

"Yes, the judge is my uncle. I had no idea he was on today. Don't worry; he doesn't hate me too much, I only seduced one of his daughters. And anyway, he's very professional, utterly impartial."

"All rise, all rise," shouts the clerk of the court. Marina is not sure her legs can carry her. The rest of her life is about to be determined by a man wearing a wig called Uncle Rupert.

"I would like to make a short speech," says Katie Tomlinson, standing up, holding a champagne glass of fizzy water, looking immaculate in a pale-pink wraparound maternity dress covering what is a barely discernible but perfectly formed bump.

They are at The Ivy in Covent Garden: Tom, Mark, Ulrika, Katie, Marina, Marina's mother and Hugo, who has been forgiven and hailed a hero after Uncle Rupert dismissed the case, dropped all charges against Marina and sent a recommendation to the Press Complaints Commission that it investigate Cameron Knight and the senior management of the newspaper.

"I would like to welcome you all here, after what can only be described as a triumph of justice. I have known Marina for a very long time and although we weren't always the best of friends, I just know she is not the kind of person to do anything underhand or knowingly illegal. Unlike some of the rest of you…" She looks around the table smiling. "I would like to propose a toast to the great British justice system, and Uncle Rupert."

"Hear, hear," says Tom. "To Uncle Rupert."

Everyone raises their glass and Marina makes a point of toasting every person there. They have all in some way helped her through this: her mother has been a shoulder to cry on, Mark and Katie came up with the QC, Ulrika has made her laugh and kept her sane, and Tom has been a rock for the last few weeks.

"Remember to look people in the eye when you're toasting," says Hugo to Ulrika. "Otherwise you get seven years of bad sex."

"Not again," she sighs. "Such a drag."

"So Marina, what are you going to do, now that you're free?" asks Katie.

"Well, Tom and I thought we might go to Rome for the weekend. I'm going to keep working on my novel…"

"You're working on a book?" Mark interrupts her. "That's great news, finally. Have you got a publisher yet?"

"It's early days. I'm told by those in the know that you have to get an agent first, otherwise you won't even get the damned thing read, so I've sent out the first three chapters and a synopsis and am waiting to hear back."

"What's it about?" asks her mother.

"It's about a foreign correspondent who gets involved

in a political scandal and brings down a government in Africa."

"So a bit like a journalist who gets involved in a journalistic scandal and brings down a newspaper?" says Mark.

Marina laughs. "Not yet, but I'll drink to that!"

They all raise their glasses again.

"What's the title?" says Ulrika.

"I haven't quite decided yet, but the working title is *Blood River*."

"Talking of names," says Tom, nodding towards Mark and Katie, "have you two come up with any ideas?"

Marina could kick him: he knows damned well they have, she told him so the other day. Amazingly, he thought there was nothing wrong with Salvador.

Katie lights up. "Yes, we have – Amelia for a girl, and Salvador for a boy."

"Well, we haven't actually agreed..." Mark begins, but she hushes him with a pat on the hand. "Mark's not that keen on Salvador, but I'm planning to talk him round."

"Salvador." Ulrika says the name slowly. "Now why didn't I think of that?"

"It's not too late," says Hugo.

"It is for you, you traitor," smiles Ulrika.

Marina laughs and leaves them to flirt. She slides into

an empty chair next to Katie. "I just wanted to say thank you Katie," she says. "As you said, we haven't always got on that well, but you came up trumps with the QC, I really appreciate your help."

Katie smiles and strokes her bump. "It was a pleasure, look I know how much you mean to Mark and the last thing I wanted was to see you behind bars. Especially now I have everything I want."

Marina follows her eyes to her baby bump. "Yes, odd isn't it, I just never wanted it, but I can see you're really happy."

"I don't want to sound like a new-age lunatic, but now it's happened my life seems to complete, it's like a dream come true. I thought I was happy when the business became a success, but now I realise that was just relief at not being a failure. This is real fulfillment."

"I really had no idea you were so keen on Mark all those years ago, I always thought it was Tom you liked."

Katie smiles. "No, I flirted with him just to annoy you, because of course you had the attention of the man I really wanted. Apart from one night when I managed to get him away from you, ply him with champagne and seduce him. It was just before the shooting, he of course regretted it immediately, which made me furious and hate you even more."

"A bit like Tom and me," smiles Marina. "Although he never even had the manners to regret it, it just seemed to mean nothing to him."

"Amazing how it's all turned out, look at him now, in love with you and chatting to your mother. As Shakespeare would say; 'All's well that ends well'".

Marina looks around the table, everyone is happy, Ulrika is howling with laughter at one of Hugo's jokes, Tom, Mark and her mother are chatting about something or other, and here she is comparing notes about her soon to be ex-husband with his future wife. She suddenly feels terribly modern and mature. And mightily relieved that she is in a restaurant sipping champagne as opposed to jail. If only she still had her column to express her feelings in.

❧ 31 ❧

"The course of true love never did run smooth."
William Shakespeare

Tom and Marina get home at about four o'clock. She feels dizzy from the alcohol but happy. When she left the house this morning she wasn't sure whether she would come back with a criminal record, or even a suspended prison sentence hanging over her. There couldn't have been a better outcome. She picks up the post from the mat, one of the letters is from a literary agency.

"Tom," she yells. "Come here, quick, there's a letter here from David Higham."

"Who's he?" shouts Tom from the bathroom.

Marina goes into the kitchen to put the kettle on. She'll need a cup of tea either way. "He's not a he, it's London's leading literary agency," she shouts in the general direction of the bathroom. As she watches the kettle boil, if only to disprove the theory that a watched kettle doesn't boil, she remembers saying goodbye to Mark today. There was an awkward moment as they went to kiss each other goodbye and their lips accidentally touched. Marina practically leapt up in the air. Mark looked serene and just smiled down at her.

"So what does David say?" Tom is out of the bathroom and standing next to her. "Are you going to steam open the envelope so you can go through the excitement all over again when we wake up after our power nap?"

"No, silly. Anyway, it might even be a rejection. OK, let's get the tea made and then I'll open it."

"How much of an advance do you think you'll get? 15k? 20k?"

"No idea. What did you get?"

"Only five thousand, but a coffee-table book of photographs is worth a lot less than a novel. OK, let's open it, come on, I can't bear the suspense any longer."

Marina slowly tears open the envelope and takes out the letter. As she unfolds it, she sees the word 'unfortunately' and knows she doesn't want to read on. Silently she passes it to Tom.

"'Dear Ms Shaw,'" he reads. "'Many thanks for submitting the first three chapters and the synopsis of your novel. When I saw it was from you, I put it right at the top of my to-read pile as I'm a great fan of your writing.

Unfortunately, as far as I am concerned, *Blood River* doesn't quite work. It is a good idea, and I see the plot has been thought out and worked on, but the actual writing lacks the vibrancy and humour of your journalistic work. I also think the title is a bit masculine for a book about a female journalist and would not really appeal to the women readers who will be your target market.

If you want to come and have a chat with me about ways to make the book more marketable, then feel free to call my assistant to set up a time to come in.

Yours sincerely

Emma Watts"

"Well, it's not ALL bad…" Tom begins.

"What? Apart from the title and the writing, which sucks?" Marina puts her teacup down. "I'm going to go for a sleep. I can't think about this now."

"Agreed," says Tom leading her upstairs. "And it's still been a good day in other ways, hasn't it?"

"Yes," says Marina. "But instead of winning the double, I've only won the Champions League."

"The what?"

"Football," says Marina, too tired to explain.

"Right, well, don't worry. You just need to put in some jokes and find a new title."

"I'm not sure it's that simple," she sighs, collapsing onto the bed.

"So Ben, the thing is, well, there's no easy way to say this," Ulrika begins. "But the fact is that the lights have gone out."

"Have they?" says Ben, looking around the kitchen.

"Not in here, you fool. The light has gone out on our marriage."

"Ah, I see. This is the 'I'm leaving you' speech I've been expecting."

Ulrika looks at the floor. She really should give him more credit than she does.

He takes a sip of his wine. "Well, I thought it was a bit odd to be offered a drink by a blonde with big breasts who normally looks like she'd rather throw a glass of wine at me. I think part of me even hoped it was a seduction ploy. Me and my irrepressible optimism."

"I'm sorry, Ben."

"Where are you going? What happens to the boys?"

"I'm marrying a man called Lord Mycroft, who has an estate in Yorkshire. The boys will come with me, but I'm not going to be a bitch about you seeing them, of course…"

"Big of you," he interrupts.

"Ben, I want to make this as painless as possible for them, and for that to happen, we have to be on good terms."

"Yes, well, husbands don't normally take well to being told their wives have been having an affair, are marrying another man and taking their lovely children with them. Have you any idea how much I'm going to miss them?" He stands up and starts pacing around the kitchen.

"I don't want to be a weekend dad, Ulrika, I want to see them every day of their childhood, I want to watch them grow, not be amazed at how much they've grown every few weeks. This isn't what I planned when I married you."

"And I certainly didn't plan to live in penury with your mother watching our every move. Or for you to get so FAT."

Ben shoots her a look.

"OK, Ben I'm sorry, that was cruel. Let's just say that neither of us got what we wanted from this marriage and it's better to call it quits."

"I wonder if the boys would agree to us giving up so quickly."

"I think the boys will be fine," says Ulrika. "We will have to make sure they are."

Ben turns to her. "Please just think about this Ulrika. I know things have been less than ideal, but I'm getting back on top of things. I got that consultancy deal in Guildford and I am on the hunt for more of the same. I thought we could get a dog, the boys love Sam so much, and I could go for runs and get back into shape. The fact is I've been so de-motivated, almost in a sort of lethargic haze, partly because I didn't want to face up to things, but I've got a grip now and I still think we could make a go of things. I don't quite know when we started hating each other, but could we not try to reverse things, or even start again? I mean now you've got such great tits and all that…"

Ulrika laughs. "Now I have big tits you'll forgive everything? I knew they'd come in useful."

Ben smiles. "I loved your old tits, Ulrika, like I loved the old you. I just want her back."

Ulrika looks away from him. The old her is no longer around. She has new breasts and a new life.

"Ben, let's try to move on, please. And try to stay friends."

Ben sighs. He recognizes that hard look. Reminiscent of Margaret Thatcher during the miners' strike. "So when do you leave?"

"There's a pre-divorce engagement party on Thursday

night, at his club. You're more than welcome to come along…"

"I suppose I should meet my sons' future step-father," he says. "I'll be there."

It finally happens on a beautiful morning in late May on the Spanish Steps in Rome. Tom and Marina sit down, having had a long walk through the Villa Borghese earlier that morning. Tom wanted to get up early to take some pictures of the pine trees and the shadows that form underneath them. Marina thought she had never been anywhere so beautiful; the mixture of nature and ancient Rome, the statues, the winding paths among the green lawns enchanted her. As they walked down towards the Spanish Steps they had a view over the city and Tom pointed out the most famous landmarks to her.

They had arrived the night before, taken the Leonardo Express into town and a taxi to Tom's apartment on the Via Margutta, a street made famous by the fact that Picasso once had a studio there for a few months. It is a cobbled street that hasn't changed much since Picasso was there, except possibly for the addition of a vegetarian restaurant and a beauty salon. Marina felt like she had landed in another world; the sounds, the smells, the colours of Rome were all intoxicating.

They had eaten in a restaurant called Nino's a ten-minute walk from his flat; prosciutto and melon, followed by hand-made fettuccine with a tomato and basil sauce that was almost sweet. The Italian waiter didn't bat an eyelid when they ordered two starters, but he was somewhat surprised at Marina's ability to drop bits of melon in her lap.

The wine was a robust red, and Marina felt truly relaxed for the first time in several weeks. Even the agent's letter failed to upset her equilibrium. After all the other two were still to respond, and if the worst came to the worst, she would just have to re-think her first three chapters. At least the agent liked the plot.

And at least she had started writing. It was such a relief not to have that nagging voice in the back of her head telling her to get on with her novel.

Tom's flat was small and cluttered, but the location made up for that. It had one bedroom overlooking the Villa Borghese park, a bathroom and a sitting room that also served as a kitchen, dining room and office.

The following day they are taking a walk around town. Rome is an amazing city for just walking in, you can waste hours wandering around the piazzas, drinking coffee and watching stylish Italians. And on the Spanish Steps where they sit down for a break, Tom finally tells Marina what she has wanted to hear since she was a teenager.

"I love you Marina," he whispers in her ear as they watch two doves in the fountain down below bathe and splash each other with water.

Marina leans towards him, and although on the surface she is happy, somewhere deep inside her a switch is flicked, like a light going off.

❦ 32 ❦

"A woman is like a tea-bag. You can't tell how strong she is until you put her in hot water."
Nancy Reagan

Of all the things she has designed; shoes, bags, dresses, underwear, even jewellery, this nursery is the most difficult. Of course not knowing whether it's a girl or a boy doesn't help, but life holds few surprises and Katie Tomlinson wants this baby to retain his or her mystery until the last possible moment.

Maybe she should call Mark, but being a medical man, he doesn't really care. Anyway, it's not really up to him. She feels very much that this is her baby; maybe all mothers feel like that? How much involvement does the father have anyway? OK, so it's his sperm, but it's her egg, her body, her caesarian scar. Happily, even though she is now five months in, she has yet to have a stretch mark. She covers herself every day with gorgeous oils to avoid them; even if all the research says that stretch marks are something hereditary, she's not risking it. And the oils make her feel good.

Katie Tomlinson adores her bump. It is the most satisfying accessory she has ever owned – never out of style, endlessly fascinating and a source of constant comfort.

She loves the feeling of the baby kicking inside her. She can't believe she almost missed out on this whole experience, and she is so grateful to Mark for that. But why is he dragging his heels over this divorce? Now Marina's court case is over, they just need to get on with it.

Her parents are delighted she is pregnant, and happy that the father is a respected surgeon and not some Russian opera singer or, even worse, a rapper or a penniless author. But they would be even more delighted to see Katie walk down the aisle in a white dress – once her baby bump had gone, of course.

Now it is too late to arrange the kind of wedding that would be acceptable among their circle of friends. A pregnant bride is worse than no bride at all. And they can fudge over the exact timing of their wedding when the baby is older. Once they're married no one will question whether it happened before the birth, or after it. Or maybe they should do a quick registry office thing and then go for the white wedding when she's lost the baby weight, not that there will be much of that. She has never felt in better shape. She's doing pregnancy yoga every day and going for long walks around Hyde Park, imagining what it will be like when she has a buggy to push around.

She walks around the empty former spare room, mentally placing a cot, a changing table and other bits of furniture in there. She looks through the colours on her colour chart. Maybe a peaceful green? Or should you never make design decisions when you're pregnant, rather like avoiding clothes shopping during your period?

Her mobile phone rings. It's Mark.

"Hi darling. Glad you called, I'm in the nursery, what do you think on the colour of the walls?"

"Why not just wait until we know whether it's a boy or a girl? He or she won't care if the room is ready the minute they pop out. And it'll only take a week or so to do. Then we can get it utterly perfect in pink or blue."

Katie makes accepting noises.

"Anyway I called to tell you we've been invited to Ulrika's pre-engagement party, Thursday night next week. You free?"

"Sure," she says, wondering how he can mention the word engagement without cringing. Surely he must know she is waiting to hear him propose every minute of the day?

"OK, great," he says. "I'll tell her we'll be there. See you later on. There's a Chelsea match on, hope I make it home in time."

Katie hangs up. Peaceful green it is.

"Hello, Marina?" She recognizes the voice as a significant one but just can't place it.

"Yes?"

"It's Les, Les from *The Chronicle*."

Of course. Les Misérables. How could she fail to identify those cheery tones? "Les, how are you?"

"Oh, you know, ticking along. Anyway, I wanted to say, sorry about all the palaver you went through, hope you're feeling OK?"

"Fine thanks Les, all fine."

There's a moment's silence. "Look, I'm calling to say that there have been some developments at the paper."

"Really?"

"Yes, er, Knight has been suspended, pending an investigation and, er, well yours truly is in charge for the moment."

"That's great Les, you must be thrilled."

"Well, up to a point, it's a lot of work. I don't have a deputy yet, though I do have someone in mind. In fact that's my next call after you. Anyway, listen up Marina, would you come back? I really enjoyed your column and we've had a lot of readers asking where you got to."

Marina thinks for a moment.

"Obviously you'd come back on full pay and benefits, love. We might even be able to squeeze a Christmas bonus in."

"OK Les, it's a deal. See you tomorrow. Is my desk still free?"

"Not been touched. That's my girl, see you in the morning."

She hangs up and immediately calls Tom, who is in Rome on a fashion shoot.

"Guess what? Les Misérables just called and I've got my job back!"

"Whoa, wait, who the hell is Les whatever and what job? The one on the paper?"

"Yes, the columnist job. Les was the deputy editor and is now the editor, Cameron Knight has been suspended, and Les just called to offer me my job back."

"What did you tell him?"

"I said yes of course."

"Without talking to me?"

For a moment Marina is too stunned to speak. What the hell is he talking about? What's it got to do with him?

"Why should I have spoken to you about it? It's my career."

"Of course it is, but if we're going to plan a future together then I would have thought these are decisions we should be taking together. I was hoping you might move to Rome at some stage."

"Move to Rome? But my career is here," she gasps. "My life is here."

"Just like my career is in Rome, along with my life, apart from you."

Marina is silent. So is Tom.

"I see your point," she says eventually.

"Look, let's talk about it when I come over for Ulrika's party, shall we?"

"Yes, let's," says Marina.

"OK, bye, love you."

"Love you too, bye," she echoes, but her mind is already elsewhere. Rome. He thought she would move to Rome? Should she? Isn't this what she always wanted? And Rome is wonderful. She need never live in London during the cold winter months again. But is it what she wants? Is Tom what she really wants? She has wanted him for so long it's almost become an unchallengeable fact, but when she does start to challenge it, what happens? It's almost as if she doesn't want to go down that road for fear of what she will discover.

Her thoughts are interrupted by her phone ringing again. It's Hugo.

"Hey Scoop, great news, you're back! I'm so chuffed, it's just great."

"Thanks Hugo. Wow, news travels fast. How did you hear? I've only told one person."

"Just got off the phone with old Les Mis. Cheery as ever that chap. Anyway, I have some even better news for you. Not only are you back, but so am I, as the fucking Deputy Editor. Can you believe it?"

"Well done!" she laughs. "I'm thrilled for you. Come along to Ulrika's pre-divorce party next week and celebrate with us all. You never know, Ulrika might even be on for a final fling before she settles down for good!"

"Thanks Marina, I'd love to," he stops for a moment. "You know the Ulrika thing was just a bit of fun. But it will be really good to see you all."

Tom Stamford feels deflated after his conversation with Marina. He has sensed her slowly slipping away from him over the past few weeks and can't understand why. This is the most serious relationship he's ever been in, and he doesn't have much experience in dealing with long-term girlfriends. But he knows that she makes him happier than anyone else he has ever been with and that he wants to make things work. He can even envisage settling down and having children before it's too late. He knows the children issue was one of the main reasons she split up with Mark, but all the female friends he has consulted assure him that when a woman finds the right man, she will want to have children with him. And isn't he the right man for Marina? Hasn't she been after him for more than 15 years? So what can be going on? He was amazed she would even consider staying in London instead of joining him in Rome. Surprised that she wasn't one hundred per cent enthusiastic about moving in with him and sharing his life.

His phone rings. It's Carla. They have a weekly 'chatting about Ollie' session whenever he is not in London.

"I'll be a little late, but order me a beer," she says.

"Great. Can we talk about Marina, as well as Ollie? There's something going on, and I just can't get a handle on it."

"Sure thing *caro*, see you in fifteen minutes, usual table."

He hangs up. It's odd – without Ollie he really has no

male friends to speak of, maybe in part because another close male friend would feel like betrayal.

"By the time you swear you're his,
Shivering and sighing,
And he vows his passion is infinite, undying —
Lady, make a note of this:
One of you is lying."
Dorothy Parker

As he gets out of the car he is greeted by a familiar flash of light bulbs. Of course he knows they're not for him, but they blind him just the same.

"Katie," calls a reporter, "any idea if it's a boy or a girl?"

"You'll be the first to know," she quips, as she poses for the media wearing one of her maternity creations, a bright-red cocktail dress cut on the bias, with an elastic front for her bump.

"He probably will be," says Mark under his breath.

They walk into the Regency Club, which has probably

not seen as much glamour nor had as much attention as this since it was first opened by George V in 1895.

Katie, as always, has timed her arrival to perfection – just early enough not to be rude but late enough to ensure most of the guests are settled in enough to watch her come in. Until he met Katie, Mark was totally unaware of the complexities of stardom – socialising, the media and so forth. And now he feels he knows more about them than he ever wants to. He is happier dealing with real pressure, like saving lives, than the perceived pressure of showing up in the right pair of shoes. But she is the mother of his future child, and probably his future wife. So he needs to respect her world, in the same way that she does his. He also needs to do something about divorcing Marina and marrying Katie. He knows she is expecting him to propose every minute. It hasn't helped that Ulrika is throwing a pre-engagement engagement party. For some reason he is still reluctant to sever all ties with Marina. Even if he knows it is the right thing to do.

He spots Marina in a corner talking to Tom and joins them.

"Hi, I saw your column this week. Great news you got your job back. How did that happen?" He kisses Marina hello and grabs a glass of champagne from a passing waiter.

"Thanks. Les Mis took over as editor and made me an offer I couldn't refuse," Marina laughs.

"What, he said he would smile once a day?"

She laughs again.

"No, seriously it's great news. Hey Tom, how are you?"

"Good, thanks," says Tom. Marina feels herself stiffen. She hates that Americanism. A person is not good, a person is well. Unless they are a saint. Like Frank Lampard.

"How are you? How's the world of the emergency room?"

"Pretty quiet recently, actually. Just hope it stays that way for September."

"Is that D-Day. Or Salvador Day?" asks Marina.

"Hopefully Amelia day," laughs Mark.

"We should get planning our own sprog," says Tom. "We could call him El to go with Salvador."

Marina freezes. She sees Mark look fleetingly pained and then he's over it and back to the banter. How could Tom be so insensitive? He knows that the fact that she doesn't want to have children is one of the reasons she and Mark split up. Luckily Ulrika comes over and distracts them.

"You look amazing Ulrika," says Mark. "Not so much the blushing bride as the hot babe."

"Thank you Doctor, I aim to please. My parents have even showed up, along with my soon to be ex-husband and my ex-lover, who by the way tells me he is now Deputy Editor of *The Chronicle?*"

"Yes," says Marina. "I think he was hoping the news might give him a right to touch up your new tits before they go and live in Yorkshire."

"I told him I'd fuck him again once he becomes Editor. You've got to give a man a goal in life."

"Where is the lucky groom to be?" asks Tom.

"That," says Ulrika, "is a very good question. If he doesn't show up soon, his new knockers may very well be donated to a pair of more punctual hands, the bastard. Loved your column by the way, Mina. I always thought celebrity chefs should shut up and get back to cooking. I mean who gives a flying fuck if they do or don't like each other, the twats."

"Thanks. It's good to be back, fabulous to have a platform to rant from every week, and to get paid for it."

"I guess that's how London cabbies feel," says Mark.

Marina laughs, Tom looks puzzled and then the penny drops. Marina reasons that he's probably been out of London for too long.

Ulrika grabs a glass of champagne. "Good health everyone, champagne for our friends…"

"Real pain for our enemies," Mark and Marina finish off in chorus.

Ulrika laughs and then looks down at her bbm, which has just beeped. She goes pale and lets it fall to the floor. Mark recognises the signs and grabs hold of her before she collapses in a heap.

"Shit, Ulrika, what is it?" says Marina, picking up the bbm and looking at it. There is a message from someone called LM. Lord Mycock, she presumes.

'Can't face it darling, after all, I find I'm not the marrying kind. Enjoy the boobs, with my blessing, they look great.'

Ulrika is just coming round as Ben appears, he has been entertaining Kitty with tales of the boys. "What's going on?"

"He's not coming," Marina tells him. "He's fucking well blown her out, the bastard."

Ben kneels down in front of Ulrika, who has started sobbing. He gently strokes her hair. "Don't worry babe," he says. "I'll look after you. Mark, I've got the car outside, can you help me get her to it please?"

"I'll come with you," says Marina. The two men lead Ulrika outside and Marina follows carrying her bbm and clutch, an engagement present from Katie.

"Here's the car," says Ben.

Ulrika gasps. Some colour returns to her face. "It's my old Range Rover. Where the hell did you find it?"

"I bought it back from the showroom," says Ben. "They hadn't sold it. I actually paid less for it than we sold it for – one upside to the economic downturn."

Ulrika manages a smile and gets into the front seat.

"Shall I come with you darling?" asks Marina.

"No, please don't. Just go inside will you and tell everyone what happened. I mean don't tell them the c*** chucked me, but tell them we have decided to split up. Mutually decided. Please apologise to Kitty and my parents, tell them I couldn't face seeing anyone. Then drink as much champagne as you possibly can. It's on that fucker's account."

"Understood," says Mark who has moved next to Marina. "We will do our utmost."

"Here's one I made earlier," says Ben, handing Ulrika an opened bottle of Moët. "I took the precaution of stealing it, to help you get over the shock."

"Why are you being so nice?" asks Ulrika. "I was dumping you to marry someone else, you moron."

"I told you, I want to get my hands on your tits."

"No chance," says Ulrika, putting her seatbelt on and swigging some champagne. Mark smiles and closes the car door.

"We'll see," says Ben, and they drive off.

"Wow, that's one persistent bloke," says Mark. "Talk about fighting for your marriage."

"Yes, something we never did," says Marina looking at him.

"Well, we don't have kids, so I guess there was less point," he says slowly.

"We should still have fought," she says. She can't quite believe she's saying it; the champagne has loosened her tongue. Does she mean it?

Mark stares at her. She can almost see his mind catching up to where hers is.

"Is it too late?" he asks.

She shakes her head slowly, unable to unlock her gaze from his. Her voice sticks in her throat, and it's just as well, because a very pregnant Katie is suddenly there, asking if everything is all right with Ulrika.

*

Tom is nervous. He knows what he has to do. The advice from Carla was to propose. No woman wants to discuss a future, with or without children, before she has a ring on her finger.

"She is married," he pointed out. "Just not to me."

"That's just a technicality. Surely divorce is just a matter of time. People get engaged all the time nowadays while they're waiting for their final release papers. Just go for it, then you'll see where you stand."

He had planned to propose to her as they strolled through the streets looking for a taxi. He had thought of several options but always came back to the conclusion that it should be somewhere simple. He didn't want them to be one of those couples who were asked years later 'where did you propose?' and the man told some convoluted story about a Ferris wheel or a yacht or some fancy restaurant. No, the occasion and their feelings were special enough; it would happen somewhere simple.

He had thought that the celebration of another engagement would be perfect, but now that seems to have gone tits-up so to speak, so he needs to gauge Marina's mood carefully. He doesn't want to pick a bad moment for the most memorable question he has ever asked a woman. He will know when the moment is right; he just has to seize it.

Marina walks back into the room and grabs a glass of champagne from the nearest waiter, which she downs quickly. She can feel the butterflies in her stomach already and she hasn't even got to the mike. She squeezes her toes and walks resolutely across the room, desperately focusing on not tripping up. She finds the microphone the future bride and groom were supposed to use to make their speech. She switches it on and taps it lightly. The assembled crowd is already aware something is up, having seen Ulrika practically carried out. Mark has gone to tell her parents the news.

"Ladies and Gentlemen," she begins, rather squeakily. "I'm afraid I have some rather sad news. Er, Ulrika and Lord Mycroft, that is, David, have decided not to go through with their pre-divorce engagement. In fact they have decided not to get engaged at all. They have split up. But, the good news is…"

She is suddenly interrupted by Tom grabbing the microphone from her. "The good news is, we have another pre-divorce engagement to celebrate." All his good intentions of a subtle engagement are suddenly swept away. This is the moment. *Carpe diem.*

There is a murmur from the crowd. Marina feels a slightly panicky feeling creep into her every pore. No, he couldn't be thinking of…

"I have been waiting for a suitable moment to ask this wonderful woman to marry me, even though she is still technically married, but if Ulrika and Lord Mycroft can do it, then why not us?"

The crowd livens up. There are a few wolf-whistles and an air of anxious anticipation. It reminds Marina of that tense moment before a penalty is taken in a football match to decide the outcome of a crucial game.

"Marina Shaw," he says solemnly before getting down on one knee, "will you make me the happiest man alive and marry me?"

He points the microphone towards her. Marina looks at his expectant face, and then the sea of expectant faces, all of them willing her to hit the back of the net. This is what she's always wanted, isn't it? Then why doesn't she feel an overwhelming urge to shriek 'Yes!' as loud as she can? Is it her old 'if you want me you can't be any good' hang-up surfacing? She has to fight that demon.

She takes the mike and nodding, says: "Yes."

Tom leaps up and hugs her and champagne corks pop from all corners of the room. He hugs her tightly and whispers to her he's going to make her the happiest woman in the world.

Out of the corner of her eye, Marina sees Mark walk outside, closely followed by Hugo Willoughby.

34

"The soul is healed by being with children."
Old English proverb

Marina has managed to get Tom to agree not to plan their wedding until she has at least started her divorce proceedings. Just the fact that she has done nothing at all during the four months since she and Mark split up is a mystery to Tom, and understandably so, but she tells him she was waiting for a good time to discuss arrangements with her soon to be ex husband.

In her yoga class with Ria, Marina tries to relax and focus on the aim of her class, which is to forget all about the things going on around her. They are practicing yoga nidra, a form of meditation, and she has been told to imagine a perfect, safe, comforting place, the idea being that you get into a meditative state and totally relax.

"Say to yourself, 'I will not fall asleep', and focus on your special place," Ria says in her soothing voice.

Normally Marina falls asleep immediately but today she is determined to stay awake; after all, what's the point in spending ten quid to fall asleep? There are two places her mind wants to take her to. One is the Spanish Steps with Tom after a long lazy lunch at Nino's. They are walking hand in hand, it is late afternoon and the sun warms their faces. The other is home, to her sofa, with Mark, a bottle of wine and a Chelsea game that is about to begin. Even better, the Chelsea game is over and they have thrashed Man U 7-0.

OK, control that mind, that's utterly ridiculous. You're supposed to be in love and you're thinking about a Lampard hat trick? And anyway, Mark is with Katie now, and they're expecting a baby in a few months' time, for goodness' sake.

Marina eases her brain back to the Spanish Steps and her future husband. She sees the two of them there, holding hands, kissing. Then the frame freezes. What's next?

She wills there to be an easy, comfortable sequel, a life of harmony – walking back to his flat on the Via Margutta, chatting and planning dinner, maybe making love on his bed that creaks ever so slightly when you move too fast. But where would she fit into his life there? Where would she work, write her book that nobody wants to publish? She can't see herself there, but she doesn't know whether it's just a question of logistics or something more serious.

To her relief, Ria starts talking again and tells them to focus on relaxing each and every part of their bodies. By the time Ria gets to their legs, Marina is asleep.

Ulrika is in the bath with Archie and Felix. They are looking at her, rather quizzically.

"You may well look in amazement, boys," she tells them. "I'm afraid it's all downhill from here. Sadly, at the age of only two years old, you have shared a bath with what is probably the most gorgeous female form you will ever behold."

Archie picks up a plastic dolphin and throws it back in the water.

"Yes, I understand your fury," says Ulrika. "And I don't blame you for it."

"Daddy," says Felix.

"No, this is mummy," says Ulrika, pointing at herself. "I know you haven't seen much of me lately, but that's all going to change now."

She gets some soap and starts washing them both. They squeal as she splashes them with water. "Yes, I was going to take you to live in a vast stately home in

Yorkshire, but sadly that didn't work out. So, for the moment, we'll just have to stay here. And then, well I don't really know what happens next, but I'll look after you, that's for sure."

"Mummy," says Archie.

"Mummy," repeats Felix.

Ulrika starts to cry. Tears roll silently down her face, which she splashes with water so the boys won't notice. She takes their faces in her hands in turn and kisses them on their noses. They squeal again.

"How could I have thought anything is more important than this?" she says to herself as her twins fight over a plastic dolphin.

Suddenly there is a scurrying sound and the door opens. Almost immediately a small, brown fur ball comes charging in. It stops in the middle of the bathroom mat, pees on it and then starts chasing its own tail. Archie and Felix stand up and cling to the edge of the bath, both jumping up and down with excitement. Ben strides in after the puppy.

"Do you mind?" shrieks Ulrika, trying to cover herself.

"Don't mind me, I've seen it all before," smiles Ben. "Actually, come to think of it," he pauses for a second, "I haven't. They look great by the way, really natural."

"Pass me a towel, pervert, and what the fuck is this

thing?" she says pointing at the puppy, who is now trying to jump up and lick the boys' faces.

Ben passes her a towel, puts the mat in the washing basket and then gets the boys out of the bath. They run down the corridor to their bedroom with the puppy following them.

"That, " says Ben, "is my new fitness trainer. I'm going to go for walks and runs with him every day, to lose my puppy fat while he gains his."

Ulrika wraps the towel around herself. "Well, we'd better make sure your new personal trainer isn't peeing on the carpet in the boys' room," she says before walking out of the bathroom.

"I know you love him really," says Ben after her, letting the water out of the bath.

Ulrika doesn't answer but is surprised to find herself smiling.

❧ 35 ❧

"May the Lord give His angel charge over you,
to guide you in all your ways."
Psalm 91:11

Brompton Oratory, London, August 14th 2011

"Amelia Sarah, I baptise you in the name of the Father and of the Son and of the Holy Spirit. Amen", says the priest.

There is a collective sigh of relief as most of the congregation imagines what the rather aged and traditional-looking priest would have made of the name Salvador. The newly named baby starts crying when the priest pours water on her head.

Marina wonders how much the christening robe cost. It looks like it took years to make. Ulrika's main emotion as she watches the proceedings is fury that she wasn't able to secure the Oratory for the christening of the twins, and she wonders how much Katie had to contribute to the Brompton Oratory Development Fund in order to do so. Had Katie known what these two women were thinking, she would have been extremely pleased. Engendering jealousy in friends is one of her main hobbies, and something she has always been extremely good at.

The congregation is made up of Mark and Katie – the latter in a stunning cream and black Chanel suit (there are certain days when only haute couture will do), the godparents Paolo, a celebrity chef, Mary-Jo, a Hollywood actress, and Charles, Mark's boss and friend. Paolo and Mary-Jo are travelling only with their celebrity status; Charles has brought his wife Victoria along. Then there's Marina and Ulrika, who arrived together because Ben and Tom are working, one in Guildford and the other in Rome: "Which just about sums up the difference between them," Ulrika told Marina earlier.

Outside chauffeur-driven Mercs are waiting to take the christening party to a smart new pub cum restaurant owned by the celebrity chef, called The Hansom Cab. There they will be met by around seventy friends and acquaintances, all of whom are invited for lunch.

As they emerge from the church there is a flurry of activity from the gathered press.

"Surely there must be more interesting things going on in the world than the christening of some random baby?"

says Ulrika to Marina. "What's wrong with you guys?"

Marina sighs. "You would think so, wouldn't you? But throw in the two famous godparents and it's an irresistible combination for our celebrity-obsessed readers."

"Well, maybe now they can't just tap their phones they'll have to do some reporting," says Mark who has joined them.

"Oh yes, what's happened on all that? Have you single-handedly changed the world since we last spoke?" asks Ulrika.

"Not quite, but the government has got involved and is setting up an inquiry into press practices and possible changes in the law," says Marina. "It's not all down to me though. There's another newspaper being sued for invasion of privacy by the family of a missing schoolgirl whose phone they hacked. So it all basically just came to a head and someone decided it was time to act. Luckily for me."

"And what's happened to that fuckwit editor whose decision it was to make you the scapegoat?"

"Cameron Knight? He's still being investigated but I shouldn't think much will happen to him. He'll just retire quietly to his country mansion. With all the people he's done favours for in the past I'd be surprised if he gets thrown in jail."

They pile into the back of the sleek white cars and are whisked off to the restaurant. Ulrika sits in between Mark and Marina, entertaining them with her latest scheme to leave her husband by seducing the celebrity chef.

"Just imagine," she says, "I would never have to cook again. And he's so Byronic."

"Moronic did you say?" asks Mark. "Sounds just like your type."

"Very amusing. You may mock, but you've landed your millionaire. I still have my work cut out. By the way, did you have a say in the godparents at all? I didn't realise you were an intimate friend of Paolo the chef and that blonde Hollywood star with the fake breasts. Correction: rather obviously fake breasts."

"Never met either of them before in my life," says Mark. "Katie did let me have one, Charles, who is in the car behind with his wife. But she really seems to have taken this whole baby thing over single-handedly. Maybe that's just the way she does things, but I can't say I've felt very involved in any of it."

"Are you planning to make an honest woman of her?" asks Ulrika.

"Yep, just as soon as Mina and I have got our divorce sorted out. And we're making progress, aren't we?"

Marina nods.

"Bloody irritatingly, you'll probably both be remarried before I am," says Ulrika.

"I think Katie wants to get on with it. I mean, we haven't talked about it, but I know she is keen for Amelia's parents to be married, as am I," says Mark.

"Were you at the birth?" asks Marina.

"I was there, yes, but only because I insisted. Katie's theory is that most relationships flounder after childbirth because the man has seen the object of his affection pushing out this enormous head and looking frightfully inelegant. I pointed out to her that as she had booked a C-section in order to avoid the birth possibly clashing with anything more important, I would be watching her lying on an operating table looking serene in green as opposed to pushing."

"And did it live up to expectations?" asks Marina.

"It was an incredible feeling seeing her for the first time, holding her. She was tiny, so vulnerable but so angry, screaming her head off. She's got good lungs. Yes, it really did live up to expectations."

"Will you have any more do you think?" says Marina, looking across Ulrika at him.

"Don't be ridiculous," Ulrika interrupts. "Women like Katie only ever have one child. They're too worried about stretch marks and droopy tits to risk it twice. I would only have had one, but two of the little blighters popped out at once."

"So you won't have any more?" Mark asks her.

"Good Lord, no. I've done my procreative duty."

Marina looks out of the window.

"Don't worry, Mina," says Mark. "There are enough of us at it for you to be exonerated."

"Oh God yes," says Ulrika, flicking her blonde hair. "Sorry, I didn't mean to be insensitive, so unlike me."

They all laugh. Marina feels truly relaxed and happy for the first time in months. No court case hanging over her, her old job back, Ulrika on fine form and added to all that, she and Mark can finally talk about children without arguing.

❧ *36* ❧

"I write entirely to find out what I'm thinking."
Joan Didion

Marina wakes up with an uncomfortable sensation that something is terribly wrong. Then for a split-second she manages to convince herself that it's just a strange dream, before she tries to sit up and collapses back into bed in a heap. Selected flashbacks pass through her mind, like the highlights of a football match.

Football match… Yes, that's where it all started to go wrong. She and Mark had been overheard bemoaning the fact that the first Chelsea fixture of the season was about to begin.

"Are you two Chelsea fans?" the celebrity chef asked.

"Yes, huge Chelsea fans," Marina replied.

Minutes later they left The Hansom Cab restaurant in the celebrity chef's chauffeur-driven Range Rover and were whisked to Stamford Bridge where they were escorted up to the VIP box by a girl in Chelsea-blue lycra.

"This is like winning *Jim'll Fix it*," joked Mark as they were served a bottle of champagne and told to enjoy the match as guests of Paolo's dear friend and business associate, the club's chairman. But it was a pathetic start to the season – Chelsea played Stoke City and were held to a goalless draw.

After the match they were invited to the restaurant Paolo owns just next to the stadium. More champagne had flowed; they had to drown their sorrows over the poor start to the season.

Alone, they talked about everything from Chelsea's next fixture to their impending divorce and how much more relaxed Katie was finally becoming and how much motherhood had mellowed her.

"We should really be getting back to the christening party," Marina said at one stage. "You're the father of the baby. You'll be missed."

"I'm having too much fun here," Mark replied. "And anyway, I really don't think I will be missed. Katie is very independent, and surrounded by celebrity friends. She'll be fine."

Marina nodded and took another sip of champagne. She felt so comfortable just sitting there chatting; she didn't want to go back to the party either. They had got through another two bottles of champagne before they finally decided it was time to head home.

"I'll drop you off," Mark told her. They got in the taxi and fell about laughing as they both tried to give the address at the same time.

"This is one of those things which will make us realise how drunk we must have been when we remember it," laughed Marina.

"If we remember it at all," said Mark.

They started kissing on the doorstep to their old home. After a few minutes Marina told Mark to pay the taxi and come inside. He didn't argue.

Marina is woken from her reverie by her phone ringing.

"Fucking hell, you won't believe who I ended up in bed with."

"Morning, Ulrika."

'So, go on, guess?"

"Paolo the Byronic celebrity chef," says Marina.

"Nooooo," shrieks Ulrika. "You'll never guess."

"Hugo?"

"Wrong again. All he does is talk about you, terribly dull."

"Lord Mycroft? The Hollywood actress? Both of them?"

"No no no. OK, you're never ever going to guess because it's the last person on earth I ever imagined I would end up in bed with. Ben."

"Ben?"

"The same. Amazing eh? Just imagine, I ended up in bed with my husband."

Marina sighs and takes a swig of water. "So did I."

Katie looks at Mark sleeping beside her. Heaven knows what time he got in. He wasn't there at midnight when she and the star of the show, little Amelia, came back.

The day had gone off so well. Amelia made just enough noise to be noticed and admired but slept through most of the delicious late lunch that then flowed into drinks and dinner. The press were given just enough to reinforce her image as a style icon now turned extremely yummy mummy. She was photographed with the handsome, Byronic Paolo several times and is looking forward to seeing the pictures in the papers later on.

Katie rolls over and gets up. She slides on her silk dressing gown and walks into the nursery, where Amelia is fast asleep. She sits down on the chair next to her cot and looks at her. She is so beautiful, so serene, so innocent. She remembers her mother once laughingly telling her that kittens are such time-wasters, because you end up playing with them for hours. It was one of the few times her mother actually spoke to her, because normally she was too busy organising charity events, or going to dinner parties, to notice Katie.

Katie can see how easy it would be to while away hours watching Amelia sleeping, or eating, or just being. Every time she looks at her, she is filled with happiness, a kind of deep, honest happiness that she rarely feels. She has spent so many years creating a perfect image, a perfect company, a perfect persona, that she has lost touch with her real feelings. These quiet solitary moments with Amelia are slowly making her realise this and making her increasingly determined to be herself and a proper mother to her. Which also involves having a proper father. She has been neglecting Mark recently and she needs to rectify that; they need to become a family, a loving, stable family. For the first time in her life, Katie Tomlinson realises she needs to change her priorities.

Marina looks at her BlackBerry. She half expected a message from Mark, or at least some sign that it actually happened, but there's nothing. She gets up, her head spinning, and goes to the bathroom. The reflection that greets her in the mirror is worse than she expected. Her eyes are bloodshot, her hair is tousled and her chin is bright red. There was a lot of snogging, she now remembers. How come they never snogged when they were married? They seemed to have lost touch with the fact that they actually enjoyed kissing each other, what with all the arguing about babies and everyday life.

She splashes her face with cold water. No difference. A cold shower is the only option. Maybe it will clear her mind too, because there is no doubt she has some serious thinking to do. Today may not be the day to decide whether or not she should break off her engagement but whatever else happens she has a column to write.

After her shower she throws on some clothes and make-up, paying particular attention to her beacon chin, and then goes downstairs. She will pick up some breakfast from the canteen. She needs to get away from the house and all the memories of last night, which are leaving her feeling partly ashamed, partly exhilarated and partly sad.

There is a letter on the doormat from another agent. She rips it open.

'Dear Ms Shaw," it begins. 'We regret to say…' She skim-reads it. Another rejection. It's going to be a long day.

The boys are racing around the kitchen after the puppy, and Ulrika is nursing an Alka Seltzer. The morning sun is piercing its way straight through the kitchen window and into her brain. For once she wishes it were raining. Ben walks in and says good morning, then sits down at the kitchen table as if nothing has happened. He offers Ulrika some coffee and starts leafing through the paper. How can he be acting so normal? The last time they were at this kitchen table, somewhere around 1 o'clock in the morning, they were naked, on top of it. Ulrika had come home from the christening after drinking champagne all evening with the celebrity chef and some other posh friends of Katie's. Ben had been up watching some golf tournament from the States. They had drunk a glass of wine or two and chatted, and then she had decided to show him her new tits. And then they had ended up on top of the table. They had also slept together for the first time in weeks, in their bedroom; Ben had been consigned to the spare room since Lord Mycroft appeared on the scene.

Ulrika sneaks a peek at him. He's cool as you like; there's no sign of anything at all. What's his game? Why isn't he all over her? Was she no good? She tries to remember the details of their lovemaking but has more of an overall image, of it being frenetic and passionate and rather good. She does remember the new breasts making her feel very sexy and even more confident than usual.

Ben gets up and kisses her on the top of her head. "Do you want me to drop the boys at nursery on my way to Guildford?" he asks.

She shakes her head. "No, I'm not going to work today, I feel too rough. I'll sort them out. Thanks."

"OK," he smiles at her. "I'll be back this afternoon. Maybe we could have an afternoon kip?"

She smiles back and looks up at him. "Good idea," she says.

He walks towards the door and turns just before walking out. "Nice tits by the way," he says and then he's gone.

Marina is at her desk, the Word document opened and saved. 'Column August 16th 2011', she writes, then stops. She takes a sip of her coffee and a bite of her low-fat blueberry muffin. Then she begins:

'Last night I ended up in bed with my husband. This might not sound significant, but it is. You see my husband and I are separated. We split up several months ago because I fell back in love with the first love of my life. My husband then started a relationship with another woman, and they had a baby. It was after said baby's christening that we ended up in bed together for the first time since the split. Add to all this the fact that a few weeks ago my first love asked me to marry him and I accepted, and you have a pretty messy situation.

What was I thinking of? How could I possibly seduce the father of a child on her christening day, drag him back to my (our old) home and lead him upstairs to our old bedroom? What kind of a woman does that? One with no morals, you will be saying. A hussy with no sense of what's right and what's wrong.

As I sit at my desk, I am asking myself the same question. The sort of woman who does something like this is not the sort of woman I am. She's not the sort of woman I want to be. How could I have behaved so badly?

I could blame it on the champagne. There was a lot of champagne involved. I could blame it on the disappointment of Chelsea drawing the first game of the season to a lesser team. But the real reason I ended up in bed with my husband is that I wanted to. Which is strange, because when we were still together, it was pretty much the last thing on my mind. Which might be one of the reasons we split up.

Why was my husband suddenly more attractive to me last night than before we split up? Because he was no longer familiar? Because he belongs to someone else? Because he was more like a lover than a husband?

Maybe it was a combination of all three. But what I want to know is this: how do you keep that lover element alive in a marriage? Because maybe if we had been able to keep that alive, I would never have felt the need to run off with my first lover and my husband and I would still be together. And the divorce rate in the UK would be a lot lower than it is.'

She leans back in her chair with a sigh and reads through the text once more. As she thought, writing has made things a little clearer, but she still has to work out what to do. The first thing is to book a flight to Rome to see Tom. OK, she and Mark didn't actually have sex – they sobered up enough to remember they had other commitments. But still, what happened was not good. And what about Mark? She checks her phone. He really is taking the lover thing a bit far; so far she has not had a peep from him. It's bloody cheeky, really. The least you can do if you end up in bed with a girl is to bbm her the next day. And it's quite unlike him.

She reaches for her coffee, almost spilling it in the process. Maybe it's partly to do with the hangover, but she can't get any clarity on her feelings. Everything seems wrapped in clouds, so unclear. She gets a piece of paper and writes the names Tom and Mark at the top of it. Underneath Tom she writes the word 'lover', underneath

Mark she writes 'husband'. Under lover she writes 'sexy' and under husband 'safe'. If Tom becomes the husband, how long before he goes from sexy to safe? And last night, wasn't that sexy? Under the word sexy she writes 'exotic'. Under safe she writes 'friend'. Then under exotic she puts the word 'future' and under friend the word 'past'. Is that what she wants? Tom to be her future, Mark to be her past?

"Morning Marina." Suddenly Hugo Willoughby is behind her, smiling broadly. She knocks her coffee over the piece of paper from the shock of hearing his voice.

"Oh sorry," he says. "Didn't mean to frighten you."

"Don't worry, I always knock my coffee over anyway," she says, grabbing some tissues to wipe it up. "Where are Flora and Jo by the way? I haven't seen them since I got back."

"They won some competition to go to Canada on a skiing holiday and were walking down a road when they got taken out by an out-of-control snow-plough."

"Nooo. Dead?"

"Stone-cold."

"Crumbs."

"I know, it's a shame, but there it is. Makes you think eh? *Carpe diem* and all that. Anyway, just wanted to see if you could write something linked to the Prince Harry and

Chelsea split for the column tomorrow? You didn't have anything else planned, did you?"

"No," smiles Marina. "I was actually thinking about doing a personal one à la Liz Jones, but have decided against it."

"Good decision, leave the reader guessing. You don't want to let it all hang out. They will be interested, but then they will resent you for it, rather like a bloke you shag on the first date," says Hugo.

"Good advice." She smiles up at him, waiting for him to leave.

He shuffles a little uncomfortably. "How are things by the way?"

"Fine thanks. Ulrika's living with Ben again. Looks like they might sort things out."

"I wasn't asking about her," says Hugo. At that moment Les Misérables calls him into his office.

He walks away and Marina looks down at her list. The coffee has made the ink run and the words are blending into one another, rather like her thoughts.

༄ 37 ༄

"The natural state of the football fan is bitter disappointment,
no matter what the score."
Nick Hornby

Mark has been in surgery all morning. Thankfully it was nothing complicated, but it was enough to take his mind off the fact that he was very nearly unfaithful to the mother of his child last night.

But technically, can one be unfaithful with one's wife? he asks himself as he washes his hands. Katie was so sweet this morning, telling him all about what happened after he and Marina went off to the match, how Amelia had charmed everyone and been so good. He felt so guilty he half thought about telling her what had happened, but then he decided against it. Something like that can never be unsaid and he was still so confused about the whole thing that he wouldn't be able to answer any of her questions anyway. Not while he was still trying to answer them himself.

What had last night meant? Was it just a bit of drunken fun, or should Marina and he think about getting back together? What about Katie, though, and even more importantly, Amelia? And anyway, what's to say that Marina wants him back? She has Tom now.

"Morning Mark." Charles was standing next to him. "Lovely day yesterday, thank you."

"Pleasure, thank you for coming."

"I'm not used to hanging out with the glitterati, makes our jobs looks a bit humdrum, don't you think?"

"Or rather more meaningful, depending on how you look at it."

Charles laughs. "You and Marina seem to be getting on well, which is great. No need for bitterness, is there?"

Mark catches his breath. "Not at all, no, it's not as if there is an injured party."

"Precisely, you're both settled with other people, no need to be immature about it all. Where was her man though? Can't recall meeting him."

"He works in Rome, he's a photographer, he had a big assignment for Italian *Vogue* he couldn't miss."

"Rome? How exotic. So will Marina move there?"

"I'm not sure. She has her job here of course, and her friends."

"Yes, it's a long way from Stamford Bridge too," laughs Charles.

"Precisely, I can't see her lasting long."

"Maybe the new chappie will have to move to London."

"Maybe," says Mark.

Charles's pager beeps and he runs off. Mark looks at his BlackBerry. No word from Marina, but then she will be expecting him to contact her. He probably should, but to say what? Thanks for last night? He can't imagine what she will be feeling about what almost happened. Is she regretting it? Maybe she's not even thinking about it; maybe she just thinks of it as a minor blip and will move on from it straight away. Maybe it was just a minor blip and he should move on too.

As soon as Marina has finished her column she goes on the Ryanair website to look for a flight to Rome. There is one that evening. She emails Tom to tell her she is coming over and goes home to pack.

Ulrika calls her as she is getting out of the Tube.

"I had sex with Ben again. My husband is my lover. I can't get over it. When are you seeing yours again?"

"I'm not. I'm going to Rome to see Tom. Hopefully once I see him, all will become clear and I will realise that my little liaison with Mark was just a mistake and that we really were right to split up."

"God, you sound terribly grown-up about it all."

"I am Miss Mature. No, seriously, I have to be mature, there's a child involved here, and Katie would be devastated. Added to which, we did split up, partly because I was still mad about Tom, and he was seduced by Katie, so where have those feelings gone?"

"Have they gone for you?"

Marina shakes her head. "I don't know. I mean it's certainly not as exciting as it was in the beginning, but is that just because it's been a few months? I was so sure to start with and so desperate for him to love me and then once he did, well…"

"You went off him."

"Nooooo," Marina remonstrates. "It wasn't that clear cut. But yes, in a way I think I have. It's like that Russian opera."

"What Russian opera?"

"Onegin something, all about a young girl who falls madly in love with this cad and then years later he falls in love with her, but it's too late, she belongs to someone else."

"Sounds dreadful. And you don't belong to someone else."

"I know, but you get the general idea."

"You're comparing your life to a Russian opera. Sounds extremely depressing, and very foreign."

Marina's phone beeps. "Hang on Ulrika. Shit, it's Mark, call you later," she hisses and hangs up.

"Hi," she says, rather too squeakily for her own liking.

"Hi Mina," says her husband.

"Mark."

Silence. "Look, I'm not saying last night meant anything to you at all," he says. Marina gulps, barely able to breathe. "I hope it didn't Mina, because I am committed to Katie and Amelia. I mean not that it wasn't fun, of course it was, and I loved seeing you, it was, well, just like old times, but…"

"Better," they both say together.

"Yes, better. But it can't happen again. You've got Tom and I've got Katie and Amelia, and we created this situation and it's not fair for us to just un-create it on a whim."

"No, you're right. In fact I'm going to see Tom now."

"That's great Mina, and I'm going to propose to Katie tonight and as soon as our divorce papers come through I'll marry her."

"But we can still be friends?"

"Of course," he says. "Don't be silly, we'll always be friends."

"We'll always have Stamford Bridge," jokes Marina.

"You said it. Fucking Stoke, as Ulrika would put it."

Marina laughs and says good-bye. Then she calls Ulrika back to relay the whole conversation to her.

"So now what?"

"I go to Rome and decide what I feel when I get there and see Tom."

"Don't you think you should decide how you feel before you see him?"

She packs her bag in a daze. Ulrika is right. She really needs to think things through before she gets there. Why did this important decision have to come on a massive hangover day, when thinking is painful as well as practically impossible. She walks into her bathroom to pack her sponge bag. She has liked living alone; she never feels lonely. She enjoys the luxury of having the bed to herself, of not having to stay up late if she's tired or please anyone else. If she agrees to marry Tom, which in theory she has already, she will no longer be living alone. They will be together, either in Rome or here. But that's not a terrible thought at all, and it maybe would be a lot better than solitary spinsterhood.

What has she done? She had a perfectly nice husband and life, apart from the fact that he wanted children and she didn't, and she threw it all away for Tom. But isn't Tom what she's always wanted? She tries to conjure his image up in her mind: his floppy dark hair, his cheeky grin, his broad shoulders. He's gorgeous. So what the hell is wrong with her?

She looks at her reflection in the mirror above the sink. "What do you want?" she asks it.

"What all women want," replies a voice in her throbbing head. "Something else."

❦ *38* ❧

Katie would reflect afterwards that for a girl who had known more exotic locations than most, being proposed to in the hospital café had a certain romance to it. OK, so it was certainly not the most glamorous of locations. The table was even a bit dirty, and the rest of the clientele could hardly have been more drab.

But it was in this café, Mark reasoned, that some of the most significant events of their short relationship had happened. It was here that Katie told Mark about Ollie, and it was here she had tried to confess her age-old crush on him before his pager went off.

"So I think it's only fitting," Mark tells her, taking her hands across the coffee-stained table, "that another significant event happen here."

He clears his throat. Katie looks up at him, half

anxious, half expectant. Just for a second she is worried he might be going to finish with her.

"Katie Tomlinson," he begins then pauses. "Katie, I think you're lovely. Will you marry me?"

As Mark and Katie leave the hospital café, Marina and Tom are sitting in a café in the Piazza del Popolo almost 2000 kilometres away in Rome. It is busy, full of diners enjoying watching *la passeggiata* over a coffee after dinner. Marina looks around her; could she be one of them? They're all laughing, gesticulating and chatting.

Rome is a stunning city. Marina could work here; she could freelance for the British newspapers, although she would lose her column; they wouldn't let her do that from anywhere abroad on the basis that *The Chronicle* readers wouldn't be able to relate to a 'foreign' columnist.

She wishes she could write about the way she is feeling now. It would help clear her mind. She is torn on so many levels. But the main question is: does she want to live in this city with the man sitting opposite her stirring his coffee?

"How was the christening?"

"Good thanks. Mark and I ended up at Stamford Bridge. We watched Chelsea versus Stoke."

"How come?"

"One of the godparents is a friend of the club's chairman. He arranged it."

"Didn't Katie mind you two absconding?"

Marina takes a sip of her coffee. She is beginning to feel normal, finally. "It's not as if we ran out of the church or anything. We left after lunch. It was great, Frank Lampard was playing. I love watching Frank."

"Who's he?"

"Doesn't matter," sighs Marina. "Just a Chelsea player."

"You seem a bit distracted," says Tom. "Are you OK?"

She has two options: to lie, or to tell the truth. Unlike many women faced with her situation, she opts for the truth. Even if it's not strictly *la verità vera*.

"Tom, I'm not happy. I mean I'm not as happy as a woman about to marry the love of her life should be. I am filled with doubts, with angst and this horrible sensation that it's wrong. Last night I got drunk and almost ended up in bed with my husband."

Marina pauses to look at Tom, who looks like he doesn't believe her. He laughs. "You're joking, right?".

She shakes her head. "Tom I have always thought I loved you more than anyone, more than anything. You were that unattainable ideal that I longed for and fought for and would have done anything for. I thought that if we were together my life would be complete, that I wouldn't want anything else. But that's not the case."

Tom nods slowly. "The irony is that for me it is the case. I mean finally I had the feeling that this meant something, that I wanted it to develop, that I wanted to have children with you, grow old with you."

Marina winces. She suddenly feels panicked, constrained. Like she just wants to get out of there.

"Marina, what is it?" asks Tom, looking at her.

"Nothing, sorry, nothing at all. I just… it's difficult. Tom, I wanted this to work so much, so much that I destroyed my marriage for you. It really hurts that it hasn't. It feels like I've failed."

"Is there really no hope Marina? This all seems so sudden, I mean I only proposed a few weeks ago, and you said yes, and now you're saying it's all over? I mean I can cope with the Mark thing. Nothing happened, after all."

Marina winces again as she has a flashback to the night before and she and Mark ripping at each other's clothes as they kissed on the stairs leading to the bedroom.

"For the first time in my life I really care about someone, and it's a feeling I've gotten used to. I love you Marina. I just regret I didn't realise it all those years ago when you were so crazy about me."

Marina hangs her head. More than anything she wants

to be able to tell him that it's all fine, that she is still that girl who is madly in love with him and they will grow old together. But she can't.

"I'm sorry Tom."

"I just don't understand. You spend all those years in love with me, and the minute I love you back, you run a mile."

Marina looks at him. He grabs her hands that are resting on the table. "Marina, look at me, I'm still the same man; nothing has changed."

Except for the fact that you love me, thinks Marina, gently easing her hands from underneath his.

When she gets on the plane, she writes her column for next week.

"First love never dies. I wrote in this column almost a year ago to the day. Such a lot has happened since then, I hardly know where to begin. But what I can tell you is this: I was wrong. First love is an illusion. First love is not to be trusted.

Shortly after I wrote the column, my first love and I got together again, which meant the end of my marriage. OK, maybe my marriage was on the rocks anyway, but seeing 'Tim' as I will call him triggered something in me that I couldn't control.

The fact is I made a mistake. I should have controlled it. Because a few months on, it's over. It was great, it was exciting, it was sexy, but ultimately it was not the right thing. We were not destined to have a long-term relationship. What I have learnt is that my whole 'first love' experience was more to do with me than it was him. You see I fixated on Tim all those years ago in part because he was unavailable, because he was aloof, because everyone else wanted him. That is what teenage girls do; they go for totally unsuitable types. Which is what Tim was. I say was, because now he is eminently suitable. And what-is-more, he loves me. Which is hopeless. Because I don't want Tim to love me. I want him to stay the way he was – a fantasy, an ideal, a first, thwarted, agonizing, inaccessible ideal. As a husband, or even a long-term boyfriend, he loses his allure.

How pathetic, I hear you cry. Just because he wants her, she now doesn't want him. Yes, it probably is pathetic, and I have learnt my lesson too late. My husband has had a baby with another woman and they will be married in a few weeks.

But at least I now know that first love does die. And actually, when it does, it's a bit of a relief."

39

"When you are a mother, you are never really alone in your thoughts.
A mother always has to think twice, once for herself
and once for her child."
Sophia Loren.

Four months later, Mr and Mrs Mark Chadwick are watching Amelia sleep. They are standing over the cot, with their arms around each other, gazing at their little girl.

"It's amazing isn't it?" whispers Katie, snuggling closer to her soon-to-be husband. "You really can't understand what all the fuss is about until you do it. I mean no one can describe this feeling to you, this feeling of utter, over-whelming and unconditional love."

Mark kisses her head. Somehow he did know it – that's why he was so sure he wanted to do it. He is very sorry his marriage to Marina is over, and he still has some feelings for her, as the night of the christening proved, but he wouldn't have missed this for anything.

"I've been thinking," Katie continues. "I want to be a proper mum to Amelia. I want to be there for her all the time, not just when things happen to be under control with the business. And I want to be a proper wife to you, not endlessly flitting around the world." She goes quiet for a moment.

"Go on," says Mark, encouragingly.

"Well," Katie looks nervous. "I never thought I'd hear myself say this, but I think I should sell KT."

"Really?" says Mark, turning to look at her. "Are you sure? But you love your work."

Katie looks at him and smiles. Then she looks down at the sleeping baby. "Not as much as I love Amelia," she says. "Or you. Or the thought of giving Amelia a little brother or sister."

Marina has spent the last few months working on her forward bends, her columns and a new novel. *Blood River* has been consigned to the bottom drawer. She can feel this new novel in her bursting to get out. She can't wait to write about all that has happened during the past year, the feelings she has been through, the breakdown of her marriage, the realisation after all these years that Tom is not the right man for her.

The night she got back after splitting up with Tom, she was depressed but full of inspiration. She started the novel on the plane ride back from Italy. When she got home, she wrote for three more hours, finishing a bottle of wine in the process, before sending what she had done off to Emma Watts at David Higham and then collapsing exhausted into bed and sleeping through the night for the first time in months.

A few months on she is still single, but not unhappy with life. She wakes up most mornings looking forward to the day ahead. She works hard, writes (the novel is going well; Emma has asked for the first three chapters and a synopsis and is confident she can sell it to a publisher) and sees friends. She still watches all the Chelsea games, which is odd without Mark, but at least she can drool over Frank Lampard as much as she likes and Hugo Willoughby has been keeping her company at a few of them.

As New Year's Eve approaches, she is gearing up for what will be a difficult time. Christmas was easy: she just worked and got double money. But she needs to stop thinking about New Year's Eve last year and comparing how solitary this one will be, even if she ends up at a party with hundreds of people.

Katie realises as she puts in her silk dressing gown and closes her Louis Vuitton suitcase that for the first time ever she actually doesn't want to go. She is dreading the first-class flight to Miami and the connection to Necker Island. She is not looking forward to the chauffeur-driven car from the airport to Richard Branson's home. And she is having panic attacks about how much she is going to miss Amelia and Mark as she networks furiously and tries to sell the business to Mr Big from New York, who is also flying in for the New Year's party.

She has had an initial conversation with him and they are in agreement so far. Their respective lawyers are working on drawing up the documents, but he wants to sit down with her "face to face, in a relaxed environment". Mark will stay at home to look after Amelia. She will only be gone for four days, and then she will start the New Year as a stay-at-home mum.

The whole concept makes her laugh. She used to despise women who didn't work; in her view they were boring creatures to be avoided at all cost, with nothing interesting to say. How the worm has turned, her father would say. But what's boring about babies? To Katie there is nothing more fascinating than the miracle of life that she has created – along with some help from Mark, obviously, although in common with most new mothers she does firmly believe that Amelia is more her achievement than his.

She knows she will have to fight this feeling if they are to have a future together; Mark is very much a hands-on father, unlike her own father. Which in theory should make her happy, because there is nothing as depressing as feeling one is repeating one's own parents' mistakes.

Hence the trip. Her BlackBerry beeps. It's Cherry telling her the car is waiting outside. She sighs and sends her a reply asking her to send the driver in to get her bags. She takes one last peek into the nursery where Amelia is asleep, kisses her softly, mouths goodbye to the nanny who is sitting on a chair watching the baby, and then walks downstairs.

❦ 40 ❧

"Football is a game of two halves."
Jimmy Greaves

New Year's Eve 2011

Marina has everything ready before the match. Aston Villa at home. Kick-off 3pm. She has decided to make the match the focus of her New Year's celebrations. After last year she has no real desire to go partying. For her New Year's Eve is no longer a time for celebration.

She wonders what Mark is doing. He's probably at some swish event with Katie. They are in touch most weeks, mainly to discuss the latest football news. Ulrika is having a dinner party, to which Marina was invited, but she decided against it. Sitting around feeling like Bridget Jones with a load of married couples from the country is not her idea of a good time.

"I don't blame you," Ulrika said. "As if this time of year isn't dull enough. But at least two of the men are vaguely shaggable so I shall plonk myself between them and flirt my way into 2012."

Hugo Willoughby called to ask her to the game, and she was tempted to go, he's such good company, but she just felt she needed this New Year's Eve to be a time for reflection, and it's hard to be reflective among 40,000 chanting football fans.

The novel is going really well. She has had an encouraging email back from Emma Watts at David Higham saying she thinks there might be a bidding war between two publishers for it. So she may not be starting the New Year with a man, but at least she will have a publisher. Some might argue the latter are harder to snag.

She puts on the TV for the pre-match build-up and pours herself a glass of Laurent Perrier Rosé. "Cheers," she says raising her glass towards the television. "Here's to a good 2012 for us both."

The rosé is cold and bubbly. It seems odd to be drinking alone, especially champagne, but it's not as depressing as she had imagined. In fact, can Laurent Perrier rosé ever really be depressing?

The match kicks off. Marina stares intently at her team. She loves the blue of the kit, the anticipation of the game, the excitement of the unknown. It brings back so many years of memories, of victories, defeats, heroes and heartbreak. Some women go shopping in their spare time, or get their nails done. For Marina, a good weekend has to include a Chelsea game. Even if they're not playing well, which is the case at the moment.

It's the first half. Aston Villa concede a penalty. Didier Drogba takes it. He scores. The commentators are apoplectic. It's his 150th goal for the club. Marina jumps up from the sofa and punches the air. "Go Chelsea," she yells, raising her glass once more towards the TV. Her BlackBerry beeps. It's a message from Mark: "Drogba is a legend."

Marina laughs and responds. "Agreed. Where are you?"

He replies that he's watching the game with Amelia at home; Katie is in the Caribbean at some celebrity-studded party. "Come over," she tells him. "I have pink champagne and HD."

She's not quite sure why she invites him, but there is no reason not to, and anyway he's got Amelia with him, so what can possibly go wrong? "We'll leave at half time," he responds immediately.

Tom is sitting on the sofa in Carla's flat, his head in his hands. She is sitting next to him, stroking his back. She thinks back to last year when Ollie was on the same grey sofa, just before his mother and brother came to take him back to England to rehab. Now she has another vulnerable man in the same position. She can't fail again. Tom has been over most weeks since Marina finished with him. He was in shock to begin with, then in mourning. But Carla's theory is that he was mourning more than his love life. It's almost as if all the sadness over Ollie came out as well. He was inconsolable, questioning everything about his life and his future.

He has been better in recent weeks, but New Year's Eve is particularly difficult. It brings back all the combined memories of Marina and Ollie; the beginning of his relationship with Marina and the end of Ollie's short life.

She runs her hand up and down his back, comforting him. She feels him begin to relax underneath her touch. She moves her hand up to his head and runs her fingers through his hair and down again, caressing his neck. She registers the surprise in his body, but he doesn't move away. Carla carries on moving her hand more slowly this time down the length of his spine. When she gets to his waist he turns to face her. He looks at her questioningly. She stops for a moment, worried she may have gone too far. But Tom smiles and kisses her; she leans back onto the sofa, pulling him down on top of her.

Afterwards they have a bath together and drink

champagne. It is New Year's Eve, after all. Tom grins at her across the white rose-scented bubbles.

"Well, an unexpected end to what was going to be a terrible day," he says, raising his champagne glass to hers.

"I agree," says Carla, giggling. As she laughs her plump breasts move on the surface of the water like apples in an apple-bobbing tub. Tom is struck by how gorgeous she is. He probably never looked at her in that way before because of Ollie. Her wide smile, her dark, short curly hair, now wet and scraped back, her smooth olive skin and round brown eyes.

"I always wondered what those magnificent breast would feel like," he grins.

She smiles.

"Shall we do it again?" he asks, gently moving next to her and kissing her. "By the way, I didn't think to ask before, but are you on the pill?"

"No," she says putting her glass down on the side of the bath and running her hands through his hair. "But if we have a boy, we could always call him Ollie."

Tom smiles and pulls her towards him. "Good idea *cara*," he says before kissing her again.

Marina has to make a quick decision. Either she misses the end of the first half to change out of her tracksuit and quickly wash her hair, or she does it at half-time, and risks him showing up when her hair is still wet. But if anything significant happens and she misses it, he will be extremely suspicious. The last time she missed a Chelsea match was during her Finals. She opts for a quick shower and hair-wash immediately with her BlackBerry on ChelseaFC twitter feed.

By the time she is out of the shower, Villa have equalized. Now she'll have to watch the goal somehow before he gets here. She gets her laptop fired up and searches YouTube while she's drying her hair, almost breaking her laptop by smashing the hairdryer into it. Then she realises that she can watch the goals during half-time, while putting on her make-up. But not too much make-up – she doesn't want to look like she's made an effort. Although she could say she has plans for later. What kind of utter loser wouldn't have plans for later?

And what to wear? Start with the underwear – that's key, according to some dreary article she read last week about French women. Matching of course. If you get that right, the rest will follow.

Suddenly she stops mid hair drying. "What the hell am I on?" she shouts. This is her ex-husband coming over, with his five-month-old child by his new wife. And she's worrying about what knickers to wear?

She slumps onto her bed. It's ridiculous. She needs to pull herself together. What on earth is she thinking? Mark is a friend now, and that's all he will ever be – a very good friend. What happened that night of the christening all those months ago was a mistake, they both acknowledged that. It's time to move on.

She stops drying her hair and gets dressed. She opts for black underwear – nothing special, just plain old M&S – black jeans and one of the cashmere jumpers Katie gave her, just to remind her what a nice person Katie can be and how she should erase all impure thoughts about Mark from her mind. Maybe Lampard will come on in the second half and make that easier.

She moisturizes her skin, curls her eyelashes, brushes some bronzer over her face and applies mascara and lip-gloss. Shame she hasn't got anywhere to go, she thinks, looking at herself in the mirror before heading downstairs again. She doesn't look half bad. Must be all the creative juices flowing.

As the second half begins the doorbell rings. Mark kisses her hurriedly on the cheek and rushes in to where the TV is. "Have we scored again?" he asks, taking off his coat and sitting down on the sofa. "Oh good, Lampard and Torres are on."

"Nice to see you too, " she laughs. "Make yourself at

home, why don't you? Where's Amelia?"

"She fell asleep in the car, so the driver is going to keep driving around until she wakes up. She had a bad night. How are you?"

"Fine thanks," says Marina passing him a glass of champagne. "Is this safe?" he grins, looking up at her from the sofa.

"You're not breastfeeding are you?" she replies sitting down too. Mark laughs.

"I've missed your sense of humour," he says, turning to face her. "Cheers, here's to 2012."

"To 2012, may it bring us the double."

"Unlikely, but one can always dream."

Amelia makes an appearance ten minutes before the end of the match, just before Aston Villa score to go into the lead. Five minutes later they score again. Amelia sits propped up on the sofa between them. Now and again Marina steals a glance. She really is a cutie, with blonde curly hair and rosy cheeks. Her skin looks like it's made of porcelain.

"She's almost enough to take your mind off the game, isn't she?" says Mark, catching her looking.

Marina laughs. "Yes, which is lucky, because we're playing horribly. I'll go and grab another bottle," she says. "Shout if anything happens, will you?"

As she gets up to leave the room Amelia starts crying. Marina stops and so does the baby.

"Separation anxiety," says Mark. "Comes from having a jet-setting mother, I'm afraid. Take her with you?"

Marina freezes. "What?"

Mark lifts Amelia up to her and places her in her arms. "Take her with you, she won't break. But don't drop her. Or the bottle."

Marina does as he says and walks slowly into the kitchen with the baby clutched tightly to her. She has never been so scared of dropping anything in her life, and she has dropped a lot of things.

Is this what her baby would have been like? The one she had got rid of as a teenager – Tom's baby. She has thought about the whole painful period so much over the years, and wondered what might have been. But of course she couldn't keep it. She was about to go to university, her life was just beginning, and a baby would have meant the end. And he would have run a mile. She had never told anyone about it apart from Ulrika. Not even Tom. And now there was no point.

She looks down at Amelia, who is gazing up at her.

"You're really very cute," she tells her. She opens the fridge very carefully with one hand, holding Amelia with the other arm. The girl seems to cling to her as if there were Velcro between them.

She walks slowly back into the sitting room with the champagne.

"What's the news?"

"It's all over, we were crap."

"That's not news," says Marina, sighing. "Is it Amelia?" she adds, looking down at the baby. "If you're going to hang out with your dad, you're going to have to get used to this kind of pain. And Katie will need to start caring too."

"God I hope she does," says Mark. "I'm going to need someone to console me over the next year if we carry on playing like that. Here let me open this."

Mark takes the champagne bottle and Marina watches those familiar fingers open it. It's strange to think they will never caress her again. Strange, but in a funny way it was stranger that they ever had.

❦ *41* ❧

"A bride at her second wedding does not wear a veil, she
wants to see what she's getting."
Helen Rowland

March 10th 2012 Chelsea Registry Office, 250 King's
Road, London

The guests are arriving. It is not one of the bigger
weddings to have taken place at Chelsea Old Town Hall, so
the flow of traffic on the King's Road is not interrupted.
Nor is it one of the more high profile ones. This is where
stars from Judy Garland to Patrick Viera tied the knot, and
Walllis Simpson married Edward VIII, thus preventing
him from becoming king of England.

Ben is the first to arrive with the twins. They walk up
the stairs, or rather the boys scamper. Felicia and Millie
follow not far behind, both girls excited to be invited,
mainly because Felicia has just written an article containing
the promising statistic that you are more likely to meet your
future husband at a friend's wedding than anywhere else.

They make their way to the Rossetti Room where the wedding is going to take place. Katie is already there with Amelia, they both look immaculate in next season's pastel colours. Katie did do the deal with Mr Big in the Virgin Islands and is now non-executive chairman of her old company KT, which means she is still very much plugged in, but free to spend as much time with Amelia as she wants. Old colleagues and friends are always telling her how well she looks, and how young, which she finds ironic, because she has stopped the botox and the peels. Maybe it's all the fresh air she's getting running around the park with Amelia, or maybe just the fact that she is really very happy.

Outside a white Mercedes stops and the bride gets out, accompanied by her mother and her maid of honour. This may only be a registry office event but, her mother said, there's no reason to lower standards. As they step on to the pavement they see Mark racing up the steps in front of them.

"Unlike him to be late," mumbles the mother as they start the walk up the stairs to the door. The bride is too focused on not tripping over to really care.

She is wearing a cream Chanel suit, a wedding present from Katie, and some vertiginous satin peep-toe Christian Louboutins. Her maid of honour, who is six months pregnant with twin baby girls, is walking almost as carefully as she is.

They arrive at the Rossetti Room far enough behind Mark to allow him to settle in. Marina is thrilled she has managed to walk all the way up to the lady registrar without missing her footing. Somehow stumbling after the ceremony doesn't seem as much of a calamity.

She and Ulrika stand next to her husband to be and his best man. Marina smiles at him. He smiles down at her.

"You look lovely," he mouths silently.

"Thank you," she mouths back.

"Ladies and gentlemen," begins the registrar. "We are gathered here today to join these two people in legal wedlock."

Ten minutes later they are on top of the steps outside looking out on the life along the King's Road. It is a glorious day; the early spring sunshine is warming and puts everyone in a good mood, even Les Misérables and Marina's rather sour and alcoholic Aunt Lizzy, or Bitter Lemon as she is affectionately known due to the perpetually bitter look on her face. Confetti is strewn over them as they walk down the steps to the waiting cream Mercedes. They hold hands. At one point the heel of Marina's Louboutin catches the edge of the step. Her new husband pulls her back in time to stop her falling.

"Thank you," she says looking into his clear blue eyes. "You might find yourself doing a lot of that in the future,"

"Happy to oblige," says Hugo Willoughby, kissing her gently on the lips.

They get into the car, which is taking them to the Draycott Hotel a short drive away where the wedding party will be held.

"What about the kids at the party?" asks Hugo, who has always been mildly terrified of children, "who's going to look after them?"

"Don't worry," smiles Marina. "We have this fabulous children's entertainer called Hassan the Clown coming to keep them busy. Ulrika put me on to him. Apparently he trained in the Gulf, where no one looks after their own children."

They lean back in the car, Marina resting her head against his shoulder. She thinks back to the beginning of their rather whirlwind romance, the day they had gone out to lunch together from the office in early January and he had told her how he felt about her.

"My New Year's resolution is to just come out with it," he said, looking nervously into his Vichyssoise. "Look, I've always had a real thing about you, I think in many ways you were my first love. At least the closest thing to that first love ideal, the first woman I ever met whom I thought I could spend the rest of my life with. But you were married, and then you were reunited with your first love. I suppose I went for Ulrika as a kind of substitute, although of course she is gorgeous and it was great fun. But it was never more than a bit of fun. Because I knew it was only that, the fact that she was married didn't seem to matter. But with you it would have been different, I felt very strongly that if anything started with you that it would be for always. And I'm not a home wrecker."

The more he spoke, the more it all seemed to make sense. It was as if she could suddenly see everything clearly. Of course she had always enjoyed his company, found him amusing and loved talking to him, but had not realised until then that there was so much more to him. And that he adored her.

"I love everything about you Marina: your writing, your character, the way you're always spilling things, your smile. And I never want to go to Stamford Bridge without you again," he finished off his speech. Lucky the soup had been cold to begin with. "Actually, the way we're playing I'm not sure I want to go there again at all, but you see what I mean?"

Marina looks at her new husband as they speed along the King's Road. Ever since that conversation, he seems like a different person to the one she used to know. The man sitting next to her now is miles away from the arrogant old Etonian image. He is altogether more complex than she had first thought. They have so much more in common than she imagined, even the same ambivalent attitude towards having children. Maybe that would change, but for now they were quite happy baby-sitting Amelia when needed, as well as Ulrika's boys.

Marina had not thought about remarrying so soon until Hugo proposed. They were walking through Hyde Park. It was a cold bright day and they stopped at the Serpentine to watch the swans glide across the lake.

"Do you know," asked Hugo, "that swans mate for life?"

"I do," smiled Marina. "I also know that they are related to geese."

"Oh yes, I remember you writing about geese in your column about first love. Well, I'm pleased your imprinting days are over."

Marina laughed and kissed him. "So am I."

Then he suddenly dropped to one knee and asked her to marry him. And she said "yes," without a moment's hesitation.

Both of them were slightly taken aback but it had just seemed like the right thing to do.

"Well, my parents will be relieved," Hugo joked afterwards. "I think they live in daily fear of you getting fed up of me and taking off."

The Draycott is in Cadogan Gardens, between Chelsea and Knightsbridge. It is a classic London building; you can almost smell the history. The wedding party is shown up to one of the private dining rooms where lunch will be served and the dancing will begin. Ulrika, Marina and her mother worked on the seating plan. The main problem of course was Aunt Bitter Lemon, who when sober is painfully annoying and when drunk utterly incomprehensible.

"Haven't we got some deaf old uncle we can shove her next to?" Marina's mother suggested.

Uncle Rupert of the court case was mooted as an option, but Marina refused because he saved her from having a criminal record.

"The thing about her," she said, "is that she's not even a jolly drunk, she's so bloody pessimistic. With her, the glass is always half-empty."

"With her, the glass literally *is* half empty," replied her mother, adding in a rare moment of selflessness that she would have the dreaded aunt on one side and hope she passed out early.

Marina and Hugo take their seats on the top table. Hugo's parents are with them, Marina has got to know them quite well. His father is an extremely distinguished gentleman, whom most would describe as an old school character. His mother is a petite, elegant lady with a passion for horse racing. Hugo is the youngest of three children. His brother, Harry, is his best man. Marina immediately liked him when she met him; he's like an older, balder version of Hugo, with all the charm and wit of his younger brother. His sister Cassandra is married with four children (hence the need for Hassan the Clown). She shares her mother's passion for horses and rarely leaves the Yorkshire home she shares with her stockbroker husband.

Harry's speech has gone down well; there is still much laughing from the assembled 150 guests as he raises his glass to the bride and groom. He has even shown pictures of a young Hugo in Chelsea strip, which is about the first time ever Marina has ever contemplated a child of her own. But then she reminds herself that they are rarely born wearing Chelsea blue and snaps out of it.

The dancing begins before the cake is cut. Ulrika

manages to look gorgeous in a designer maternity dress, despite a large two-baby bump.

"Thank God Ben can now afford to buy me decent clothes," she whispers to Marina as they take a break from the dancing. "I can't tell you what a difference it makes to the way you look, not to mention the way you feel about your husband when you know your credit card is going to work every time you hand it over."

"I hate dancing," says Aunt Bitter Lemon who has just joined them. A rather suave Italian waiter approaches them and offers them a drink. Aunt Bitter Lemon takes two gin and tonics.

"I'll have some sparkling water," says Ulrika, looking him up and down. "Sadly I'm off booze, and games." The waiter smiles back at her and pours her some water.

"So how do you know the bride?" Aunt Bitter Lemon asks Ulrika, while motioning for the waiter to replenish her one of her drinks.

"Oh I fucked her husband," smiles Ulrika downing her water in one.

Marina and Ulrika take Aunt Bitter Lemon's silence as a sign to escape for a pee.

"Did you see her face?" laughs Ulrika as they run out of the room and into the corridor.

"I know, I think she might still be wondering if she's

had too much gin and heard you wrong," laughs Marina. "Now where's the loo? I'm desperate for a pee."

"You're desperate! Try carrying twins that are squeezing your bladder into nothing," shrieks Ulrika.

"It's just down the corridor on your left," says a male voice behind them. Marina turns around to thank him and finds herself face to face with Frank Lampard.

She is too stunned to speak. Happily this is not an affliction that ever affects Ulrika.

"Frank!" she shrieks, "OH MY GOD. You've no idea how utterly brilliant this is. This is my best friend Marina, who is your BIGGEST fan, and today is her wedding day."

"Congratulations," smiles Frank, shaking her hand. Marina is by now beginning to wonder if she's had too much gin.

"I just know you would make her day even more memorable and perfect than it already is by giving her a little kiss," continues Ulrika. Frank is silent. "It doesn't have to be a full-on snog or anything, I mean she is married now, shame we didn't run into you an hour ago."

Frank laughs. "You a Chelsea fan?" he asks Marina.

"Yes," she nods. "A huge Chelsea fan."

"Who's your favourite player?"

"You are," she squeaks.

Frank leans forward and kisses her on the cheek. "Enjoy the rest of your day," he says before walking on.

Acknowledgements

With many thanks to my talented and industrious publisher, Martin Rynja at Gibson Square books, as well as Mary Jones for all her hard work on publicity. Thank you to all my friends, past and present, who provide endless inspiration and fodder. Please keep up the good work. Finally, huge thanks to my husband, Rupert, who may not have been my first love, but is by far my most significant.